BOUND BY BLOOD

BOOK FIVE
OF VIGILANTE

A BRAD MADRID STORY

BOUND BY BLOOD

BOOK FIVE
OF VIGILANTE

A BRAD MADRID STORY

GLYNN STEWART
TERRY MIXON

FAOLAN'S PEN
PUBLISHING
faolanspen.com

This edition published in 2019 by:

Faolan's Pen Publishing Inc.

22 King St. S, Suite 300

Waterloo, Ontario

N2J 1N8 Canada

ISBN-13: 978-1-988035-87-1 (print)

A record of this book is available from Library and Archives Canada.

Printed in the United States of America

1 2 3 4 5 6 7 8 9 10

First edition

First printing: April 2019

Illustration © 2019 Jeff Brown Graphics

Faolan's Pen Publishing logo is a trademark of Faolan's Pen Publishing Inc.

Read more books from Glynn Stewart at faolanspen.com

CHAPTER ONE

THE UNDERLYING ASSUMPTION of house arrest was that the person being arrested had a house to keep them in.

Since Commodore Brad Madrid normally lived aboard the mercenary destroyer *Oath of Vengeance*, a warship that spent most of her time around Jupiter, placing him under house arrest on Earth had caused the Agency—the primary intelligence organization of the Commonwealth—at least one headache.

His sympathy for their problems was limited. The Agency was one of his employers, but the decision to arrest him had been one of paranoia, not of cause.

And keeping him in house arrest on Earth *sucked*. The dark-haired mercenary leaned into the soft fabric of the lounger on the house veranda with a groan. The Agency had decided to lock him up in a safehouse on a Mexican island. From what he could tell, the covert operations organization owned the entire island, which made it perfectly secure.

Brad had been born in space and spent almost his entire life aboard ships and space stations. He regularly worked out in full gravity, but the vast majority of human spacecraft kept their gravity at seventy percent of Earth's.

Living in full gravity was *very* different from working out in it. Even if he'd wanted to run, he wouldn't have made it very far—and that was ignoring the polite-but-cold sentries who guarded the property or the tracking implant in his left shoulder.

The sun and beach were nice, he supposed. It had taken him a week of angry muttering to even begin to appreciate them, but he'd been trapped on Earth for a month now.

A month in which he'd had access to news but not communications. The entire Solar System was reeling from the consequences of his visit to Earth. The President of the Commonwealth had been revealed as a traitor and then shot down by his own allies in the courtyard of the United Nations building.

Brad had been there for all of it. Had been the man to stand on the floor of the Commonwealth Senate and accuse President Mills of trying to create a war to allow himself to seize power.

And as a reward for that, he'd been arrested. Placed in "protective custody" because the Agency had run a genetic analysis and discovered that President Mills's main ally, the pirate warlord known variously as Jack Mader or the Phoenix, was Brad's brother.

Brad wasn't even sure how that was *possible*. Certainly, he'd never worked with Mader—quite the opposite, they'd been on the opposite side of a covert war for years.

"Commodore."

Brad looked up with a sigh at the speaker. Lieutenant Florencio Araya was the Mexican Army officer the Agency had arranged to act as his jailkeeper. Araya was a squat and broad-shouldered man with sun-darkened skin, quite unlike anything Brad had encountered in space.

Outside of their hair color, the two men couldn't be more opposite. Brad was tall and slim, his skin pale from a lifetime under artificial lights.

"Yes, Lieutenant?" Brad asked. Araya might be his jailer, but the man was polite and helpful for all that.

"I think you need to see the news," the Lieutenant told him. "There's an announcement coming out of Oberon."

"Oberon?" Brad repeated. He had history with that particular moon of Uranus but he still couldn't see why an announcement from Oberon would make the news on Earth.

"Why would the news here be carrying an announcement from Oberon?"

Araya snorted.

"*Dinero*, Commodore," he told him. "Someone paid them to. Seems odd…and Oberon is out near your home, isn't it?"

Brad chuckled at the naïve lack of knowledge inherent in calling a moon of Uranus "near" to his homeport at Io, a moon of Jupiter.

"More relevant than here, I guess." His chuckle died and he nodded. "May as well take a look. The beach isn't going anywhere, after all."

———

The house might have looked like a colonial beach home from another century, but it had state-of-the-art *everything*. Including, of course, state-of-the-art security and enough controls over data flow to allow Brad to access incoming news feeds but not send out communication.

Since they'd taken Brad's wrist-comp, the ubiquitous personal computer of the Solar System, away, he needed those systems to stay sane.

They got inside in time to see the screen on the interior wall showing the promised announcement. The camera feed from the reporter passed through the garish doors of the meeting chamber of First Oberon's Council of Speakers as Brad took a careful seat. Those familiar doors were a huge bronze affair with mosaics of the original Council on them.

All of that Council were probably dead now. Outer-world politics were brutal.

The inside of the chamber, however, was almost empty. Brad had seen the wide horseshoe-shaped table and the garish paint and velvet curtains before. Instead of the seven-person Council of Speakers, though, there was a single man sitting in the middle of the table.

There appeared to only be the single camera, but it was enough for Brad to recognize that there were also a lot fewer guards than there had been when he'd met the Council of Speakers—and that the three apparently decorative women in the room were a *far* better security force than the dozen guards the Council had retained.

Once the camera reached the center of the table, Brad finally recognized the figure with a sigh. Knowing what to look for now, he could see the family resemblance. Jack Mader was slightly taller than he was but just as slim, and they had identical black hair and dark eyes.

"Greetings," Mader told the camera. "I'm sure some of those watching have met me by one name or another; my life has been a complicated one.

"Let's begin by laying out the simplest point: my name is Jack Mantruso and I am the Admiral of the Independence Militia. My organization, funded by several of the Outer World colonies as well as allies on Earth, has spent the last few years opposing Commonwealth oppression out here."

He shook his head sadly.

"I did not want to be the man who broke humanity," he continued, his voice *dripping* sincerity and regret.

Brad wanted to reach through the screen and strangle his supposed brother. He'd been born *Brad* Mantruso himself, and the concept of them being brothers might have occurred to one of them sooner if either of them had used their actual last name. Not that it would have changed where they ended up, but it would have avoided the surprise, at least.

"With the murder of President Mills and the ongoing coup on Earth, the governments and councils of the Outer Worlds no longer feel that they can trust the Commonwealth. They no longer feel that the Fleet will protect them from the pirates and slavers we have struggled with for so long.

"And they feel that we can no longer bow to a government more kilometers away than we can even comprehend."

Mantruso shook his head.

"No transition of this scale is easy and we do not expect Earth to calmly permit us to leave, but it falls to me to announce the formation of the Outer Worlds Alliance and our secession—our true and inevitable independence—from the Commonwealth of Earth."

He let those words hang on the video for several seconds.

"To secure the safety of this new nation, I have agreed to bring the Independence Militia in from the cold, so to speak. We will now become the Outer Worlds Navy...and I have, with both regret and great sobriety, accepted the position of Lord Protector of the Outer Worlds Alliance.

"I have been charged to protect these stations and settlements that will no longer kneel to the tyranny of Earth. I will not fail in this charge, no matter the cost. No matter the sacrifice.

"We are free, and I am entirely willing to water this tree of liberty with the blood of any damned patriots who'd change that."

CHAPTER TWO

WITHOUT ANY ABILITY TO communicate directly with the outside, all Brad could do about the sudden sea change in the politics of his world was to go back onto the beach and stare at the waves. A robot trundled out after him with a drink tray and he patted it gently on what passed for a head as he took the soda.

It had taken him almost as long to convince the machine to not bring him alcohol as it had taken him to start appreciating the beach. The house was not normally used as a prison.

As night fell with the usual suddenness of the Caribbean, he was still on the porch. Today, his muscles hurt too much to move around in Earth's gravity unless he needed to.

Looking up at the stars, he tried to pick out Jupiter. Home. After a few moments' searching, he concluded it couldn't currently be seen, and sighed.

"My brother is an asshole who wants to conquer humanity," he said aloud, just to get the words out. "Fuck. *I have a brother*…and he's an asshole who wants to conquer humanity."

The ocean didn't answer. There was probably at least one sentry close enough to hear him bitching out the universe, but they wisely didn't say anything.

So many years. So many dead friends. He'd spent his entire adult life fighting the Cadre and then the Independence Militia they'd spawned as a front and the conspiracy that had supported them.

And now Jack Mantruso had turned all of that into a new nation. A nation that answered only to him.

Somehow, Brad didn't think that the older Mantruso was going to just sit by and idly enjoy the nation he'd created. War was coming. A war that the Vikings, the mercenary warship squadron he'd built up from a single salvaged pirate corvette, would inevitably be in the heart of.

And he was here.

How many prisoners on Earth had a warship with a platoon of soldiers in orbit, he wondered? So far as he knew, *Oath of Vengeance* hadn't left in the last month. Her captain, his wife Michelle Hunt, had been allowed to visit him twice during that time, and he knew that the rest of his squadron was at Jupiter, repairing and waiting for new ships to come online.

But his ship and his wife remained in Earth orbit, waiting for him. The Agency wasn't going to let him leave. Not when his brother had transitioned from wanted criminal number one into the head of state of a hostile nation.

He sighed, studying the stars…and picked out the oncoming light of the aircraft before he heard it. Once he heard it, long practice allowed him to identify it as a standard orbital shuttle—and it was headed for his little island.

Brad Madrid, *né* Brad Mantruso, had been expecting them. His brother had declared his play, and the Agency was at least good enough to explain where he stood.

Even if it was effectively as a political prisoner.

———

Brad made his way carefully back into the house and started up a kettle for tea, listening for the sound of a vehicle. He wasn't entirely sure where the landing pad was on the island—he'd been in a state of shock when he'd first arrived—but it was far enough that his guest would probably take one of the handful of electric cars on the island.

He heard the whir of the car as the kettle boiled, and laid out two cups of tea as he waited patiently for the guest he knew would be arriving. It was a question of *who* would be coming, really, and the sound of a cane rapping on the front steps answered that question.

"Director Harmon," Brad greeted the head of the Commonwealth Intelligence Agency as the goblin of a man walked through the front door without knocking.

Director Antonio Harmon was, frankly, ugly. He was squat and heavyset, with a clear pot belly and unusually large ears and nose. The red tinge to his nose suggested a long-standing drinking habit, and he walked with a cane, his left leg clearly not working quite right.

"Tea?" Brad asked politely.

Harmon grunted as he took a seat at the kitchen table.

"I know damned well this place has an expensive booze robot," he replied. "Whisky on the rocks, hold the rocks."

The robot apparently heard the instruction and emerged from its cupboard a few moments later. Brad was probably anthropomorphizing the machine when he saw a degree of enthusiasm for being allowed to serve its actual purpose.

He kept the tea himself, leaning against the countertop as he studied the director.

"You don't visit without a reason," he told Harmon. "What do you want?"

"Want's got nothing to do with it," the smaller man replied, downing the glass of whisky in one shot. "It's what I owe you. You saw the news announcements, I presume?"

"About this new OWA?" Brad asked.

"Yeah. It is, as I'm sure you're surprised to hear, about as much of a democratic alliance of free worlds as *I* am a ballerina."

Brad said nothing, simply sipping his tea as he studied the man who'd ordered him detained.

"The OWA is, at best, a soon-to-be constitutional monarchy and at worst an outright military dictatorship," Harmon said flatly. "The

Cadre has to have been laying the groundwork for this for a long time. Twenty million people don't fall into line overnight, Madrid."

"That many?" Brad asked, shocked.

"The Commonwealth has its detractors and its dissidents, always has," the Director grumped. "A lot of them realized over the years that a decent solar-powered hydroponics setup and half a dozen nano-vats are all you need to set up a self-sufficient settlement in the back of nowhere. The ship to carry all that is more expensive than the gear is, so we probably see a couple of hundred thousand people a year go wandering off into the back of beyond.

"Some don't make it." He shrugged. "Others come back or join one of the existing settlements out there. Others make it work. Only reason we have anything close to a census out past Saturn is because of the Doctors' Guild."

"Why Saturn?" Brad asked.

"Stereotyped as the end of civilized land, so people go further," Harmon said flatly. "Stereotype begets reality, so the Outer Worlds were born. And now the Cadre has bound them all together at the point of a rifle."

"I'm guessing the Cadre gets subsumed now?" Brad said.

"Yeah. News I'm getting is that what's left of the Cadre is now Outer Worlds Intelligence—or has joined the Independence Militia in the Outer Worlds Navy. Our greatest enemy just metamorphized into something entirely different."

There'd been an attack early on in Brad's career where the Cadre had produced thousands of assault troops and no one had been quite sure where they'd come from. With a chill, Brad realized he now knew.

"I wonder how long this has been the *actual* truth behind the Cadre," he murmured. "Even if, say, Oberon or the other large colonies were holding out, they'd still have had vastly more people and resources than we thought."

Harmon sighed.

"Probably. The problem from your perspective, Commodore, is that there is no official inheritance process for the Lord Protectorship…and *Jack* Mantruso has no kids. Just a brother."

"You think he's going to, what, bribe me by making me his heir?" Brad demanded.

"Basically, yes," the Agency Director admitted.

"Pretty much every time the Phoenix and I have been in the same room, we were trying to kill each other," Brad pointed out. "What in Everlit makes you think I'd *want* to be his heir?"

"Not much," Harmon admitted. "But it's a risk I can't take, Madrid. Not with a key agent and merc commander, not without some kind of assurance."

"What kind of assurance do you need?" the younger man demanded. "I'm not even sure how I have a brother, let alone why I'd go try and join him."

The Director snorted.

"Your parents were the heirs to the Mantruso and Riggio crime families," he told Brad. "They married to solidify a peace agreement… then killed their *own* parents to secure their power base. Jack Mantruso was born as part of the peace agreement, the designated heir to take over the largest crime family in the Solar System.

"So far as I can tell, you came along after they actually fell in love. It's a sickeningly sweet story, but it adds up. We already knew that Conrad Mantruso was running a freighter through the Belt run as a cover. We didn't know which one…and a kid aboard the freighter definitely would have made us look for a different one."

Harmon sighed.

"I can tell you how you have a brother," he said. "I can tell you your parents died when *Black Skull* was destroyed by the Mercenary Guild invoking an overriding contract.

"I can't tell you why you never met your brother. I'm surprised, knowing what I know now, that Armand Riggio didn't show up and whisk you away."

"Because my other uncle got there first," Brad said with a sigh of his own. Boris Mantruso had basically adopted him after his parents died. He realized, now, just how much his uncle had protected him from. "I can put the pieces together now, Director, but I still don't see how that makes me a threat."

"You're not a threat, Brad. You're a *risk*. A risk we can't afford as the entire Solar System prepares to break apart and trigger a war we cannot stop."

"So, what happens to me, then?" Brad demanded.

"You stay here," Harmon told him. "For at least a few more months, until we have a better handle on what's going on with the OWA. I want to trust you, Brad. Your record justifies it...but I can't help but wonder if this is just a long game on you and your brother's part."

"Then ask bloody Falcone. She knows me."

Agent Kate Falcone had been Brad's Agency contact before he'd joined the organization himself, and had served as his sometime control, sometime partner after that.

"She does," the Director agreed. "And, to your credit, I think she'd have broken you out of here if I hadn't sent her away already. There's a lot going on and we may need you before this is done...but right now, the President is dead. The Senate is in metaphorical flames, and your *brother* just threw down a gauntlet at the feet of the entire Commonwealth.

"I need to control what risks I can, and letting Jack Mantruso's brother wander free would be a long way from that. Understand?"

"No," Brad told him. "I'm not even sure how you think this mess is going to *get* me to help you later, either."

He shook his head.

"I'll play along for now, Director, but we both know I can be out of here in under an hour if I choose to. I'm just not willing to burn bridges and leave a trail of bodies just yet."

The Director put his face in his hands to cover another sigh.

"Do me a favor, Madrid? *Don't* say shit like that. I have enough migraines as it is."

CHAPTER THREE

"It's about as bad as it can get, my love," Michelle Hunt's image said on the screen. She was only allowed down to the planet to visit Brad every so often, but she was at least allowed to send him video mail.

He just wasn't allowed to *reply*.

"OWA has everything outside of the orbit of Saturn," she told him. "Neptune, Uranus, the Kuiper Belt, the various Trojan clusters…everything. And we finally got word from the Guild on their position."

Brad leaned forward in interest.

"Officially, the Mercenary Guild has recognized the Outer Worlds Alliance as the legitimate government of the outer system. As a legitimate government, they are a recognized contractee and can file contracts with the Guild and hire mercenaries."

He could hear the *but* before she said it.

"Unofficially, the Guild has informed all senior officers that anyone who takes contracts against *either* the Commonwealth or the OWA will be stripped of their rating," Michelle said quietly. "They are going full neutral. Guild mercs like us are allowed to take contracts from either side to deal with pirates or other problems, but we are not allowed to get involved in the war everyone thinks is coming."

The Vikings were one of the few Platinum-rated mercenary companies the Guild had. The rating system had more to do with success rates and professionalism than actual firepower—a few of the Gold-rated companies actually fielded more ships than the Vikings, for example—but it also defined hiring rates.

Losing their Guild rating would *destroy* most Guild mercenary companies. There were other sources of contracts, but without the legal coverage of the Guild, well…you were a few steps away from thug and pirate at best.

"Neutrality seems to be the word of the day elsewhere, too," Michelle concluded. "Officially, Jupiter is part of the Commonwealth, but the rumors Kawa is sending my way suggest the governors are leaning towards keeping out of this.

"I don't know if the OWA will *let* Jupiter sit this one out, but I think the governors are going to try. I can't blame them, really." She shook her head. "Fifty million citizens in the Jupiter System alone, and they provide food and water for another twenty million across the Trojans, Saturn and the Belt.

"In their place, I'd look to my constituents first, too, but it leaves the Commonwealth in the lurch." The brunette spaceship captain shook her head. "For now, the Vikings are keeping their heads down. We took a lot of damage at Ceres and the two new destroyers are almost online. Sooner or later, we get our Commodore back and *then* we can decide what we do."

She blew a kiss at the camera.

"I love you," she told him. "I miss you. I'm still looking for strings I can pull to get you out of there, but I don't know how effective they are yet. I'll see you soon."

The message ended and Brad sighed, leaning against the table.

He could see the logic in neutrality on the part of the Mercenary Guild and the Jovian governors. From his own encounters with the Phoenix and the Cadre, he doubted it was going to end well for anyone, but he could see the logic in the decision.

There might be a new name and a new official existence to his enemy, but he had no illusions. It now looked like the Cadre had been a caterpillar and the Independence Militia the chrysalis…but the Outer

Worlds Alliance was definitely the same beast his enemy always had been.

The name was shinier and the ideals better spoken, but it was a "nation" built to allow a bunch of slavers and pirates to rule over people who couldn't escape them.

Sooner or later, Brad was going to find a way to stop them.

———

Brad wasn't certain how many other houses were on the island—or even where the island was other than "near Mexico." He presumed there was somewhere his Mexican Army security detail lived, but he didn't ask.

He was being cooperative so far, but after almost six weeks, he was starting to get angry. He was watching enough news to know that the Senate was almost paralyzed, still tied up in the aftermath of the President and his party being involved in a conspiracy that had seen thousands of Commonwealth citizens dead.

From the tone of the media, *somebody* in the new OWA had spread a lot of money around Earth before they'd officially taken shape. There was a lot of "cautious optimism" and "wait and see" being bandied around Earth's news.

To be fair, Brad supposed, the news didn't know that Jack Mantruso was the Phoenix. That revelation alone would probably have shut most of the pandering up. So far, the OWA and their Lord Protector had played things close to their chest as well.

If there were purges going on as the new government solidified their power, the Earth media didn't know about them.

The absence of the Council of Speakers when the Lord Protector had announced his new position was a bad-enough sign to Brad. He *knew* that collection of politicians, and they gave most politicians a bad name. They were exactly the kind of self-aggrandizing blowhards who would have wanted to be in that video, if only to attach themselves to Jack Mantruso's coattails.

If they weren't there, they had at best been rendered no longer relevant and at worst rendered no longer breathing.

"The marathon session of the Senate called three days ago to discuss the impeachment of Acting President Leigh Olson has now closed off the gallery," the news chattered behind him. "Media has only had limited access to the ongoing debate, as many of the details of President Mills conspiracy remain under a surprising level of secrecy.

"President Olson, who served as vice president under Mills for the last three years, insists she knew nothing of the conspiracy now alleged to have taken place under Mills's authority. At best, however, her critics say she *should* have known.

"And many say that there is no way the president would have come as close to success in his schemes to overthrow our democracy as he did if his vice president had been unaware. The truth to this, however, lies in the evidence that we have not yet been permitted to see."

Brad was tempted to turn the screen off...but he *needed* to know what was going on with the Commonwealth. An old friend of his, Senator William Barnes from Jupiter, had been made Speaker of the Senate after Mills shot the previous Speaker.

Barnes's first task had been to decide if the Senate would attempt to impeach President Mills's right-hand woman and successor. Right up until the moment the Senate had been called into the mammoth session the news was now reporting on, every sign had been that he wouldn't.

Brad wished he had the connections to know just what in Everdark had changed. Even if he had them, it wasn't like he could call out.

The world was changing around him, and all he had was the news and a twice-weekly video mail from his wife.

Something was going to have to give.

With a sigh, he turned the news off. The world might change before he woke up...but it wasn't like he could *do* anything about it.

CHAPTER FOUR

BRAD'S MUSCLES might still complain about Earth's gravity, but his senses had *never* been impaired by anything on the homeworld. He woke up the moment he heard the steps up to the second floor creak and realized he wasn't alone in the beach house.

He waited a few seconds, remaining still as he assessed the situation. There was at least one more person in the house...no, three. One on the stairs, two in the kitchen.

The house was old enough that the floorboards were *not* quiet, and the strangers were wearing combat boots. No powered heavy armor or anything like that, but it definitely sounded like armed men.

Or women. Those could be even deadlier in his experience...and while Brad had been permitted many amenities, the Agency hadn't allowed him a weapon. Or a nano-vat, for that matter, given that he was still more than up to using the portable fabricators to make a gun.

He suspected that the house was normally used for therapeutic rest and relaxation for agents who'd seen too much, though, which meant it had a closet full of sports supplies. Including a baseball bat that Brad had relocated to under the bedside table.

The footsteps were getting closer and he silently cursed whoever was in control of the house's alarm system. At some point in reprogramming it to keep him in, they'd clearly accidentally disabled the parts supposed to keep people out.

He slid out of bed. The baseball bat wasn't a weapon he was used to, but he wasn't a very good unarmed fighter by his people's standards. Give him a monofilament blade, a pistol or a rifle, he was as deadly as any trooper in his company.

Leave him unarmed? At least a tenth of his non-troopers could beat him up.

"House is clear," he heard someone murmur in the hallway. "One thermal signature in the bedroom."

There was a long pause, and then the stranger rapped on the door.

"Commodore Madrid?" a young male voice called through the door. "I know you're not supposed to have any weapons, but your posture suggests otherwise. May I suggest that we *not* come to blows? My boss would be *pissed*."

"Who in Everdark are you?" Brad demanded.

"Lieutenant Edward Jenkins," the speaker responded. "Black Spade Charlie Actual."

Black Spade…the man outside his door was Secret Service. Brad shifted his grip on the baseball bat. The Secret Service had been Mills's hatchet people and his go-betweens with the Cadre as he'd set up his plan.

He heard Jenkins sigh through the door.

"Look, I need to clear the house as safe," the Secret Service officer told him. "Just you in there?"

"Yeah," Brad conceded.

"And I'm guessing that's not an explosive, a firearm or a mono-blade you're holding, is it?"

"No," Brad allowed.

"Then I'm going to call the house clear and tell my boss he can come in. How about you put on some clothes and meet us in the kitchen in five minutes?"

"…I can do that," Brad said after a moment.

"Okay. Just do me one favor."

"What's that?"

"Tell me where the *hell* the coffee machine is in that over-smart monstrosity?"

———

By the time he was dressed and slowly heading toward the main floor, Brad's curiosity had overcome his fear. The presence of Black Spade agents was strange enough. Once he'd fully woken up, he remembered that Black Spade was the callsign for the President's personal security detail.

He couldn't think of any reason that President Olson would be there, especially since she'd been facing impeachment when he'd gone to sleep, but he wasn't the President of the Commonwealth.

There had to be a reason.

Part of the answer was provided when he reached the stairs and was waved past a pair of Secret Service agents. There were two people sitting at the kitchen table and neither was Leigh Olson.

He didn't recognize the woman but she was a tall and white-haired Admiral of the Commonwealth Fleet. That narrowed it down, since there were only four full Admirals in the Fleet—and meant that she was Admiral Violet Orcho.

Brad *did* know the man. He was a tall man with deep mahogany skin and short-cropped steel-gray hair. And when Brad had gone to sleep, he had been the Speaker of the Senate, not the President of the Commonwealth.

"Mr. President," he greeted William Barnes with a small bow. "I'm not familiar with Commonwealth succession rules, but I'm guessing that President Olson was successfully impeached?"

"She was," he confirmed. "A number of Secret Service agents decided to come in from the cold a few days ago. Their testimony and evidence are helping us put a lot of people behind bars...starting with Olson.

"And since I was the Speaker and no new Vice President had been appointed since Mills death, that made me President." Barnes shook his head. "Technically, it's two years until the election. I'll probably accelerate that, but we can't afford questions of chain of command while we're at war."

"We are at war, then?" Brad asked quietly.

"There's no question," Admiral Orcho noted, her voice crisp. "We don't know when the OWN will make their first move, and public sentiment is such that *we* can't initiate the first offensive."

"Director Harmon is digging into the flow of money to see if he can find out just *why* our media is being so wonderfully friendly to your brother's new empire," Barnes added. "I suspect some interesting tidbits are going to fall out of that."

Brad winced.

"Can we *not* call that asshole my brother?" he asked. "That relationship is causing me enough problems without being reminded of it."

"That's fair," Barnes allowed. "We're here to short-circuit at least some of those problems, though."

"Can I go?" Brad asked bluntly.

"It's more complicated than that, but basically, yes," the President told him.

"How complicated can it be?" Brad asked. "At some point this becomes illegal detention, after all."

"Protective custody," Orcho told him. "I didn't like it, but I understand where Harmon came from. The President, however, knows you better than either of us—and I'll be damned if I'm starting my relationship with my new boss by arguing with him."

"The Admiral has her own reason for being here," Barnes said. "Your detention is lifted, but I have a favor to ask, one that means you don't get to go to your ship right away."

"I've seen my wife twice in almost six weeks. I haven't seen my crew or my people at all. I have an entire company of mercenaries who I need to make sure haven't burned a planet down in my absence," Brad replied. "What favor do you think outweighs that?"

"You're also a reserve Fleet officer," Orcho noted. "A legal fig leaf to cover your use of nuclear weapons in the past, but we now find ourselves desperately short of flag officers we can trust...and almost entirely lacking in flag officers that anyone outside the orbit of Mars will trust."

Brad stared at them in silence.

"This war is going to pivot on Jupiter and Saturn," Barnes said quietly. "I was one senator, Brad. One Senator for an entire planetary system and millions of people. The Jovian governors had quietly informed the Senate that they will not permit the Fleet to refuel or anchor in Jupiter space for the duration of the conflict.

"They don't trust us. Very shortly, however, they're going to *need* us —and if we're to meet them halfway, we need to have officers they can trust."

"Your reserve status has been activated, Commodore," Orcho concluded, sliding a box across the table. "There's a suitcase with a uniform that should fit you in the front hall, and these are your insignia."

Brad opened the box. As a mercenary Commodore, he hadn't gone in for much insignia—everybody knew who the Commodore of the Vikings was.

The box contained matching sets of a single gold circle, designed to be magnetically attached to the collar of either a dress uniform or a combat vac-suit.

"Normally, refusing to be activated in time of war is a felony," Barnes said gently. "On the other hand, normally a reserve officer gets *paid* and you never did—not by Fleet, anyway. If you want to walk away, Brad, I'm the President of the Everdarkened Commonwealth. I can make it happen.

"But I'll be blunt, old friend: if you walk away, neither the Agency nor the Fleet will be able to trust you again...and we need you."

"Nasty choice," Brad muttered...but he picked up the insignia. "Can I at least call my wife before I get to work?"

———

The uniform wasn't a particularly good fit. Unlike his Vikings uniform, it had clearly been pulled out of a storage rack somewhere. Modern technology and fabrics allowed it to be adjusted in several places to fit better, but Brad could still tell the difference.

Once he was showered, shaved and dressed, however, he certainly looked the part of the rank. He'd carried the title of Commodore as a mercenary for years. How different could being a Fleet Commodore be?

Barnes had even extracted his wrist-comp from the Agency and he linked it into the planetary network to place a call to Michelle.

"Captain Hunt," she answered crisply, then saw his face on the screen. "Brad! Did they let you go? Are you out?"

"Yes, yes...and no," he told her. "I assume you know about President Barnes?"

"Yes, that's why I was hoping you'd get free," she admitted. "I've been bending his ear as our Senator for a while on getting you out!" Michelle paused. "What do you mean, 'and no'?"

"They activated my reserve Fleet commission, love," he told her. "Technically, I can't say no, though Barnes would cover for me if I did. But...they need me, love. Or someone like me, anyway.

"More importantly, *Jupiter* is going to need me here, in this uniform," he said quietly. "Our planet. Our people. I owe them, more than anything."

"If you're in the Fleet, though, what happens to...us?" Michelle asked. "What happens to the Vikings?"

There was another question in there, too, and Brad thought it was *far* more important.

"I'm pretty sure Fleet officers get leave to visit their spouses," he told her. "We won't be in each other's back pockets as much, which *sucks*, but I'm not letting you go, my love. Not now, not ever. Hear me?"

Stress that he didn't think Michelle had realized she was holding released from her face, and she smiled at him.

"Good man," she allowed. "And the company?"

He waved a finger in her direction.

"Boom. You're now a Commodore, too," he said with a grin. "I'd like you to hang out in Earth orbit until I know what they need me to do and, well, I've had a chance to visit, but you're now in charge of the Vikings."

He paused.

"I'm looking forward to my first dividend payment that *I* didn't have to work for," he concluded with a grin. "But I'll visit as soon as I can. I suspect I'm about to get tossed on a shuttle with Admiral Orcho, however, so I don't know when that will be."

She exhaled a long sigh and nodded.

"I'll take care of our people," Michelle promised. "Our nest egg, too. I have one big requirement in return, though."

"Anything, Michelle," Brad said quietly.

"You protect my husband's ass," she ordered. "Clear? I'll let you get away with this for now, but you're coming home, you hear me?"

"Loud and clear, Commodore Hunt!"

CHAPTER FIVE

WITH ONE FINAL HANDSHAKE, President Barnes was whisked away by his escort onto his shuttle. That left Brad standing next to Admiral Orcho, wondering just what in Everdark he'd signed on for.

"Fleet shuttle is already on its way," the Admiral told him. "My apologies, Commodore, but you're not going to get much time to enjoy your liberty. We're heading straight for orbit."

"I'm aware I traded a prison of one type for a prison of another," Brad noted. "But the President knows exactly which of my buttons to push. We go back a long way."

"So do you and Fleet," the Admiral said. "My inbox exploded for a few days once the rumor of your detainment hit Mars and Jupiter."

"Is anyone left at Jupiter?" Brad asked, listening for the sound of an incoming shuttle.

"Unavoidably, but we're doing our best to honor the Jovian Council's request," Orcho told him. "We've got personnel on the various gun platforms in the planetary system, but we've pulled our fleet back."

"How far back?" Jupiter had various guard and militia forces that were more powerful than many suspected and was home to multiple mercenary companies. They were still utterly outclassed by the kind of strength Brad knew the Independence Militia had possessed.

He didn't know what kind of firepower the Outer Worlds Navy had, but it seemed likely they'd absorbed both the Militia and the spaceborne elements of the Cadre.

"We can only play so many games," Orcho admitted. "We've got a force in the leading Trojan cluster, at the invitation of the Board that runs Serenade, but that's it. Most of the ships have been pulled back to Mars or are even on their way here."

"I don't think anything in Earth orbit is going to matter much," Brad pointed out. "Or Mars, for that matter."

"I agree," she said, raising her voice slightly to speak over the engines of the descending shuttle. "However, we need to reorganize, assess the loyalties of our remaining captains and officers, and prepare for the coming storm.

"Earth and Mars are secure. There's nowhere better to do this."

"Remaining captains?" Brad asked. "I didn't think there'd been any fighting yet."

The shuttle's engines grew louder and Orcho shook her head.

"You'll be briefed at Orbital Command," she shouted. "We're still waiting on some final pieces."

The shuttle swooped in for a landing and Brad looked at the swept-wing spacecraft with undisguised longing. He'd put up with a *lot* of bullshit to get out of Earth's gravity well.

"All right, sir," he told the Admiral. "I look forward to seeing what you want me to do."

She snorted.

"I'll remind you of that in a few weeks," she told him. "We're the military, Madrid, not mercenaries. *Hurry up and wait* is a legendary phrase for a reason."

———

As the shuttle passed out of Earth's gravity well, it switched over to artificial gravity. At the standard seventy percent of a g, Brad felt his muscles truly relax for the first time in weeks.

"I am not going to miss Earth's gravity," he admitted aloud. "The beach was nice, but I wasn't enjoying weighing half again what I was used to."

"It shouldn't have taken you much longer to adjust," Orcho told him. "Our bodies evolved for it and we can tell, even if you spent your entire life off of Earth."

Brad shook his head.

"Intellectually, I get that," he admitted. "But it's not a theory I'd choose to test."

Orcho chuckled as the shuttle slowed to dock with Orbital Command.

"Fair enough, Commodore. We're not going to insist you spend any time on the surface, that's for sure."

Brad followed her out onto the main boarding area and she waved a noncom over. The man had clearly been waiting for them, as he had a datapad he handed the Admiral as soon as he'd saluted.

"Chief Hespeler, can you see Commodore Madrid to visiting officers' quarters and get his gear settled?" Orcho asked, her voice distracted as she scanned through the datapad.

"Can do, sir. Do you need him anywhere after that?"

"Do we have a flag officers' briefing scheduled today?" the Admiral asked as she read the report.

"Not booked yet."

"I'll get in touch with Captain Hardy and *get* one booked. Keep in the loop," Orcho ordered. She checked the time. "Forty-five minutes, if I can pull it off. Make sure Madrid makes it."

She turned to Brad.

"Looks like we're throwing you in the deep end, Commodore. Welcome to the Commonwealth Fleet. I'll be briefing everyone shortly."

They traded salutes and she disappeared at a brisk pace as Brad watched her go.

"You get used to her," Chief Hespeler told him from over his shoulder.

"I'm used to being the one in charge," Brad admitted. "It's more than Admiral Orcho I need to get used to."

"You're the merc they drafted, right?" the Chief asked.

"Roughly. Where are these quarters?"

"This way, sir," Hespeler said. "You took Andre on after the idiots fired her, right?"

"Captain Brenda Andre?" Brad asked.

"Yes, sir," the Chief said as he led the way.

"Yeah. She's a damn fine officer, saved my life both in Fleet and working for me."

"I served under her," Hespeler replied. "I doubt the news of your activation has made it out yet, but I suspect I'll be getting a note from her shortly. If my old skipper went to work for you, the least I can do is make sure you land on your feet."

"It's appreciated, Chief," Brad told him. "Let's get this show on the road, shall we?"

———

"Attention!"

The single word barked by the Marine standing by the entrance to the briefing room brought the officers to their feet.

Brad was half a second or so behind the rest. He hadn't expected quite so much formality out of a briefing where he was, so far as he could tell, the most junior officer present.

There were three full Admirals, six Vice Admirals and five Rear Admirals in the room, representing at least two-thirds of the Admirals the Commonwealth had.

Possibly more. Brad was only aware of three Admirals of any rank positioned away from Earth.

The other missing Admiral was Violet Orcho, and she entered through the door to face the standing crowd.

"Cut the mickey mouse," she snapped. "You should know better."

Several people chuckled and Brad realized that the level of formality *wasn't* required. It was more on the order of a running joke between Admiral Orcho, the current Chief of Space Operations, and her senior subordinates.

"If any of you didn't know who Brad Madrid was *before* the last two months, you were falling short on your job," Orcho told them all, gesturing at Brad. "If any of you don't know who he is now, you're damned incompetent and can turn your stars in right now. Anyone?"

There were no chuckles this time, but no one took Orcho up on her statement, either. It sent a chill down Brad's spine to realize that even *before* he'd walked into the Senate and helped accuse President Mills of treason, his Vikings had been a big-enough deal that the Admirals should know who he was.

"The reason I called this meeting on this short notice is because we got final confirmation seventy minutes ago of our worst-case scenario," the Admiral continued after a moment. "Task Group *Immortal* left Ceres on schedule, headed to Earth; however, they detoured approximately thirty-four hours later."

Brad swallowed. He'd seen Task Group *Immortal* heading to Ceres after his own engagement there. It had been an impressive force. Three cruisers, twelve destroyers, thirty frigates...and *Immortal* herself, one of only three battleships ever built by the Commonwealth Fleet.

The battleships were far larger and more powerful than required by any task the Fleet had expected to take on. All three were almost fifty years old, though his understanding was that they'd been kept well upgraded over those years.

The fact that the Fleet had three battleships and no potential enemy had any was one of the things underlying the assumption that the Commonwealth's core worlds were secure.

But if *Immortal* had detoured...

"We have no confirmation of just what happened," Orcho noted. "I'd like to think that Vice Admiral Wu remained loyal, but that would mean he is now dead.

"Task Group *Immortal* has defected to the Outer Worlds."

The room was silent.

"That...quadruples their cruiser strength?" someone asked quietly.

"We know that three cruisers would have ended up in Independence Militia hands without Commodore Madrid's intervention," Orcho pointed out. "We have no data to suggest that any others *did* end up in those hands, but I was uninclined to assume that we had a monopoly on heavy warships.

"Nonetheless, I would guess that Task Group *Immortal* doubles their cruiser strength. A much-lower impact on their destroyer and frigate strength, simply because they had more of them to begin with.

"The key, however, is *Immortal* herself. While we continue to outnumber the OWN in every class of heavy warship, they now possess a battleship—a class of ships we assumed to be our monopoly."

"Wait," Brad interrupted. "You mean the OWN actually outnumbers the Fleet in some types of warship?"

Orcho sighed and tapped a command. A display of icons appeared on the wall, laying out the estimates of the OWN's fleet strength.

"We still have two battleships to their one and thirty-plus cruisers to their four-to-six," she explained. "We have eight carriers, but we have no idea how many the Alliance has. At least one, probably more. Both we and the OWN field around a hundred destroyers; but the OWN is believed to field over three hundred corvettes and frigates. To our two hundred and ten."

And since most of the OWN's destroyers and lighter warships had been built by the Fleet's own suppliers, their ships were newer and more advanced on average.

"We have the advantage of superior fixed defenses in most locations and the fact that we can be relatively sure that both the Mercenary Guild and the Jovian Militias will *eventually* come in on our side," Orcho noted. "That will even the odds, but until the OWN makes their move, we are at a disadvantage."

"I can't believe Jupiter betrayed us like this," one of the Vice Admirals groused.

"Why not?" Brad asked. "What has the Commonwealth done recently to suggest that Jupiter gains from backing us?"

"Are you serious?" the woman demanded.

"Deathly," he told her. "Over the last few years, the Commonwealth has pulled back fleets and resources, leaving the Jovian planets to their own devices. They've only ever been given one Senator on Earth and have generally felt forced to go their own way.

"They don't *think* of themselves as part of the Commonwealth, not truly," Brad explained. "So, they see the OWA as a threat to the Commonwealth, not to themselves."

He held up a hand before anyone started shouting.

"They're *wrong*," he said calmly. "The OWA is simply the final form of the threat we've faced all along. The Phoenix—this Lord Protector—has been leading the Cadre for years now. The Cadre, the Independence Militia, the Outer Worlds Alliance…it's all one thing. Funded by President Mills, organized by the Phoenix, supported by piracy and slavery.

"They're going to come for Jupiter. They're not going to just settle in the outer system and live their quiet lives. The Lord Protector wants to be emperor of all mankind."

"I should note, if anyone is feeling questionable, that *no one*, in this entire Solar System, has spent as much time fighting the Cadre as Brad Madrid and his people," Orcho reminded the other admirals. "There's a reason we activated his reserve commission. He knows this enemy."

"So, what would you suggest, then?" the same Admiral demanded.

"Saturn is the key," Brad said quietly. "The Cadre developed methods of small-scale fuel refining, but those won't suffice for fleet movements. Raids, even with carriers or cruisers? Yeah.

"Not fleets. Not assault operations. Not a *battleship*. They need fuel and they need vast amounts of it—which means either massive distributed operations…or Saturn or Jupiter.

"Jupiter is badly positioned for them to hit *without* holding Saturn; plus, Jupiter is far better defended. Saturn, on the other hand, is probably the most lightly populated place in the Solar System.

"We need to reinforce Saturn's defenses as soon as possible."

One of the full Admirals chuckled.

"You were right, Orcho," he noted. "All right, Madrid. If we send that kind of force, will you command it?"

"Yes," Brad confirmed without hesitation. "I have friends out there. I owe them."

CHAPTER SIX

FROM THE SPEED OF EVENTS, Admiral Orcho had figured she wasn't keeping Brad as a Commodore for long. She'd given him the insignia, but he was barely out of the flag officers' briefing before she handed him new insignia.

"Here, you're a Rear Admiral," she told him. "With me, Madrid."

"You had these on you already?" he asked.

"Tradition says I can't bring you in at higher than your Guild rank, and Guild regs only make you a Commodore," she said crisply as she led the way into the labyrinthine administrative sections of Orbital Command. "But I need you as a task force commander, not a squadron leader."

"I see." Brad was feeling more than a bit lost in the rush, but he was willing to see how things shook out.

Orcho led him through a door marked with her name into an office that was doing its best to pretend it was floating on an ocean on Earth. All four walls and the ceiling had been configured to show what looked like a live feed from a sunny day on the surface.

The Admiral's desk and other office paraphernalia were in the middle of that illusory ocean. She took a seat and gestured him to an available chair.

The apparent open space was enough to make Brad's hindbrain shiver. Stepping from the corridors of a space station into an open area of this size usually meant you'd done something very wrong.

"We've been assembling a task force to send out as a show of strength," she told him as he carefully sat down. "It wasn't expected to fight *Immortal*, but nothing in space was. I was leaning towards Saturn as the destination, but there were other options in play. Both of the main Trojan clusters of Jupiter, for example."

"And now?" Brad asked carefully.

"You made a cogent argument, one that put together the kind of data a native of the mid-system would know instinctually and my collection of Earth and Moon-born flag officers wouldn't," Orcho told him. "I've known for a while that the lack of true spaceborn officers in our higher ranks was going to come back to bite us...but there was only so much even I could do."

One Admiral of four, Brad reflected, was effectively only one *vote* of four for a lot of the decisions around running the Fleet.

"We're giving you what's being designated Task Force Seventeen," she concluded. "The numbering is basically random, don't worry. You'll get both of the *Tremendous*-class cruisers, but we're still sorting out what else I can break free.

"I can promise you'll get at least one more cruiser, but beyond that, you may well only have destroyers and frigates."

"Depending on what I'm expected to do, that should be enough," Brad said slowly.

"Officially, your mission is to defend Saturn," Orcho told him. "Unofficially, that mission is secondary to the preservation of your command, Admiral."

"Sir?" he asked.

"You heard the same numbers everyone else did," she said grimly. "For the first time, the Commonwealth Fleet faces a fundamentally equal opponent. I don't think Mills's little plan called for that to happen—a few defeats, maybe, but he didn't want a *real* threat to the Commonwealth.

"He wanted to be in charge when the dust settled, after all."

"So, we can't afford to lose the task force," Brad concluded.

"Exactly." She shook her head. "It's worse than we're going to let most people know, too. But if I'm sending you to the heart of the fire, you need to understand how bad off we are."

"What do you mean?"

"*Immortal* was the most updated of our three battleships," Orcho told him. "Assuming equal escorts, *Immortal* would probably defeat *Eternal* in a straight-up fight."

Brad winced. *Eternal* was the battleship guarding Mars and, like the other battleships, had basically been regarded as invulnerable.

"What even most of our flag officers don't realize is that we never had the budget for upgrading all three battleships," she said quietly. "*Amaranthine* has never been upgraded from her original specifications, Rear Admiral Madrid. The two *Tremendous*-class cruisers that will anchor your task force could probably defeat her. She is more than a paper tiger, she is still the third most powerful single warship in the Solar System, but…"

"But she can't fight *Immortal*." Brad sighed. "Which makes *Eternal* her only competition in the system."

"Exactly. And it means that our handful of *Tremendous*-class ships are worth their weight in gold. Fifteen-centimeter mass drivers aren't fifty-centimeter mass drivers, but every system aboard them is a match for *Immortal*'s equivalent."

Immortal just outmassed them by approximately eleven to one.

"Unofficially, you're showing the flag," Orcho told him bluntly. "You're to engage and destroy any OWN force you believe you can defeat, but if the OWN deploys an equal or superior fleet to yours, you are to evacuate the civilians and withdraw from the Saturn system."

"I understand," he said. He didn't *like* it, but he understood. "What about reinforcements?"

"We're still trying to sort out who we can trust, Madrid," she replied. "A goddamn *battleship combat group* defected. Once I have crews and ships I'm certain of, we'll feed them out to you. Saturn won't be our Midway." She grimaced. "But your job is to make sure it isn't our damn Pearl Harbor."

"What about mercenaries?" Brad said.

"The Guild has declared neutrality. Good luck with that."

"The Guild won't take contracts *against* the OWN," he pointed out. "We can hire them to help provide security for the Saturnian stations. It's loophole abuse, but if the OWN moves against Saturn, the Guild can't be neutral.

"They'll probably allow it—and I *do* trust my Vikings."

"If the Guild will allow it, you can hire mercs," Orcho told him. "As many as you can. I'll even explicitly allow hiring your Vikings. That would, I'll note, normally be a conflict of interest you shouldn't engage in."

That thought hadn't even occurred to him and he nodded his acknowledgement. He still owned the Vikings, so hiring them was putting money pretty directly into his own pocket.

"I see that," he conceded. "I wasn't thinking in those terms, I have to admit. I was thinking we could trust them."

"I know. That's why I'll authorize it, this time," Orcho noted. "I wouldn't count on being able to hire them in future, though."

"Understood." Brad took a nervous look at the ocean surrounding them. "In that case, sir, it seems to me that I should be getting to my flagship."

————

Leaving his bag in the visiting officers' quarters had apparently been a near-waste of time. Brad had gone there to drop off his bags and only went back to pick them up.

The process, however, gave the Fleet time to organize his shuttle again. Apparently, someone else had been watching. A small woman with shoulder-length golden hair was waiting for him as he reached the shuttle bay. Despite her Commodore's insignia, she didn't bother to salute.

"Madrid."

"Bailey," he greeted Commodore Angel Bailey carefully. He'd worked with the Commodore off and on for years. "Shouldn't you be aboard a battleship orbiting Mars?"

"I got replaced. Something about a battleship skipper defecting," she snapped. "Any more salt you'd care to pour in that?"

He raised his hands.

"I didn't expect that," he told her. "The question was honest."

She grunted.

"You've got me in more trouble over the years than anyone else I've ever met," she told him. "You've been damn useful, too, but I can't say I'm pleased to see you in a damn *Admiral*'s uniform."

"The new President and I go way back," Brad said. "He asked. I couldn't say no."

"What millstone did they hang around your neck to try and drown you with?" Bailey asked.

Brad laughed.

"Commodore, I've known you for long enough to know that there's no way in Everdark your connections haven't told you what command they've given me. So, why are you ambushing me?"

"Because we're on the same shuttle, Madrid," she replied. "You're going to *Incredible* and then the shuttle is taking about a fifty kilometer hop over to *Bound by Blood*." Bailey shook her head.

"I'm your escort commander," she concluded. "*Sir.*"

The inflection on the *sir* told Brad everything he needed to know about Bailey's opinion of reporting to him.

"Honestly?" he said. "That might be the best news I've had all day."

He grinned as Bailey glared at him.

"We've worked together before, Bailey," he pointed out. "We've done good work. Which means I know how you operate and I know I can trust you. And given the storm of Everdarkened bullshit we're dealing with...that latter means a lot."

"I have no *fucking* clue what they were thinking to make you an Admiral," she told him. "We worked together when you were a glorified spy."

"What they were thinking is that nobody at Jupiter or Saturn is going to trust an Earthborn commander right now," Brad said. "They will trust me. That's the lever Barnes yanked to get me to put on this uniform, and it's the lever I'll yank to get you and whoever my cruiser commander is to follow along.

"You're right. I'm not a Fleet officer. I'm a businessman whose business happens to be leading a destroyer squadron. That means when you raise a concern, I'm going to listen. But."

Brad raised a warning finger at Bailey.

"I'm also in command for a reason. I know the people and the players out there—even better than you do, Commodore. You know Mars. I know Jupiter. I know Saturn. And, curse me to the Everdark, I know the Cadre."

"Things will have changed," she replied. 'They're pretending to be a government now."

"I suspect that's been in the works for as long as you and I have been fighting them," Brad said. "Some things may have changed, yes, but it's the same ships and the same crews. The same knives held to their throats to make them do terrible things."

He shook his head.

"I expect the OWN to fight more cleanly than the Cadre did, but that's a low bar. I don't expect them to fight as cleanly as we'd like. We need to be ready for them to break every rule, every expectation. Most of them are conscripts and draftees—but the rest are pirates that got stuffed into fancy uniforms."

Brad smiled thinly.

"And you and I, Commodore Bailey? We know those pirates. Are you ready to go after them under my command?"

She snorted.

"I didn't need the speech," she told him. "I'm pissed, Madrid, but the people I answer to said you're in charge, so you're in charge." She sighed. "And you're right—it helps that I know I can trust you."

"After the last couple of months, it's nice to know *someone* does," Brad replied. "Come on, Commodore. We're holding up the shuttle."

CHAPTER SEVEN

THE LARGEST VESSEL Brad had ever commanded was the custom-built destroyer *Oath of Vengeance*. *Oath* was a good hundred meters long, packing multiple torpedo tubes, gatling mass drivers and a platoon worth of combat troops.

Incredible put her to shame. Three hundred and fifteen meters long and massing over eighty thousand tons unfueled, the only reason she wasn't going to be the largest ship Brad had ever set foot aboard was because he'd visited Commodore Bailey aboard the battleship *Eternal*.

Incredible had sixty gatling mass drivers and thirty-six torpedo tubes, each equal to their counterpart aboard *Oath of Vengeance*. Unlike *Oath*, however, she also had eight dual fifteen-centimeter heavy mass-driver turrets.

Brad had come into possession of *Bound*-class ships, like Commodore Bailey's new flagship *Bound by Blood*, for his Vikings. They carried *two* of those turrets, making them the deadliest dedicated ship-killers in their weight class.

The two *Tremendous*-class ships could chew up a *Bound* or three apiece and laugh…and both of them were now under Brad's command.

He could see *Tremendous* herself in the distance, a vague round smudge past his flagship. Destroyers and frigates were scattered through the space between the two cruisers. He didn't have a rundown of his lighter warships yet, but he was hoping for as many *Bound* and *Warrior*-class ships as possible.

The *Bound*-class ships were unique, and the *Warrior*s were of the same vintage as the *Tremendous*es, brand-new ships with firepower to spare.

Which meant, of course, that he probably didn't have very many of either. He'd make do.

Linking his wrist-comp into the shuttle's systems, he confirmed that *Oath of Vengeance* herself was orbiting roughly a thousand kilometers away. He'd be able to have a live conversation with Michelle once he was aboard *Incredible*.

Updating her on everything was going to be quite the conversation. He still wasn't entirely sure just how deep the rabbit hole he'd fallen down went, but it at least looked like he was going to fall out the other end on top of some poor Cadre bastards.

"Taking us in to dock," the pilot announced. "Captain Jenci Jahoda is *Incredible*'s commanding officer. I've advised him the flag is coming aboard."

Brad looked over at Bailey.

"How much crap am I in for?" he asked.

She chuckled.

"By *crap* I presume you mean *ceremony*?" she asked sweetly. "Less than you're afraid of, but probably more than you're used to."

"I ran a mercenary company," Brad replied. "What's *ceremony*?"

———

The sound of a computer-generated whistle echoed around the boarding bay as Brad Madrid stepped onto his new flagship. Two files of a dozen Marines apiece snapped to attention, forming a path for him to enter the ship through, and a voice boomed out above him.

"Task Force Seventeen, arriving."

Brad managed to not obviously shake his head as he walked carefully between the two lines of Marines. A tall hawk-faced officer was waiting for him at the end of the file, saluting crisply as Brad approached.

"Welcome aboard *Incredible*, Rear Admiral Madrid," he said. "I am Captain Jenci Jahoda. May I present my executive officer, Alycia Nah?"

The woman next to him was equally tall, with dark skin and noticeably slanted eyes.

"Admiral," she saluted in turn. "Normally, this is where we'd introduce you to *Incredible*'s senior officers and your staff, but Captain Jahoda figured we'd reduce the ceremony."

"And you don't have a staff yet," Jahoda told him. "You have your orders, sir?"

That took Brad aback for a moment, and then he remembered that he'd been handed a paper sheet at some point in the chaos of getting him aboard *Incredible*.

"I think so," he said carefully, then watched his new flag captain manage to *not* roll his eyes too obviously.

"Tradition says you read them into the record of the ship now," the Captain said delicately.

Ceremony.

Brad found the sheet of paper a moment later and unfolded it, the formal words looking strange to him as he scanned them and then looked up at Jahoda. The flag captain gave him an encouraging nod and *Brad* found himself trying not to roll his eyes.

It seemed his new superiors had chosen his flag captain well.

Brad cleared his throat.

"To Rear Admiral Brad Madrid. You are ordered to proceed aboard the cruiser *Incredible* and there hoist your flag as commanding officer of the Commonwealth of the United Nations of Earth Fleet Task Force Seventeen.

"You are charged with the lives and mission of this task force. Fail not in this charge, at your peril.

"Signed, Admiral Violet Orcho."

He folded the paper up again and leveled his gaze on Captain Jahoda.

"I assume command of the task force," he said formally. "Is there anything else I've forgotten, Captain?"

"That will do for now, I suspect," he confirmed. "Would you like a tour of *Incredible*?"

————

By the time the tour was complete and Brad was able to drop himself into the chair in his quarters, he was exhausted. It had been a *long* day. He'd woken up a prisoner, just over thirty hours before.

Now he was a flag officer in the Commonwealth Fleet, in command of a task force being sent to protect Saturn. He didn't even know the full strength of his task force yet—he'd have to follow up with Admiral Orcho once he'd rested.

The quarters they'd stuck him in were disturbingly large to a man raised in space. The rooms were aboard a ship but were probably as large as his and Michelle's luxury apartment in the Io Shipyards.

He had a bedroom, a sitting area, an office—even a formal dining room. It was all rather excessive to his mind, but he supposed a cruiser had more space than a destroyer.

Exhaustion threatened to drag him to sleep on the chair, but he had work to do still. Dragging himself from the chair, he crossed into the office and linked his wrist-comp into its systems. The computer there happily acknowledged his authority.

It promptly proceeded to ask what background he wanted for his office. Shivering in the memory of Admiral Orcho's virtual ocean, he tapped NONE immediately.

Bare steel walls had worked for him for his entire life so far. He didn't need to add to his discomfort with his current position.

His wrist-comp already had the codes to reach out to *Oath of Vengeance* and link directly to Michelle. It took a few seconds for them to process through, and then his wife appeared on the screen.

"*Incredible*, this is Commodore Hunt how can I...*Brad*?"

"I thought the codes would have told you it was me," he said, half-apologetically. "I'm exhausted, I'm sorry."

Michelle glanced down at a screen he couldn't see.

"They did," she admitted. "I just didn't notice. What is going on, Brad?"

"Apparently, I was only a Fleet Commodore for regulation's sake," he told her. "I think I spent a grand total of twelve hours at that rank. They made me an Admiral, love. *Incredible* is my new flagship."

"Everlit," she breathed. "Guess the Vikings aren't getting you back anytime soon?"

"Not directly," he agreed. "Love, I need you to do me a favor. I don't even know who to contact for Guild operations here in Earth orbit, but I'm authorized to contract for mercenary space forces."

"We're not allowed to get involved in the war," she pointed out.

"I'm not hiring anyone to," Brad told her. "I'm hiring mercenary companies to provide security for Blackhawk Station and the other Saturn facilities."

Before they'd met, Michelle Hunt had commanded one of the diving ships at Blackhawk that entered Jupiter to steal the denser gases lower in the planet's atmosphere.

They'd survived the Cadre attack on the station, too. Brad had lost an arm there, and his regenerated limb still bothered him some days.

"If the OWN attacks, we'd be required to defend, even though we can't take contracts specifically against them," Michelle said aloud. "Clever. I'm pretty sure we have a factor somewhere in Earth orbit; I'll run down the contact information."

She studied his face.

"Have you slept?" she demanded.

"Not since President Barnes woke me up," Brad admitted. "That's where I'm headed next. But I needed to talk to you, both for work and for...personal."

She smiled.

"I'm okay, Brad," she told him. "I'll be *better* if we can steal some time together before you head off to Saturn."

"I'm explicitly authorized to recruit the Vikings, so I plan on bringing *Oath* with us," Brad replied. "I figure we can sort out *some* time together along the way."

Michelle laughed.

"We're probably smart enough for that. Go rest, my love. We'll talk once you've slept."

"All right," Brad conceded. "Take care of my people, hey? I trust you—that's why you're Commodore—but you'll allow me some worrying, right?"

"Go sleep," she repeated with another laugh. "I've got the Vikings in hand. You worry about Fleet."

CHAPTER EIGHT

INCREDIBLE'S FLAG deck was unlike anything Brad had ever seen. He'd been aboard Fleet cruisers before. He'd even been on their regular bridges, but he'd never set foot on the flag deck of a Fleet warship.

He commanded the Vikings from a glorified observer seat on *Oath of Vengeance*'s bridge, using the destroyer's regular command systems to control the small squadron.

That wouldn't work for Task Force Seventeen, and he now sat in the midst of the most advanced command-and-control systems ever devised by human minds. His chair was surrounded by screens, allowing him to check in on any ship of his command or any function he wanted at any point.

A dozen technicians and analysts worked at consoles around him. He had the access and the power to check every detail of every ship of his command, and he could already see how that could get tempting.

It was awe-inspiring enough just to look at the status reports.

Three cruisers. Twelve destroyers—four each of the *Bound* and *Warrior* classes he'd hoped for, plus four older ships. Twenty corvettes and frigates.

None of the corvettes or frigates were new ships, but he had six of the most modern warships the Commonwealth Fleet possessed. They'd done fairly by him and his mission.

And as for adding to those forces, that was what the old man on his communications screen was about.

"We both know you're playing games with the Guild's restriction," Factor Davis Anderson said bluntly. "We are not allowed to get involved between the Commonwealth and the Outer Worlds."

"I'm not asking you to," Brad said patiently. "I'm trying to hire several companies, including one I *own*, to assist in providing security for the Saturnian extraction operations. My own mission is the security of the Saturn System, nothing more.

"I have no authorization or intention of waging offensive operations." He shook his head. "I'm not going to pretend the Commonwealth doesn't regard itself as being at war, but we have recognized the Guild's decision to remain neutral."

"And if the Outer Worlds were to attack, would you expect your mercenaries to stand aside?" Anderson asked.

"Would the Guild truly want that of its people?" Brad asked gently. "I'm not asking anyone to fight a war for the Commonwealth, Factor. I'm just trying to contract additional security for Saturn.

"If the OWN attacks Saturn…do you really think the Guild is going to *stay* neutral?"

The Factor chuckled bitterly.

"You're not wrong and your contract is not in violation of the new restrictions," he admitted. "My records say that Commodore Michelle Hunt now commands the Vikings? I presume you've spoken to her already?"

"I have," Brad confirmed.

"I'll forward contract details to her. I'll touch base with home office to see what else I can find you. I'm assuming you want primarily spaceborne units, destroyers and the like?"

"If I thought there was a mercenary company out there with a cruiser, I'd offer them more money than I think exists," the newly fledged Admiral said with a grin. "I'll take anyone you can get with destroyers. If the Guild can pull together a dozen destroyers and some lighter ships, we'll pay Platinum rates for all of them."

"I understand that *Oath of Protection* and *Oath of Vigilance* should be online by the time you reach Saturn," Anderson noted. "The Vikings alone make up half that number."

"And are a Platinum company," Brad agreed. "The other restriction is that they need to be able to meet me at Mars in twelve days."

"Mars, Admiral?"

"It's closer to on the way than Jupiter is," Brad pointed out. The "geography" of the star system was predictable, at least, if not consistent. "I know the Vikings can make it. I'll take whatever the Guild can get there by that timeline."

"They won't be able to engage the OWN, Admiral," Anderson reminded him.

"If the OWN doesn't attack Saturn, I won't even want them to," Brad replied. "If the OWN actually decides to open this war, well, then a lot of things change."

"The Guild officially has no position on the conflict between the Outer Worlds Alliance and the Commonwealth," the Factor said formally. "For myself, however…good luck, Admiral. May the Everlit guide your way."

―――――

"Commodore Nuremberg," Brad greeted his cruiser commander. "It's a pleasure to meet you again."

Tremendous had shown up to perform "cleanup" after one of the more noticeable clashes between Brad and the Independence Militia. He'd destroyed three cruisers with a handful of destroyers and a stolen drone carrier, and Commodore Iris Nuremberg had come in with fire in her eyes.

He'd talked her down then, and now the heavyset older woman reported to him. The world moved in mysterious ways.

"Likewise, Admiral Madrid," she told him. "It's a small Solar System, isn't it?"

Brad nodded and gestured to the other two women on the video-conference.

"I believe you know Commodore Bailey and Commodore Hunt?" he asked Nuremberg.

"I met Commodore Hunt when I met you," she confirmed. "Bailey and I know each other."

From the way the two women regarded each other, she was as fond of Angel Bailey as anyone was. No one would begrudge Bailey's competence, but she didn't seem to make very many *friends*.

"Currently, Commodore Hunt is only directly commanding one ship," Brad noted. "We will be rendezvousing with the rest of the Vikings at Mars and hopefully several more mercenary companies' worth of ships.

"Given the Guild's position on the current situation, Commodore Hunt's command will be entirely defensive. The mercenaries' role will be to provide security for the Saturnian stations while we scout the area and watch for OWN incursions.

"If the Outer Worlds is as peaceful as they have promised, then we're going to be very bored and the mercenaries are going to make a great deal of money for nothing," he concluded. "If anyone on this call thinks that's actually going to happen, let me shatter your illusions."

He tapped a command, bringing up the image of Jack Mantruso.

"This is Lord Protector Jack Mantruso," he said, unnecessarily. "Today, at least. In the past, he went by the name Jack Mader as he worked as a Cadre deep-cover operative on Jupiter. After that, he was better known to most as the Phoenix.

"While the Outer Worlds Alliance talks a good game, they are simply the latest iteration of the Cadre," Brad concluded. "Mantruso told me himself that his goal was to conquer the Solar System, to make himself emperor of mankind.

"We won't let that happen."

"Why in Everdark was Mantruso telling you that?" Bailey asked.

"He wanted me to join him," Brad said quietly. "Despite every-thing, I think he wanted to avoid having to kill his brother."

The call was silent.

"What. The. Fuck."

Bailey's words were harsh, but they summed up Brad's own opinion of the situation.

"He worked it out about the same time as the Agency did," Brad told the Commodores. Michelle already knew. The others, it seemed, hadn't been briefed. "Jack Mantruso was born to seal an underworld alliance.

"My birth name was Brad Mantruso. I was apparently born after our parents actually fell in love. When my parents died aboard *Black Skull*, my father's brother apparently kidnapped me to get me out of the Cadre's clutches."

Brad shook his head.

"Believe me, it's quite a shock to find out that the criminal and terrorist organization you've spent your adult life fighting is the Ever-darkened *family business*. It doesn't change anything in the end, though. Mantruso won't stop until he's emperor or he's dead."

"*Our* job is to make sure it's the latter."

CHAPTER NINE

TWELVE DAYS in space was normally a chance to relax, to catch up on paperwork while keeping an eye on what was going on in the Solar System.

This time, however, Brad's every waking hour had been consumed by everything from learning just what Fleet paperwork even *looked* like to negotiating with the Mercenary Guild by recorded messages to, thank the Everlit, spending time with Michelle when he'd managed to bring her aboard the flagship.

"It's mostly the lack of Platinum ratings that's bothering me," she admitted to him as she went over the latest transmission from the Guild. If the mercenary Commodore was looking at that transmission naked in the Admiral's bed, well, no one had any illusions about Brad's relationship with the Vikings in general and Michelle in particular.

"Getting a Platinum rating is *hard*," he pointed out. "A minimum of fifteen contracts in a row with no complaints, plus at least forty contracts with no more than two complaints overall. Plus, you have to demonstrate a level of professionalism the Guild is willing to declare top-tier. *Plus,* all of your officers have to pass exams, *plus* you have to pay more money."

"You got a Platinum rating while flying a single corvette," she replied. "These guys have *destroyers*."

"And aren't willing to hand over an additional four percent of their contract revenue to the Guild," Brad countered. "I *needed* that stamp of approval. The Goldmisers and Harding's Guardians? They don't."

The Goldmiser mercenary fleet had actually *been* in Mars orbit, which made Brad's life much easier. The Gold-rated mercenary corporation was one of the few that actually mustered a heavier space fleet than his own Vikings at this point.

Six destroyers, older ships but still potent, plus four brand-spanking-new corvettes. Brad had never met the Commodore commanding that fleet, but he knew the woman's reputation as a problem child. Competent as all Everlit but hard to deal with.

There were more reasons than one that the Goldmisers weren't rated Platinum.

Harding's Guardians, on the other hand, only had two destroyers. They fielded six heavy corvettes, though, the biggest that Fleet had ever built of that class.

Harding was a giant question mark. The Guardians weren't Platinum because they hadn't completed forty contracts at all, let alone without complaint. They'd come into existence during the fleet downsizing a couple of years before when a slew of ex-Fleet officers had been looking for work.

They'd found a backer in the reprobate son of a Martian merchant dynasty. The Harding family had underwritten James Harding's mercenary company to be rid of the man, so far as Brad could tell. His kin had probably been pleasantly surprised by their return on that investment.

"Both the Goldmisers and the Guardians are Gold-rated, field destroyers and are reputed to be competent and capable," Brad continued. "If Sonja Gold is an abrasive bitch and James Harding is a remittance man who got lucky, well...my brother is the Lord Protector of the OWA."

"I can't throw too many stones from my glass spaceship."

Michelle snorted at him.

"They also are either at Mars or will be there within twenty-four hours of our arrival," she agreed. "That's worth a lot on its own. The Vikings will be there almost the same time as us. That's six more destroyers, and *I* wouldn't want to get on the wrong side of the two new *Oaths*."

Brad shook his head.

"I hate standing back and letting others run the company," he admitted. "I *trust* you—and Saburo and Brenda and the others—but damned if it still isn't hard."

"Shelly's in command of the deployment," Michelle told him. "Finally got her out of the office and onto a command deck. Gave her *Oath of Vigilance*."

Shelly Weldon had been Brad's navigator when the company had started. Her husband had been his original tactical officer, but *he'd* died when the ship Brad had given them command of had been destroyed.

Shelly had spent the time since running the Vikings' administration on Io. Brad had promised her one of the *Oaths* if she wanted it, but she'd been unsure for a long time. He was glad to hear she'd taken the ship.

"That'll give us an extra fourteen destroyers and ten corvettes," he concluded. "Thirteen destroyers, I guess, since *Oath of Vengeance* is already here."

That would double his destroyers to twenty-six and bring his corvettes and frigates to thirty ships. It would be quite a fleet he'd be taking to Saturn, even if half of it was technically forbidden from engaging the OWA.

The Guild had proven surprisingly willing to codify the loophole he'd chased, though. The companies he'd contracted were not permitted to be deployed against the Outer Worlds Navy...but they were explicitly contracted to defend the space stations at Saturn against *any* enemy.

"We're close enough to Mars I should probably get back to *Oath of Vengeance*," Michelle said regretfully. "Let you focus on your job and me focus on mine."

"I know," he told her. "I've already traded some messages with Admiral Weber. We haven't solidified numbers yet, but it's not just mercenaries we'll be picking up at Mars."

"Good. I'm having nightmares about trying to take down a battle-ship with this fleet," she admitted. "*Immortal*'s defection really messed everything up.

"I know," he told her. "I'd poach *Eternal* if I thought that was remotely possible, but there's no way the Fleet will uncover Earth or Mars now."

"Everyone's afraid." Michelle shook her head and kissed him fiercely. "It's your job to make them feel safe again, right, Admiral?"

Brad returned the kiss but sighed.

"Somehow," he agreed. "I still can't believe where I am or what I'm doing, but…we'll make it work."

"*You'll* make it work," she told him. "I know you will. And the Vikings will be with you the whole way, regardless of whose uniform you're wearing."

"Speaking of which, you should probably put *on* a uniform if you're planning on making it out of here," Brad pointed out as he gently embraced her.

"Oh, I was thinking I could take a *bit* longer," she said with a teasing grin.

———

As the distance to Mars continued to shrink, Brad returned to *Incredible*'s flag deck to study the information available to him. His fleet was currently decelerating, fusion thrusters flaring brightly as they followed a course that would slot them neatly into high orbit.

They'd be under the guns of Deimos, the outermost moon having long since been repurposed as the linchpin of the Martian defenses. There were no civilians on the tiny moon, only a small army of Fleet personnel who manned the big mass drivers that stood guard over the still-terraforming world below.

Deimos was the centerpoint, the only place in the planetary system with fixed fifty-centimeter mass drivers, but it was far from the only defenses Mars commanded. They were intermingled with the civilian platforms, almost hidden to the casual observer.

In fact, as Brad reviewed the Fleet files, he realized that many were hidden to the professional observer. He'd recognized many of the forts and weapons platforms when he'd visited Mars before, but the Fleet files told him he'd missed at least a third of them.

Mars was, in many ways, more heavily defended than Earth itself. It was certainly more *vulnerable* and there was less question of the Commonwealth's authority there. Earth's defenses were more patchwork, many still operating under the authority of the homeworld's nations.

The Martian defenses were a unified command with the defending squadron under Admiral Weber, led by *Eternal* herself. Brad's own fleet would melt like a snowball in a blast furnace if he were to challenge Mars's defenses.

It was reassuring to know that the core of the Commonwealth was secure, for now at least. He had no illusions about what would happen if Jupiter and Saturn fell, however.

The effective range of a mass driver was a few tens of thousands of kilometers at best, but that was based on active radar and ships' ability to dodge. Stations and moons didn't dodge.

Long-range mass-driver fire could gut the defenses of Mars. The collateral damage would be unimaginable, but Brad was grimly certain that Jack Mantruso would gleefully accept it.

If the OWN acquired the fueling infrastructure to deploy its full fleet against Mars, Mars would fall. Until then, however, the planet was as secure as anywhere in the star system. That was part of the argument that Brad had used to convince Admiral Weber to hand over ships to him.

The Martian Squadron was secure and supported. Task Force Seventeen was heading right to what was about to become the front lines.

"Sir." The channel to the bridge drew Brad's attention as Captain Jahoda opened a video link.

"Captain."

"Our ETA is just over twenty-four hours," the cruiser's captain told him. "We're close enough for functionally real-time communication if you need to talk to anyone."

Brad chuckled.

"I can do that math on my own, Captain," he pointed out. "I did live out here."

Jahoda winced.

"Apologies, sir. I'm used to Admirals who haven't left Earth orbit. Ever."

"That's not the best structure, I have to admit," Brad murmured.

"We've got a few space-born Commodores, but everyone higher… they're from Earth, sir. We are Earth's Commonwealth, after all."

Brad shook his head as he eyed the screens.

"I'd say that would come back to bite us, but I think it already has," he said. "No one past the Belt wants to trust the Commonwealth. It's why Mantruso succeeded in putting together his empire and why Jupiter and the Guild are trying to be neutral."

Jahoda was silent for several seconds.

"I can't say for sure, sir," he admitted. "I'm from Warsaw, on Earth. I've served on Mars, but once we head past there, it'll be the furthest I've ever been from Earth."

That would be somewhat unusual for a cruiser captain, as Brad understood it, but not entirely out of the question. Which, of course, was why the Commonwealth was in the trouble it was in.

"That might be something we'll want to look at once this is over," he said aloud. "Maybe even make sure every captain does a tour out beyond the Belt."

"That makes sense to me, sir," Jahoda confessed. "Right now, though, I'm just glad to see Mars looking hale and hearty as ever. *Eternal* and her sisters are always a sight for sore eyes."

Brad chuckled bitterly and was about to make a comment about *Immortal* when a data tag flashed up on *Eternal*'s icon on his screen.

"What the Everda—"

The sudden spike of radiation had drawn the attention of *Incredible*'s sensors as well as her Admiral, which meant that Brad had a perfect view as the Commonwealth battleship *Eternal* exploded.

CHAPTER TEN

INCREDIBLE'S BRIDGE and flag deck were shocked to silence for several seconds, then Brad swallowed.

"Captain Jahoda, get your tactical team on that right now, if you please," he ordered gently. "I need to know what happened to *Eternal*."

He turned to his own staff, a set of officers and analysts he barely knew the names of.

"Lieutenant Commander Abelli, please start working up a course to get the task force into Mars orbit as much faster as reasonably possible," he told Lieutenant Commander Wawatam Abelli, the task force operations officer. The young dark-haired man from North America got to work instantly.

"Lieutenant Commander Walter, get the rest of the task force on the coms and take us to full stealth," he continued, turning his attention to Lieutenant Nikolaj Walter, the task force systems officer. The blond German officer nodded and grabbed his headset.

"Lieutenant Commander Werner." He turned to the only woman among his three staff officers. Jan Werner handled logistics and coms for him, both of which had changed the rules on him. "Coordinate with…whoever is in charge now. I need to know we can still restock and refuel without interruption. If you can get us a sensor feed from the Deimos Array, that could buy us some more data."

All three of his officers were head-down in their consoles and conversations with their staff in moments, and he turned his attention back to Jahoda.

"Stealth mode, if you please, Captain," he said quietly.

"Already engaging," Jahoda told him. "We won't hide much. We've been visible to anyone who wanted to look for days. Adjusting our course will help but also makes us easier to detect."

The stealth mode on a modern fleet ship—or *Oath of Vengeance*, for that matter—had three components. The first was that the hulls of the ships were already coated in radar-absorbing paint and designed for low radar profiles. The difficulty in targeting with radar and lidar was part of why the effective range of their weapons was so low.

The second aspect was a series of heat sinks that could absorb *almost* all of the ships' heat production for up to twenty-four hours. More could be gained by using the third aspect and directionally venting heat at an angle you knew to be safe.

It wasn't perfect, but neither were the sensors available to them or their enemies. With them still over thirty hours' regular flight from Mars, it would hide them from anyone who wasn't looking right at them.

"What in Everdark is going on, Captain?" Brad asked grimly. "That looked like a fusion core overload."

"It wasn't," *Incredible*'s Captain replied. "We're still validating, but it looks like bombs. Fusion warheads in the fifty-megaton range, at least four of them."

"Someone snuck thermonuclear weapons aboard a battleship?" he asked.

"Yes, sir."

"Confirm that, Captain," Brad snapped. "Werner, get me the Commodores. Including Hunt, if you please."

He turned back to Jahoda.

"Keep me updated on what you…"

"*Weapons fire!*" someone on the bridge yelled, and Brad swallowed as he turned his attention back to the tactical display.

"Who's shooting?" he demanded.

There was silence on the channel as the computers calmly drew in what they could detect and resolve. No hostile icons were being added to the display, no one in Brad's task force was picking up enemy ships…but Fleet vessels were disappearing.

"Fleet is, sir," Jahoda said very, very quietly. "Multiple vessels have opened fire on the rest of the Fleet ships in orbit."

Brad was silent for a long time.

"Sir?" Werner finally said behind him. "I have the Commodores for you."

He swallowed and nodded.

"I'll take it in my office," he told her. "Keep me in the loop as soon as we know *anything*, Captain Jahoda."

————

The three women on the wallscreen in Brad's office looked various degrees of shaken. The worst was Commodore Bailey. No real surprise there, given that her previous command had just gone up in a giant ball of fire.

"Someone snuck four nukes aboard *Eternal*," Brad told them flatly. "The only reason my first guess isn't the Cadre is because the Cadre is now, apparently, Outer Worlds Intelligence."

"Same murderous fuckheads, different business cards," Bailey said harshly. "And what the *fuck* are we doing about it?"

"Right now, trying to work out what in Everdark is going on," he replied. "The last scans I saw showed the Martian Squadron opening fire on each other. I have no idea what's going on in Mars's orbit, and I'm hesitant to take this task force into it until I *do* know."

"You know these people better than any of us, Bailey," Nuremberg said. "Any clues?"

"Cadre infiltrators," *Eternal*'s former commander told them. "Or OWI, whatever we want to call them. They always did a surprisingly good job of finding the people who could be blackmailed or bought—it's where their bloody 'Independence Militia' came from."

"And since we now know they'd have had full access to the Fleet's personnel records through the Secret Service, that makes more sense than it used to," Brad said grimly. "But still, enough infiltrators to turn half of the Martian Squadron on the other half?"

"Get the right hands in the right places and you can sneak an assault force aboard any ship," Michelle pointed out. "Even a cruiser can be taken by as little as a platoon if they have surprise and proper prep."

"What about the fixed defenses?" Nuremberg demanded. "They should be doing something!"

"Doing what?" Brad asked. "For that matter, what could we do if we were there? Do you have a way to tell who are the mutineers and who are the loyalists?"

The videoconference was silent.

His wrist-comp pinged.

"Madrid," he answered.

"Sir, we have Deimos Command for you," Werner told him. "Should I hold them until you're done?"

"No," he replied. "Keep the Commodores on the line, but don't let Deimos Command know they're listening in. Then patch them through."

He turned to the women already on the call.

"Bailey, if whoever is on this call isn't who they're supposed to be, let me know ASAP," he ordered. "If I have to take Deimos and the orbital defenses away from the Cadre, this war just got a *lot* uglier."

All three women slid to the side of the screen, and the image of a command center appeared in his screen. There was a strong resemblance to *Incredible*'s flag deck, but the room was built with more space and more responsibilities.

"This is Commodore Talgat Saltanat at Deimos Command," a swarthy and broad-shouldered man greeted him. "Rear Admiral Madrid, thank the Everlit you're here."

"We're still almost thirty hours away, Commodore," Brad pointed out. "I don't think I'm doing much more than cleanup. What in Everdark is going on?"

"I don't know for certain, but a number of our crews appear to have mutinied and seized their ships," Saltanat told him. "From what I can tell, our loyalists have the numerical edge, but fighting continues on half the ships that are still under our control."

"Can you identify the mutineers?" Brad demanded.

"Some of the ships, at least," the Commodore confirmed. "The loyalists are still in my tactical net, but that net would block any attempt to fire at a Fleet vessel without counter-authorization from here. The mutineers had to cut free to launch their attack."

So, there was no guarantee that the ships *in* the network were loyal, but everyone who'd cut themselves off was a mutineer.

"Are you going to engage with the fixed defenses, Commodore?" Brad asked gently.

Saltanat winced as if struck, then sighed.

"I was trying to avoid that, sir," he admitted.

Brad glanced over at Bailey's image, and the blonde Commodore gave him a grim thumbs-up.

"My authority, Commodore Saltanat," Brad said grimly. "Summon any ship that's severed themselves from the tactical network to surrender. You are to engage and destroy any that refuse; do you understand?"

He swallowed, and then slowly bowed his head.

"I understand, Admiral Madrid."

————

The only reason the mutiny had lasted even this long was because it had taken time to identify which ships were a problem—and then because Commodore Saltanat had hesitated.

Brad could understand that—even the ships that were apparently entirely in enemy control almost certainly had prisoners aboard—but there was no way they could rescue those people.

Saltanat controlled more firepower from that one room on Deimos than the rest of the Martian Squadron combined now that *Eternal* was gone. His surrender demand alone should have been enough to end the fighting.

It wasn't.

Brad was keeping track as the message went out. It was received. And the fighting continued. Another destroyer cut itself from the tactical network even as Saltanat's message was arriving, firing into a sister ship at point-blank range.

Every second was costing lives and Brad responded to the Commodore's pained look with a simple nod.

And then nothing happened.

"Commodore?" he asked.

"We're trying, Admiral," Saltanat told him. "We got weapons lock and then...nothing. Our systems are refusing to engage. We've lost our sensor locks and none of our remote weapons are responding at all."

The Commodore winced.

"Nothing on Deimos is reporting in, either. It's like our entire weapons control software just wiped itself."

"That's entirely possible," Brad said grimly. "Find out, Commodore. Get your weapons back online."

He looked at his people as he muted the link to Deimos.

"I'm guessing everything looks intact?" he asked.

"Looks it," Bailey confirmed. "I don't know how far I trust that little—"

"Every sensor in the defensive network went down as he was trying to fire," Nuremberg told them. "He's not lying. Someone had a time bomb ticking away in Deimos Command's software."

"Blackhawk," Michelle breathed.

Brad nodded as he met his wife's eyes.

"I don't know if you two are familiar with the Battle of Blackhawk Station," he said to the two Fleet Commodores. "The Cadre used a virus to disable the Station's fixed defenses, allowing them to send in a force that was almost entirely landing ships rather than the warships they'd have needed to break through."

"More than that," Michelle pointed out. "That was their backup plan, Brad—Admiral."

It hit him like a ton of bricks.

"Everlit preserve us," he murmured.

"Admiral?" Nuremberg demanded.

"At Blackhawk Station, the Cadre used the virus to hide an approaching fleet. Disabling the defenses was the second string to their bow. The first string was getting in undetected in the first place."

The conference was silent.

"Fuck stealth," Brad finally swore grimly. "Every ship goes active with every sensor they've got. If there's a ship within a goddamn *light-minute* of Mars, I want to know about it *yesterday*."

———

The result didn't surprise him when it came in. There would be questions later around how the Outer Worlds Navy had pulled it off, where they'd refueled, how they'd got them even that close without being detected, but it was no surprise when they found the fleet.

"Forty-eight bogeys on course for Mars," Jahoda reported to the flag conference call grimly. "Still breaking down classes, but we've got at least four that are either cruisers or carriers.

"They're maybe twenty hours out. I'm betting they were counting on the fixed defenses' problem not being noticed for a while yet."

"I'm not," Brad said grimly. "Assume that the fixed defenses won't be online for at least twenty-four hours. The Martian Squadron will have smashed themselves to pieces by then. What can they do?"

"They can't take Mars," Bailey said flatly. "Not without a few hundred thousand troops, and that flotilla isn't big enough for that. They *could* wreck the fixed defenses before they come back online or…"

"Or they could punch through whatever's left of the Martian Squadrons and whatever's online of the orbital defenses and land on Deimos," Brad pointed out. "There's, what, a thousand Marines on the moon?"

"If even," Bailey told him. "Everlit, Madrid…"

"And if they take control of the orbital defenses, they might not control Mars tomorrow…but no one else will be able to relieve Mars in time to change anything," Brad concluded. "I don't see many options on our side, do you?"

Silence answered him.

"Get your navigation departments talking to each other," Brad ordered. "I want us on a course that will intercept the bastards short of Mars in ten minutes.

"Understood?"

CHAPTER ELEVEN

THERE WAS no subtlety available to Task Force Seventeen now. To intercept the Outer Worlds force before they reach Mars, the Fleet force had to accelerate at maximum.

Brad studied the vectors as they moved, and shook his head. They'd have bare *minutes* in weapons range of the enemy force. He had enough of an advantage in firepower and tonnage to make that a winning proposition, but it still meant that Mars was vulnerable.

It would take him an extra day to get into Mars orbit after the fight, but the OWN fleet would be there six hours after they clashed. That eighteen-hour gap worried him.

"If we can't take them out in the firing pass, the Martian Squadron is going to have to deal with them alone," Michelle told him quietly.

They had a private channel in the middle of the battle preparations. Brad was now at the point where it was down to his subordinates to execute his orders, and Michelle had one ship. *Oath of Vengeance* could fight above her weight class, but she didn't require that much attention from her Commodore in the hours before a battle.

"We should be able to do enough damage to let the Squadron handle the leftovers," he told her. "We can't count on Deimos

Command to get the remote platforms back online, but I expect the Commodore to get *Deimos's* guns in action."

He smiled coldly.

"I wouldn't want to tangle with those mass drivers, and I'm perfectly happy to let the OWN throw themselves at them."

"That's still a risk," Michelle said quietly. "There is another option."

He looked at the screen she was on and at the mercenary warship behind her. The back wall of *Oath of Vengeance*'s bridge was emblazoned with a larger-than-life-sized mural of a Viking warrior: Vidar, the old Norse silent god of vengeance.

The symbol of his mercenary company.

"Where are the Vikings?" he asked. "What about the Goldmisers and Harding's people?"

His wife grinned.

"Vikings can get to Mars about two hours before the OWN flotilla will," she told him. "Harding's Guardians are coming in from a different angle; they'll get there earlier. Our Vikings could actually come into *our* little scuffle if we asked them to."

"We can't," Brad replied. "We've been playing fast and loose with loopholes already. I can't order the Vikings to directly engage an Outer Worlds force." He sighed. "I probably should order *Oath of Vengeance* out of the line, for that matter."

"Anyone wants to tell me I shouldn't go into battle alongside my husband can go fuck themselves," she said harshly.

"The Guild isn't any more sure of who the bad guys are in Mars orbit than we are," she continued after a moment. "Doesn't help that Commodore Saltanat ordered a full lockdown of civilian shipping to keep the situation under control. The Goldmisers can't leave dock without violating a Fleet order."

Brad considered the situation. Those extra destroyers could save Mars, but the Guild was still officially neutral. On the other hand, it would still be almost six hours before the two fleets opened fire on each other.

"I think I need to talk to Factor Kernsky," he said aloud. Sara Kernsky was an old friend of his, the Guild Factor who'd first brought him into the Guild…and now a senior Guild Factor on Mars.

"You should have her contact information," Michelle told him. "I'll forward it over anyway. Just to make sure they haven't changed it on us."

"Thanks, my love," Brad said. "As usual, you're the clever one."

She was still laughing when she closed the channel to let him call Mars.

———

Brad knew Mercenary Guild protocol well enough by now to know that the number he'd been given *should* have connected him to a receptionist. It would have been Sara's own receptionist, a trained bodyguard and security professional trusted to screen the Factor's calls, but it shouldn't have put him directly through to her.

Instead of the receptionist, however, the screen instantly connected to a luxurious but windowless office. It was prestige on Mars to be deeper into the underground tunnels, and the Guild was nothing if not prestigious, after all.

The walls were bare stone but had been worked into a series of friezes around bookshelves carved from actual wood. Like the office on Ganymede where he'd met her years before, this space spoke clearly, if silently, of the wealth and power of the Mercenary Guild.

The redheaded woman behind the solid wood desk had aged a bit since they'd last met. There were streaks of silver visible in her hair now, but she was still just as bright-eyed and beautiful as she'd been the first time they'd met.

"Brad," she greeted him. "I was expecting you to call sooner or later."

There was enough distance between Task Force Seventeen and Mars to build a few seconds of delay into the call. Not enough to interrupt a live conversation, just enough to be noticed.

"It's nice to know that being a Fleet Admiral hasn't made me any less predictable," he said. "I see the Guild is treating you well."

"It's a living, especially if you don't care which particular rock you're living on," Kernsky agreed. "Much as I'd love to catch up over a bottle of wine, I can't imagine this is a social call...*Admiral*."

Brad's own video feed would be showing *Incredible*'s flag deck, swarming with personnel as Brad's orders were being carried out.

"It's not. I need an exception to the Guild's neutrality policy," he said calmly. "The Goldmisers are locked down in orbit by a Fleet order that I can overrule. The Vikings are a few hours out, as are Harding's Guardians. All three of those companies were supposed to accompany me to Saturn.

"Now I need them to defend Mars, but there's no loopholes or games I'm willing to play, Sara," he told her. "In six hours, the Fleet will engage the Outer Worlds Navy flotilla heading for Mars.

"They can't evade us, but we don't have enough of an edge to guarantee their destruction or surrender. The survivors of their force are going to reach Mars, Sara. And the Martian Squadron is tearing itself apart."

He shook his head grimly.

"That mess will be over soon enough, I hope, but the Squadron won't be in a position to defend Mars, and the fixed defenses have been disabled.

"I need to contract with the Guild, with any ships you have at Mars or that can get to Mars in the next few hours, to engage and drive off whatever remains of the Outer Worlds force."

Sara was silent for a few seconds.

"I can't authorize that," she finally said. "An overriding contract requires at least four director-level Factors, Brad."

He blinked.

"I'm not asking for an overriding contract, Sara," he pointed out. "Just the authorization to hire Guild companies to specifically defend Mars against the OWA when the Guild's formal policy is not to take contracts in this war."

"Brad...the OWA just attacked Mars. That neutrality policy isn't going to last out the fucking *day*," she told him. "An overriding contract will be harder, but authority to hire Guild companies to engage the OWN? You've got it.

"I thought you wanted to commandeer the entire Guild, like we did against *Black Skull*."

Brad chuckled. There wasn't a lot of humor to it, but it was honest.

That whole story had an entirely different meaning for him now that he knew his *parents* had died aboard the pirate cruiser.

It was an ugly mess.

"I might still," he told her. "But right now, I just want to post an open contract for mercenary ship companies to engage the OWN in defense of Mars. Can I do that?"

"Yes." Sara appeared to look past Brad's shoulder and smiled. "I was going to say have your staff draft one and send it over, but they look busy. I'll have *my* staff send you something for your approval in the next twenty minutes, and *I'll* start calling everyone with a damn spaceship near Mars.

"Got a budget, Admiral?"

"Sure. What's Mars's GDP again?" Brad asked bluntly. "Platinum rates for anyone willing to engage the OWN. Mars will not fall."

"We'll back you up, Admiral. You have my word."

————

A quick text message later and he confirmed that the Goldmisers were free. He wasn't contracting them to get involved in the ongoing mutiny, but getting them into space was a good starting point.

"Well, *that* certainly had an effect," Werner noted a few minutes later.

"Would you care to share, Lieutenant Commander?" Brad asked delicately.

"Your orders broke free the merc companies in orbit. Went from just the Fleet duking it out with each other to six destroyers and eight corvettes jumping out. I don't know if they were supposed to get involved in the mutiny, but, well…"

Werner put a recorded message on Brad's screen.

The woman in it kept her head shaved to show an intricate abstract tattoo that started at the base of her neck and encompassed her entire head. There was no specific image in the swirling lines of blue and gold ink, but Brad suspected most people *still* found it intimidating.

"Fleet mutineers, this is Commodore Sonja Gold of the Goldmisers," the tattooed woman barked in a slow accent. "I don't know what your bullshit is, and I don't care. The next ship that fires on a Fleet vessel inside my range envelope finds out why everyone is scared of me; am I clear?

"Any of you want to live through this bullshit, cut your engines and transmit your surrenders. I'll leave cleanup to your own damn Marines, but fuck with me or fuck with Mars and you'll meet my mass drivers."

Brad snorted.

"If I wasn't married, I think I might have just fallen in love," he said aloud. "Any takers on her offer?"

"Surprisingly, yes," Werner told him. "Looks like a bunch of mutinying destroyers and corvettes in her line of fire are standing down."

An explosion marked Brad's screen and he quickly checked.

Someone had decided to test Sonja Gold's resolve. A Fleet destroyer had already been in the process of an attack run on a badly damaged cruiser, and her captain had decided to finish the job. Eight torpedoes flashed toward the cruiser, more than enough to finish her off.

Gold's people had been watching, however, and a curtain of mass-driver fire filled the space between the two ships. None of the mutineer's torpedoes survived—and by the time the last one had died, a dozen mercenary torpedoes had caught up with the mutineer destroyer.

Mixed in with a storm of gatling mass-driver fire, the destroyer's defenses were overwhelmed and she came apart in a ball of fire.

"More surrender signals," Werner concluded. "It looks like about a third of the mutineers near Gold just laid down their arms. The rest are getting a sharp lesson in how much more experienced mercenary ships are than most of the Fleet."

"I'd feel better if the cruisers weren't busy duking it out above Mars's north pole," Brad replied. Gold was able to intimidate the lighter ships, but four of the Martian Squadron's cruisers had established a mutineer formation above the ice cap and were in a close engagement with five loyalist ships.

The mutineers had started the fight, giving them enough of a surprise to help even the odds. Brad didn't expect them to *win*, but it was also clear there weren't going to be many functional cruisers left from the Martian Squadron when this was over.

The most important result from that for *him* right now was that he couldn't let any of the heavier ships from the OWN flotilla make it through. The mercenaries could fight off destroyers and lighter ships, but even a single cruiser or carrier could devastate the forces in Martian orbit.

The Commonwealth was winning this mess...but if Brad wasn't careful, that victory could end being even more Pyrrhic than it was already looking.

CHAPTER TWELVE

"WELL, that answers the question of whether or not any of the big boys are carriers," Brad noted calmly as a swarm of new icons speckled his display. "Do we have a number on the drones?"

The Commonwealth Fleet had tried, *hard*, to keep the existence of the drone carrier program secret. There was a lot of concern around the idea of even semi-autonomous weapons platforms, and the drones ran their own heuristic AIs.

Unfortunately for that secrecy, the people who'd built eight of the ships for the Commonwealth had proceeded to build an unknown number of them for the Independence Militia, which meant that the Outer Worlds Navy had them.

"We've got sixty Javelins on the screens," Lieutenant Commander Abelli reported. "They don't seem to be holding any back, which would make two carriers."

Brad nodded absently as he looked over the energy signatures.

"That fits," he concluded. "Four ships bigger than the rest, two of them bigger than the other two. I was hoping for at least one *Warrior*, but it looks like I'm not that lucky."

It was hard to tell solid details at this range, but they could pick out which ships were bigger than the others. A *Warrior*-class destroyer wasn't as big as a drone carrier, but she'd be bigger than anything else the OWN could field.

"We're calling it two cruisers," Abelli confirmed. "No classes, but I'm *reasonably* sure they're not *Tremendouses*."

"And the destroyers don't appear to be *Warriors*," Brad agreed. "Which, given that we know the Independence Militia had more *Warriors* than the Commonwealth Fleet, tells me something interesting."

"Sir?" the operations officer asked.

"The Lord Protector sent an expendable fleet," Bard told him. "No *Warriors*. No *Tremendouses*—and I'm pretty sure the bastard has at least two more of those we've missed. There might be some *Invictus*-class corvettes, but I wouldn't put money on it."

They'd still be modern ships, but they wouldn't be the absolute top-of-the-line ships that the Cadre had convinced one of the Fleet's main providers to build for them.

"Second-line ships, ships they can spare, with a pair of *Spearthrowers* to stiffen it up." Brad shook his head. "If everything had gone according to plan, it would have been more than enough. But I'm guessing the plan was set into motion before anyone knew Task Force Seventeen was going to be going via Mars."

"Those drones will be in range in under ten minutes," Jahoda noted. "Our anti-torpedo suite is only really designed to handle *maybe* twenty incoming weapons at once. How many can those Javelins put in space?"

"One each," Abelli replied. "If they throw them at one of our cruisers, that's sixty torps at a single target."

"Can the laser suite cover the other cruisers?" Brad asked. The *Tremendous*-class ships were piloting a brand-new anti-torpedo system based around lasers.

"No," Jahoda said grimly. "The system doesn't have the coherence for long-range engagement or the targeting flexibility to hit anything that isn't coming straight at us. We can cover them with our mass drivers, but that's it."

"Well, then, I suggest we target those Javelins before they can launch," Brad said. "The fifteen-centimeter guns are overkill, but we've got ammunition to spend. We'll reload at Mars before we move on.

"Order all ships to target the drones with everything and fire at will."

"We're outside of range," Jahoda objected.

"We're outside of range of ships with live crews," Brad replied. "Those drones are remote-controlled with AI subroutines. I'm betting that they don't dodge as well as a warship does...and if they do, all we've lost are a few rounds we can replace."

Those rounds weren't free, Brad knew, but they were a *lot* cheaper than cruisers, and the Fleet had lost several of those today.

He wasn't willing to lose any more.

He felt *Incredible* shiver under his feet as her heavy mass-driver turrets rotated. She could only bring thirty or so of her standard octo-barrel gatling mass drivers to bear, but she was designed so that at least six of her eight turrets could bear on any target.

Even with the recoil-absorbing systems and automatic thrust adjustment for firing, the big ship jerked underneath them as twelve fifteen-centimeter mass drivers fired. The thirty standard gatlings maintained a continuous fire as Brad's fleet walked mass-driver fire across space.

The drones were still over thirty thousand kilometers away. It took a full minute for the mass-driver fire to reach them, a minute in which they *were* evading—but as Brad had chosen to gamble, they were evading in a consistent pattern that the Fleet computers had already resolved.

A third of the drones vanished in a single salvo, and Brad watched in satisfaction as the mass drivers continued to walk their fire across the robotic spacecraft.

Anything that missed the drones was a threat to the OWN fleet behind them. He wasn't likely to hit any of their ships, but he wasn't going to turn down any luck that came his way today either.

"Remaining drones are launching torpedoes," Abelli reported. "I'm reading...twenty-one inbound. Target is...*Istanbul*."

Someone on the other side was being clever. They'd recognized that

Brad had two *Tremendous*-class ships—and that his third cruiser *didn't* have the same anti-torpedo suite.

"Fleet is to redirect standard mass drivers to cover *Istanbul*," he ordered calmly. "Heavy drivers are to maintain fire on the drones until they're gone."

The drones had their own mass drivers, too. Standard fifteen-millimeter guns in a four-barrelled arrangement, they were about as light a weapon as qualified as a real threat in the battlespace.

Of course, they *did* qualify as a real threat and warning icons started to gleam on his lighter ships. None of them were more than "ablative armor expended" so far, but it was only the beginning.

Every strip of ablative armor Brad's ships expended against the drones was a defense they weren't going to have in an hour when the real battle started.

"Last drone is down," Abelli reported. "Torpedoes neutralized. No damage to the fleet."

Brad nodded his acknowledgement.

"They should have held them back," he said quietly. "Used them in conjunction with the rest of their fleet—but sending them in ahead is *our* deployment doctrine." He shook his head. "It makes sense when you've got a carrier facing off against a destroyer or two, but it's the wrong doctrine for a fleet action."

Which made sense, of course.

The Solar System had seen very few fleet actions yet, and none involving both cruisers and carriers.

Brad Madrid was going to be in command of the first.

———

Brad was convinced there had to be something he could do to minimize his losses and make sure he smashed the OWN force. Every ship that made it past Task Force Seventeen was going to be a headache at Mars.

"Current vectors are giving us a nine-minute engagement window starting in thirty-two minutes," Abelli told him. "I'm not sure how much damage we're going to pull off in that."

He nodded silently, then glanced at Werner.

"Get me the Commodores," he ordered.

His call apparently wasn't a surprise to either of his Fleet subordinates. Both Nuremberg and Bailey were on his screens in seconds. Michelle had spent most of the trip linked with him, so he wasn't surprised to get her instantly, either.

"Thirty minutes to contact, people," he told them. They almost certainly already knew, but he wanted to be sure they were on the same page.

"I know what I'm thinking, but if you've got any brilliant ideas, I'm listening."

"We're already decelerating to draw out the engagement time," Nuremberg replied. "Otherwise, the only clever idea I've got is to ignore the carriers."

"Agreed." The carriers weren't defenseless, but with their drones gone, they had fewer weapons than most of the destroyers on the board. They were better armed than the corvettes that made up the majority of the OWN's numbers, but there were still two cruisers and fifteen destroyers that were bigger threats.

"The only previous cruiser-on-cruiser engagement was the Augustus Logistics Facility," Bailey said flatly. "We had three cruisers. The Cadre had one. We lost."

"They opened that one with a long-range nuclear bombardment," Brad pointed out. "We've scanned for heat shields and radiation signatures, Bailey. No one is sneaking up on us this time. It's a straightforward, head-to-head fight."

"Kill the cruisers and the destroyers," Bailey told him. "Corvettes, even carriers, the mercenaries you recruited can clear up. They can't fight cruisers, and the fewer destroyers we leave them, the better."

"Agreed." Brad nodded sharply as his thoughts fell into place. "We can't change the vector of the engagement at this point, so what's left to us is target prioritization and our own positioning.

"Let's start by pulling the corvettes and frigates back," he ordered. "They're too fragile to take cruiser fire, and each of them still has a dozen Fleet personnel aboard. We'll use their torpedoes for long-range fire, but they'll operate their mass drivers in pure missile-defense mode.

"Move the cruisers and destroyers together, like this." Brad was moving icons on a display as he spoke, sending his data over to his subordinates. It was a dome shape in space, with his three cruisers holding the top of the formation and the destroyers spreading out as a "skirt" beneath them.

"The cruisers can take hits from even fifteen-centimeter guns. Nothing else can, so we offer them up as a target," he said bluntly. *"Tremendous* and *Incredible* are our toughest units. If they want to focus fire on us, let them. We can take it—and I intend to cut off their heaviest firepower immediately.

"We hit the cruisers first. Torpedoes, heavy mass drivers, light mass drivers from the destroyers and cruisers. Everything we've got. Nukes first," he added after a moment. "How many do we have?"

He'd only used nuclear weapons once before, and he'd stolen those from the Cadre—who'd stolen them from the Fleet, the only people *supposed* to have them.

"Not many," Nuremburg told him. "The destroyers all have four. The cruisers have twenty each."

"We use them all in the first salvo," Brad ordered. "I'll lock in my authentication codes before we reach range." He shook his head with a shiver. "We can't run radiation scans in mid-battle. Assume any torpedo they fire at the cruisers is a nuke. We have the firepower to stop their torpedo salvos, so let's make sure they don't hit anybody."

"That'll require focusing the destroyers' mass drivers on defense," Bailey pointed out.

"Agreed. We'll use their drivers in the first pass, but once there are torpedoes heading our way, only the *Bound*s are to continue offensive mass-driver fire," he confirmed. "We'll pound them with the fifteen-centimeter guns until we're out of range or they roll over."

"And what happens when they do something you don't expect?" Bailey demanded.

"They *will* do something we don't expect," Brad said quietly. "That's war. When it happens, we improvise."

———

In Brad's experience, nothing *ever* went according to plan.

It was a surprise, therefore, when the battle started exactly when expected. There was no attempt by the OWN to evade. They couldn't really, in any case, and had already adjusted their course to cut the engagement time to a minimum.

"Fleet is firing," Abelli reported calmly as *Incredible* shivered around them. Torpedo icons appeared on Brad's display by the dozens, joining the vaguer icons representing mass driver fire.

The sensors couldn't track individual fifteen-centimeter projectiles, let alone individual fifteen-*millimeter* rounds. They could project where the heavy mass-driver rounds were, but for the smaller guns, the computers just drew in lines of fire.

An eight-barrel gatling mass driver fired a slug every one point five seconds at five hundred kilometers per second. There were hundreds of the weapons in each fleet, and the faint lines the computers drew in could easily have blocked out Brad's entire display if they'd been marked more clearly.

"Incoming fire. Hostiles are focusing heavy mass drivers on *Istanbul* again," Abelli confirmed. "Any orders?"

"Nothing new," Brad said quietly. *Istanbul* was already falling back inside the dome formation, forcing the incoming fire to pass her sisters. At that range, they *could* use radar to locate the heavy rounds.

And what they could locate, they could shoot down.

"Enemy torpedoes are inbound as well. They'll arrive just before ours do. Target is…unclear."

Brad grimaced. *Unclear* wasn't what he wanted to hear about weapons that were almost certainly carrying nuclear warheads.

"*Clarify* that," he ordered. "Then shoot them down."

The Fleet's focus on defense was showing. The cruisers on both sides had taken heavy mass-driver hits, but they *could* take them. Cruisers were built to take a beating and keep shooting. That was why—

"Torpedo hit! Nuclear detonation!"

Brad's gaze snapped to the screen showing his own fleet, and swallowed hard.

The Alliance commander had clearly decided they couldn't take down the Fleet cruisers with their laser defensive suites. Instead, they'd set their torpedoes to look like they weren't targeting anyone specifically.

Until the last moment, when they'd flung themselves at Bailey's destroyers...and revealed that the OWA disagreed with Brad's assessment on the value of sending nukes at destroyers.

Seven of his destroyers were gone, obliterated in balls of thermonuclear fire. *Bound by Blood* and *Oath of Vengeance* were still clear, he realized with relief, but half of his heavy escorts were gone.

"Good hit, good hit!" someone else snapped. "We got the cruisers, they're *gone.*"

He yanked his attention to the enemy fleet as *his* nukes hit home. He'd fired over fifty thirty-megaton warheads at the two cruisers. It wasn't clear how many had made it through, but most of them had died during their flights.

Enough had survived. Both Alliance cruisers were gone, obliterated by one of the few weapons they couldn't take multiple hits from.

"All right," he said grimly. "They've got their pound of flesh. Now let's teach them the *cost*. Focus fire on the destroyers. Let's work our way down the list until there's nothing left!"

CHAPTER THIRTEEN

WITHOUT THE FIREPOWER of the cruisers, the second-rate enemy ships weren't able to effectively strike back at Task Force Seventeen. Brad's ships took a little more damage but in the process eliminated both of the carriers—a strategic rather than a tactical victory at this point—and all of the enemy destroyers, and damaged most of the smaller ships.

With that accomplished, he ordered their ships to turn around and make best speed for Mars. As Brad had expected, the fighting there resolved itself before they'd made it even halfway back to the Red Planet. The loyal forces carried the day, but the cost in ships and lives was bad.

None of the defecting cruisers had survived the fight over the north pole, but only three of the loyal ships had made it through, all damaged. Maybe half of the other combatants were still operable in some form or another.

The combat in Mars orbit had been the equivalent of a knife fight in a suitcase. No one escaped uninjured, and far too many of the survivors might still bleed out.

The Goldmisers, reinforced by Harding's Guardians and the Vikings, either destroyed or captured the remainder of the smaller ships that had rebelled, but the once-powerful Fleet presence at Mars was now shattered.

How exactly that had happened was a question that still needed to be answered. If they could do it at Mars, they could do it at Earth. And if Earth fell this way, the Commonwealth was done. He'd sent a message saying so to Admiral Orcho as soon as he'd turned his ships for Mars.

When she finally replied to him, Orcho looked even worse than he felt. The distance between Earth and Mars precluded a two-way conversation, so her call was only a report to bring him up to speed.

She sat behind a large desk with the flag of the Commonwealth draped across the wall behind her. In contrast, she almost drooped with exhaustion.

"God, Madrid, this is a frigging disaster," she said, rubbing her face. "Worst case, I expected you to take some hits at Saturn. I figured we had a solid base of defense at Mars. That's gone and so is Saturn.

"The first-rate OWN ships showed up at Blackhawk Station right at the same time the second string tried to jump Mars. They were far more successful, though we don't have any real information yet. All we know for sure is that they won. They've got control of Saturn."

She pinched the bridge of her nose between her thumb and forefinger. "Your warning about traitors in the various ships here at Earth was timely but would've been useless if I hadn't taken some precautions of my own.

"I'd already been removing questionable officers, so that gave me a leg up in making sure none of the ships just took off. I had my engineers put hidden controls in the fusion plants to make sure no one got very far.

"Honestly, I'd already made my move before you'd called. As soon as I got the first reports of intership fighting at Mars, I killed every fusion plant here at Earth. Turns out they'd planned the same here, but that's really hard when you can't maneuver and fight effectively and a dozen known loyal ships are waiting to stomp on you."

There was a long pause there, allowing him to digest just how bold his brother's plan had been. He'd come within a hairsbreadth of clearing the board of his most powerful enemies in one move.

"My forces here will take weeks to get back online," Orcho said in a low voice. "I can't trust anyone, really. How many people did that bastard Mills and his Secret Service lackeys get onto my ships?

"As best I can figure, based on some last-minute shuffling of crew, they pulled the mutinous elements off your ships as soon as I started forming Task Force Seventeen so they could have the best shot of repeating what happened at Mars here at Earth.

"My guess is that they expected the force you trashed to kill you with a surprise attack and wanted their people to be ready to use the chaos of the aftermath to do the same here on Earth. If they'd pulled it off, Jupiter could be captured at their leisure because they'd already have won the war."

With a deep sigh, she shook her head. "Director Harmon is trying to figure out how that was done, but I don't hold much hope of him identifying the responsible parties. Someone erased the personnel computers and all the backups. Even the ones off planet and the backups at Mars. That wasn't supposed to be possible, but they did it anyway.

"What it means is that we don't know who ordered what, which people might be dirty, or even which ones might not even be Fleet.

"The rot went right up to the top. Hell, Admiral Annenberg tried to *kill* me when I dropped the hammer, and I've known him since we went to the academy together. He was my *friend*!"

That last brought tears to the woman's eyes, but she wiped them away angrily. "Anyone I leave in command, or with the ability to seize control, could literally stick a knife in my back with no warning what-soever. Anyone at all.

"I'm doing what I can, moving *everyone* around to different ships and breaking up established command teams, but that's going to play merry hell with even the capabilities of my remaining loyal people.

"The bottom line is that I'm not going to be sending you any rein-forcements. Not when they could be traitors. You're going to have to fight the OWA with what you can scrape together at Mars and Jupiter, if you can manage to convince them to actually participate in their own defense and allow you to help them."

She sat up straighter and stared at the video pickup. "To do all this,

I'm going to need you to up your game. You've pulled off a miracle, but now I need more. No one else has a chance in hell of making this work.

"As of this moment, you're a full Admiral and I'm putting you in command of the newly formed First Fleet. You can have any elements you can recover from the disaster at Mars. Welcome to the big league and good luck. If you fail to stop your brother and his henchmen, the Commonwealth is doomed."

———

Admiral Orcho had obviously also sent a message to Captain Jahoda, because the flag captain showed up at Brad's office a few hours later with a small box in his hand.

Brad eyed it suspiciously. "What's that?"

The other man smiled humorlessly. "Something you'll need, Admiral. Props are very important in this kind of play."

He handed the box over and Brad opened it. Nestled in the velvet interior were the rank insignia for a full Fleet Admiral. Four stars to replace the two he currently wore.

"You have the oddest things stored away, Captain," Brad said wryly. "Were you expecting to need these?"

Jahoda chuckled and shook his head. "Not at all. I had someone in Engineering whip these up. I suspect they melted something down, formed them and coated them with what they had. Most likely all of this from the damage control supplies. They look shiny enough, but you'll probably want to get an official set at some point."

"Screw that," Brad said firmly, plucking the stars out of the box and starting the process to swap them out with the previous set. "These came from my crew. Their support means a lot more to me than how shiny they are. Thank them for me. It means a lot."

"Already done. I also made certain that they knew I wanted them to pass the word around about what they'd done. You're new to Fleet command and this might otherwise slip under your radar, but this is their way to show you're theirs and they are yours. Until this battle, you commanded this ship and this task force, but they weren't yours. Now they are and you're theirs."

As soon as Brad had the new insignia in place, the flag captain straightened, snapped to attention and rendered Brad the sharpest salute he'd ever seen. "It is my great pleasure and honor to command this ship under your flag, Admiral."

Brad rose to his feet and returned the salute as best he could. "Thank you, Captain. I'd like the names of the engineers who created this for me. I want to personally thank them.

"Of course. I'll have my yeoman send that to you at once. Now, if you'll excuse me, I need to return to my bridge and get *Incredible* ready for whatever surprises are left in Mars orbit."

Once the other officer was gone, Brad sat again and rubbed his face with his hands. What they knew about the other half of the Battle of Mars was bad. Nothing good was waiting for them there.

Well, he had to base his plans on the worst-case scenario anyway. If anything was better than expected, he'd take it, but he couldn't count on it. Defeating the OWN forces at Saturn, especially with the battleship and its support group out there somewhere, was going to be damned hard, but they had no choice other than to fight them.

First, though, he needed to salvage what he could at Mars to make First Fleet more than a paper tiger.

————

Brad brought the task force to battle stations before they entered weapons range of Mars, including the defenses at Deimos. Yes, those were supposed to be in friendly hands, but the targeting systems were still locked down by the infected computers. It was always possible they'd open fire with no warning and no ability for the Fleet personnel to stop them.

All that caution proved anticlimactic. No one opened fire and the captured Fleet ships sat quietly under the guns of the surviving loyal units and the mercenary forces. Not that Brad expected much resistance from them, since there were armed and armored boarders on the traitorous vessels seeing that the bad seeds were taken off and located somewhere they couldn't cause any more damage.

Knowing his enemies, Brad had insisted that the prisoners be locked up somewhere that they couldn't be killed by an unexpected outside force. He actually wanted to get some questions answered this time.

That place ended up being Deimos base. Or, rather, one of the older segments of the base that was no longer used for operations. It was isolated from the sections of the base that controlled the defenses and could be sealed off by dumping the air from the connecting tubes.

As protection for the prisoners, Brad had ordered his ships to both position themselves to defend the base and to send down Marines to guard them. They'd take no unnecessary chances this time.

Rather than go down to meet with the commanders, he decided he'd use his rank and have them come to him. Being a cruiser built to house a flag officer, *Incredible*'s wardroom was large enough for everyone. Barely.

More than one person had complained that they had plenty of work that required them on their ships—and they were right—but Brad needed to meet each of them face to face. These commanders were key to his success in fighting the OWN, and he had to form the right kind of bond as quickly as possible. He had to know he could trust each and every one of them.

Once that was done, he had to go down to Mars and convince Sara Kernsky to go to bat for him with the other Mercenary Guild directors. He'd need that overriding contract if he was to have any hope of pulling this off.

That supposed he was even able to convince the political leaders in the Jovian system to support him. The OWA would waste no time in moving on Jupiter and the Trojans now. They had to secure those colonies or they'd have enemies at their backs while they fought for the Inner System.

Brad put his head in his hands as he sat at his desk. He was there alone because it wouldn't do to have the commander of the fleet waiting in the conference room as his subordinates straggled in. He'd arrive when they were gathered, to assert his command position.

A rap at his door brought him upright. A check of the clock told him it was still far too early for his aide to be coming for him. There was something else wrong.

"Enter," he said, preparing for more bad news.

One of the Marines guarding his door stuck his head in. "Commodore Hunt to see you, sir. She said she has an appointment." The last part was said with a bit of a smirk.

"I do," his wife said as she breezed past the guard. "And this is an important strategy meeting. We're not to be disturbed unless someone starts shooting. We'll need a ten-minute warning before the meeting is ready to start. Clear?"

"Yes, ma'am," the Marine said, seemingly ignoring the fact that she wasn't in his chain of command, or even Commonwealth service at all.

Michelle faced Brad as the hatch closed behind her. "How long until you have to be in the wardroom?"

He did some mental calculation. "It'll be an hour before everyone is aboard, I think."

She smiled and headed for his desk, already working at her uniform tunic. "That'll work. I need to make sure my husband is relaxed for this important meeting. It wouldn't do for him to be wound too tight."

He wanted to argue, but her mouth claimed his and his resistance vanished. They'd fought and could've died. There was time to live before he planned the next stage of the war.

CHAPTER FOURTEEN

"ATTENTION!" the Marine at the wardroom hatch shouted as Brad walked past him, almost causing him to twitch in surprise. Everyone seated around the conference table rose to their feet, the Fleet officers at once and the mercenaries a few heartbeats later, and waited for him to sit at the chair at the head of the table.

"As you were," Brad said. "There's no need for that. We've got a lot to discuss and I don't want to have ceremony get in the way. Please be seated."

He caught Michelle's eye as she sat a few seats to his right. His wife's knowing smile might be lost on all the other officers present, but he felt his face heating just a little.

She'd slipped out of his office when the Marine guard had given them the ten-minute warning, so that they'd arrive separately. All right and proper.

He had to admit that he was a lot more relaxed than he'd been an hour earlier. He felt ready to take this challenge on now. He still might not win, but he'd give it his very best.

Commodore Talgat Saltanat, the commander of Deimos Command, sat at the other end of the table. He was the senior surviving Mars Command officer. Commodores Bailey and Nuremberg sat across from

Michelle, while Commodores Sonja Gold and James Harding sat to either side of his wife.

The remaining seats were filled by senior Fleet and Mercenary Guild captains, including his own—rather, Michelle's—Vikings. They were a steadying sight. He'd held any number of briefings with those faces around his table. He knew without question that he had their support.

The rest? Well, time would tell.

"For those of you who don't know me, my name is Brad Madrid and I'm in command of First Fleet," he said as he looked around the table, meeting each person's eyes for a moment. "If you don't know what that is, I'm not surprised. It didn't exist a few hours ago.

"I've been tasked with picking up the pieces here and putting together a force to challenge the OWA ships that took Saturn, and you all are going to help me make that happen."

"With all due respect and so on," Gold said, "that's crap. From what I hear, those damned pirates have a battleship and as much force as we had before all these Fleet idiots started shooting their friends. Exactly how do you hope to pull that off, *Commodore* Madrid?"

More than one person started to tear a strip off the abrasive mercenary officer, but Brad pounded his fist against the table to distract them.

"Yes," he said into the suddenly tense silence. "I was a mercenary Commodore like you just a few weeks ago. Since then, I've trashed an OWN task force that could've scrubbed Mars clean of defenders. I didn't ask for this job, but I've got it and I'm going to make it work. *Commodore.*"

Rather an angering the woman, his response made the corners of her lips twitch up. "I see. Thank you for the explanation, *Admiral.*"

"Well, I don't see," Harding said in a much less challenging tone. "The points my associate raised are still on the table. How do we possibly take on a force like that? If any of the Fleet ships in orbit here are undamaged, I'm not aware of that fact. Some of them are in pretty bad shape.

"How can we win that kind of battle? I'm a mercenary and I'm not throwing my ships into a meat grinder. You hired us to defend Saturn.

Well, that's off the table now and we have no authority to attack the OWA. In fact, we have specific guidelines not to take a contract to do so. The Mercenary Guild is neutral."

"I have every expectation that that set of circumstances will change very shortly," Brad said in far more conciliatory tone than he felt. "I'll be heading down to Mars to see Factor Kernsky as soon as we finish here, as a matter of fact.

"As for the rest, you're asking the wrong question. What you should be wondering is how your people will survive the purge that's coming if the OWA wins this fight. If you think Jack Mader—the leader of the Cadre, no matter how he changes his name or title—is going to allow armed forces not under his direct command to exist, you're mistaken.

"He'll disband the Mercenary Guild and confiscate every ship with a weapon in this system. He'll press every surviving mercenary and Fleet crewman and officer into service, unless he decides to space the ones he doesn't think he can trust. And I guarantee that he won't trust anyone at this table."

He let that sink in for a few moments before he continued. "Even if you decided you weren't going to fight, Commodore Harding, it's already far too late to save yourself. The key now is to find a plan that has the best chance of working, no matter how bad the odds stacked against it.

"Because make no mistake, we're not only fighting for our lives but for the lives of everyone in the Commonwealth. The Phoenix has no mercy in him. He wants to rule humanity with an iron fist while crushing any resistance under hobnailed boots. We have two options: stop him or die trying."

———

That seemed to settle the meeting down. No matter what the Fleet officers thought, they weren't going to show dissension in front of the mercenaries.

"Commodore Saltanat," Brad said. "What is the status on rooting out the virus in your controls?"

The officer smiled grimly. "Now that we know what to look for and don't have to work while everyone is shooting, I think we'll have the platforms back under control in a few hours. We have the mass drivers on the moon under manual control at the moment and are relying on Commodore Gold's ships to provide us warning if anyone is sneaking in.

"The logs aren't going to help determine who did this, but I've implemented safeguards to require a number of trusted people to oversee any updates and to check one another. They got us once, but they won't manage it again."

"We thought that after they did this at Blackhawk Station," Michelle said. "Yet I'm almost certain we'll find out they did it again when they made this new attack."

The Fleet officer didn't quite sniff, but he managed to look down his long nose at her. "That was a civilian group. We're a lot more organized in Fleet. Now that we know this is possible, we'll be on our guard."

"Will we?" Brad asked. "We reported what the Cadre did at Blackhawk Station the first time, but they still pulled it off on Deimos today."

Saltanat frowned. "I never saw a report about anything like that."

"It probably never made it out from Earth," Bailey said. "Those bastards have been suppressing information that could've made a difference against them for a long time."

"We can't control what's happened in the past," Brad said. "Let's focus on moving forward. Do we have any idea how they got nukes aboard *Eternal*?"

The other officer shrugged. "We haven't got a clue. They should've been able to detect something like that, but someone on the inside must've cleared the way for them. We've been hunting for any of her crew that was off the ship during the blast, but most of them have vanished."

"We need to make sure that doesn't happen to any of our other ships," Nuremberg said tiredly. "Or to Deimos. Everdark, to any of the cities down on the surface."

"We're going to have to rearm," Bailey said. "We used every nuke we had."

"We've got reloads for you," Saltanat said. "I suggest we only send people we trust to bring them back to the ships. I already took the liberty of securing the facility holding them even more tightly than it was before, just in case someone might want to blow it up."

"We'll also want to check each warhead before we move it," Michelle said. "It wouldn't shock me if someone sabotaged a few to blow up when we tried to load or fire them."

That produced a long silence in the wardroom.

"I hate being that paranoid," Nuremberg said. "Still, I suppose it's warranted."

"What about our current force?" Brad asked, moving things along. "How many ships do we have left in each class out of the Mars force?"

"The Martian Squadron has three cruisers, thirteen destroyers, and forty-five corvettes and frigates," Saltanat said. "All are damaged to one degree or another. Some of them were recaptured from mutineers, thanks to Commodores Gold and Harding as well as the Vikings. We can repair the worst of the damage, but I wouldn't call them fully combat-capable."

"My ships didn't take too many hits," Gold said with more than a hint of superiority in her tone. "Even for mutineers, I expected better of Fleet."

"You're a jackass," Harding said, frowning at the woman. "Seriously, can you debitch while we try to save our asses?"

"Stop!" Michelle said, holding a hand up to the mercenaries at her sides. "We have zero time for personalities. Do I need to put someone in the corner?"

Gold blinked at Michelle, opened her mouth to say something, but stopped. When she finally did speak, it was in a calmer tone of voice. "Sorry."

For a moment, Harding didn't seem to realize Michelle had meant him too—and then Brad met and held his eyes.

"Sorry," the younger mercenary muttered.

It didn't sound as if either of them really meant it, but Brad bulled ahead before the mercenaries could derail the meeting. "We'll repair what we can here and reload all the spent ordnance. We'll have time while I try to get the Mercenary Guild fully onboard and convince the Jovian governments to get off the fence.

"We'll also need to question the prisoners. I damned well don't expect much out of that, but someone we took knows something useful, and we have a very short window to get it out of them. I hate to say this, but they're mutineers. Does that give us some leverage to compel cooperation?"

Nuremberg's eyes narrowed. "They might be bastards, but we can't treat them like pirates and space them. As much as I want to, they're allowed a court-martial. That isn't happening right away. Everdark, if we lose, it might not happen at all."

"Which doesn't mean they have to know that," Bailey said with an evil grin. "If we get a bunch of them in a room and lead them to believe we're treating this like piracy, we can hustle the most obnoxious ones out and put them in solitary. If the rest happen to think we spaced them, well, that would be an unfortunate misunderstanding."

That made Brad chuckle. "Then I think *you* should deal with them. As they were stationed here at Mars, they already know and fear you, if they have any sense at all. Make them sweat and get me any useful information you can, Commodore Bailey."

"You bet your ass I will," she said grimly. "They helped kill my ship and my crew. It doesn't matter that I'd been moved; they were mine. No one takes what's mine without paying for it."

He nodded. "Then we all have things to do. Keep my staff updated on your progress and I'll make sure the information is passed back about what we're going to do and the timeline in which we're going to do it. Dismissed."

As they started filing out, Brad stopped Jahoda. "A moment, please, Captain."

When they were alone, Brad closed the hatch. "We have one other major problem to solve and I'm going to need your input for that."

"Anything you need, sir," the man said, standing at ease.

"Three of the Martian cruisers survived, but the Commodore commanding the group didn't. I want to get your honest opinion about your executive officer."

Jahoda nodded, a look of understanding on his face. "Commander Nah is one of the finest officers it's ever been my pleasure to command, but wouldn't it make more sense to have one of the surviving cruiser captains take command? Alycia doesn't have the experience to guide three cruisers into battle."

Brad smiled a little. "No, I didn't think she did, but I suspect she'll do fine as my flag captain, Commodore."

The other officer blinked. "Excuse me?"

His smile widening at the other officer's reaction, Brad pulled the same box Jahoda had given him earlier from his pocket and handed it to the man.

The Captain—now Commodore—opened it with a look that mixed confusion with consternation. Inside sat the Commodore's insignia that Orcho had given Brad just a few weeks earlier.

"I've already spoken with Admiral Orcho and she's approved your promotion. You're the best man to lead my second cruiser group, Commodore Jahoda. Congratulations. We'll go surprise Captain Nah now, if you'd like to give her your old insignia."

The other man smiled, still obviously shocked. "Nothing would give me more pleasure. I'll do my best for you and the Commonwealth, Admiral."

"I know you will," Brad said, clapping a hand on the other man's shoulder. "Let's hope our best is good enough."

CHAPTER FIFTEEN

ONCE HE HAD everything moving in orbit, Brad took a shuttle down to Olympus Mons City. This visit was far different from the last time he'd been there. For one, he wasn't sneaking in with Kate Falcone. This time, he was coming openly and in force.

He'd wanted to do something low-key, but his officers wouldn't hear of it. With everything that had happened so far at Mars, it was far too likely that the OWA had forces lurking around that would love to be able to decapitate First Fleet, figuratively speaking, and decapitate Brad, literally.

So, rather than taking a shuttle down in relative anonymity, Fleet descended on the spaceport in force. First came a wave of Marines strong enough to hold off even the most determined ground attackers. Second was a screen of small craft that could intercept any attempts to shoot down Brad's shuttle. Only with them in place was he allowed to proceed.

He'd have argued that that was too much, but he knew from past experience that it wasn't. The Cadre had managed to attack him in places that he'd never have thought possible. If they took him out, the Commonwealth's last chance to convince the Jovian system to join them might die, too.

Michelle was waiting for him when he stepped out of his shuttle.

"How do you ever get any privacy?" she asked as she fell in beside him as he walked toward the ground cars waiting nearby. "Do they send in Marines to clear the bathroom and provide overwatch while you take care of business?"

"Only on days where they think there won't be any trouble," he said as he held the door open for her. "But all kidding aside, I did find out that they make sure I'm protected at all times, even when I'm in a safe area."

Once they'd put their seatbelts on, the driver joined a convoy of other cars and left the spaceport.

"What does that mean?" his wife asked, turning to face him.

"Just that they take care to have the areas I'm in under continuous observation, except for my bedroom and bathroom."

She frowned for a second before her eyes bulged. "Are you telling me they had your office under surveillance when we…"

He gave her a long, sad look and then grinned. "No, that's off limits, too."

Michelle smacked him hard on the arm. "That's not funny!"

"I disagree, though I won't push my point of view too far because I certainly don't want to make you mad enough to not do it again."

"You make me crazy," she said with a huff. "What's the plan here? We got the word from Factor Kernsky that the restriction on taking contracts against the OWA has been rescinded. You can hire anyone you like. What's next?"

"Have you ever heard of an overriding contract?" he asked. "As someone relatively new to mercenary work, I'm betting not."

She shook her head. "What's that?"

"When the Mercenary Guild decides they're going to call every unit in and go after something together. Every ship, every trooper. They drop whatever they're working on and the Guild puts everything they have into kicking someone's ass.

"The last time it was used was when they went after the Terror and his cruiser *Black Skull*. They killed the ship and got his bosses—my frigging *parents*—but not the man, sadly. I want them to do the same now. We need them."

"But you expect resistance."

He nodded. "No one wants to willingly stick their hand into a meat grinder. Factor Kernsky said that it takes four director-level Factors to declare an overriding contract, and after the last time, I wouldn't be surprised to see that the OWA took steps to make sure that wouldn't happen again.

"Either they'll have moved behind the scenes to see that people less inclined to do something like that are in positions of power, or they'll kill the Factors before they can come to a decision. We've seen them do stuff like that before, and I'm hoping we can get a favorable ruling before they do it again."

———

Once they'd arrived at the Mercenary Guild offices and were ushered inside, Sara Kernsky met them in a conference room rather than her office. She had several other people with her, and her expression was grim.

After they'd declined refreshments, the Factor got right to the point. "I tried to get the directors to invoke an overriding contract and they refused. Well, *refused* is perhaps too strong a word. They dithered."

Brad frowned. "Don't they understand the danger we're all facing?"

"If they don't, it's not because I failed to tell them in every way I could think of. What do you know about the Guild directors?"

He shrugged. "Not that much. You said they were director-level Factors, which is the first I've really heard of them. As a mercenary commander, I never really had to deal with anyone higher in the hierarchy than someone like yourself."

His eyes narrowed. "Unless you're a director-level Factor and I didn't know about it."

"I'm getting up there in seniority, but that's not the kind of club that allows just anyone in. There are five director-level Factors. You almost certainly haven't met any of them because they don't do contract work once they join the board.

"Personally, I think that's a mistake. They lose the bond that joins them with the mercenaries that we represent. That kind of insulation is never a good thing."

"So, they turned you down?" Michelle asked. "What does *dither* mean in this case?"

"That they want to discuss the problem at greater length," Kernsky said with a hint of disgust in her voice. "What I really suspect is that they've been in contact with the OWA and have let them blow sunshine up their skirts."

"In other words, you think they've cut a deal to stay out of the fight," Brad said, feeling himself sag a little. "You think they've been paid off?"

She shook her head. "Not in so many words and I could be wrong. We're based out of the Jovian system, so they might be allowing the governments there to make them more cautious. I just can't tell from here. That's why I'll be going with you when you set out for Jupiter."

He raised an eyebrow. "You think you can knock heads in person?"

"I'll bet I can. Some of these people have to understand the risks of what's going on. I'm sure you've already gotten word of what happened at Saturn. They ambushed Blackhawk Station in a very similar manner to how they almost did the last time.

"This time, they made it in and locked everything down. They're bringing in their fleet to fuel up, and that means an attack deeper into the system isn't too far away. They've trashed Mars, and Earth is in disarray. How juicy of a target does that make the Jovian system?"

"But they don't need to," Michelle objected. "They've already declared their neutrality. Why pick a fight that you don't need to?"

"The Jovian systems can change their minds any time they choose," Kernsky said. "There are a lot of ships in Jovian space. The OWA has to realize that the only chance they have of outright victory is to take them out along with the Commonwealth.

"There's an old Earth saying by Benjamin Franklin: 'We must, indeed, all hang together or, most assuredly, we shall all hang separately.' The longer they wait to deal with the Mercenary Guild and the various forces in the Jovian system, the better the chances are that their enemies will realize their peril and make common cause. It's going to take everything we have, combined with what Fleet has left, to deal with the OWA."

Brad nodded. "I got word just before I came down that Task Group *Immortal* showed up at Saturn. This is going to be a major push when they launch their attack. The only Fleet forces that can meet them are mine, and even with every ship I can scare up here, I'm going to come up short.

"Sara, I want your honest opinion. Do you think you can convince the Mercenary Guild to commit to an overriding contract?"

The redhead shrugged. "I don't know. Two or three of the directors? Yes. One is a certain no vote, and I'm sure he's in the OWA's pocket. The last vote is a wildcard. That's why I need to be there in person to make our case.

"What about the Jovian governments? Do you think you can bring them around, Madrid? If we don't get everyone onto the same page, it won't matter whether or not the Mercenary Guild joins you."

"I still have to make a call," he said. "I doubt it's going to be easy, but I've got to try. I hope you're packed, because we need to get a move on. As soon as First Fleet is ready to go, I'm setting out for Io."

"I'm packed and ready to go, along with my staff. If you've got room, I'll ride back up with you."

————

Once he was back aboard his cruiser, Brad retired to his office and composed a message to Governor Ilene Johnson of Io. He'd helped rescue her son from slavers back when he'd started out as a mercenary, and Jack Mantruso—though he'd been called Jack Mader then—had once been her special assistant.

If anyone was willing to give him a chance, it would be her.

As soon as he was facing the camera on his desk, he started recording.

"Governor Johnson, this is Brad Madrid. I realize that we've settled all our debts, but I need to impose on you for a favor. By now you've heard about Blackhawk Station. You know who leads the OWA better than anyone alive, including me. You have to know he'll come for Jupiter.

"The Jovian governments are right to be angry with the Commonwealth, but you can't let your righteous indignation become a suicide pact. You know me. You know that I'm one of you. Can you get me a hearing with the other leaders where I can try to at least convince them to see the threat?"

He took a deep breath and let it out slowly. "I sure hope so, because I'm leaving Mars with my fleet in a few hours. I can't let that bastard come for you without fighting him. As they say, it's always easier to beg forgiveness than to ask permission, but I still hope to have your blessing to at least be there when the hammer falls. Madrid out."

Almost as soon as he'd sent the message, there was a rap at his office door. A Marine stuck her head in. "Commodore Bailey to see you, Admiral."

"Send her in."

A grim-faced Bailey strode into his office a few moments later. "Do you have any booze? I need to wash the nasty taste out of my mouth."

He gestured toward the small bar that had come with his office. "Pour me something as well."

She chuckled as she poured two glasses full of amber liquid. That was more than three shots, so he'd be careful to sip his slowly.

Once she'd handed him his glass, she took a seat across his desk and downed half of hers. "I think I have the basic outlines of what happened. I had to pretend to make a few salutary examples before the buggers started talking to save themselves from their own supposed summary executions.

"They were all compromised one way or the other or weren't even Fleet to begin with. Whoever managed this used every string she could to get as many people on board the ships of the Martian Squadron for this. None of them really knew there would be others. In fact, only the leaders knew they would be seizing Fleet ships and when."

Brad took a sip of his whisky and nodded. "Operational security would be important with something like this. You said they had people from outside of Fleet? How did that work?"

"Boarding parties led by actual Fleet officers. If they didn't have enough people on a ship to take it over, they brought in help at the last second. Almost none of them knew what was planned, and by the time the shooting started, it was far too late to object that it wasn't what they were hired for.

"Which, by the way, was piracy. Each group was told they were taking over a merchant ship. Boy, were they surprised when they found out the truth. Some of them fought back when they did—even though they were willing to be pirates, they had some kind of soul. Or sense of self-preservation, I suppose. I made notes when I found any of that kind."

None of that really surprised Brad. He'd known all along that it had to be something like that. He agreed with Bailey that whoever had orchestrated the attack had been damned good.

"Did we get any of the leadership?"

She shook her head. "No. None of the people behind the attack participated in it. This was to sow chaos, not actually win the fight. They didn't care what happened, so long as Fleet ships were damaged or destroyed."

He nodded. "We'll let Fleet security handle the prisoners. We have more important fish to fry. Are your ships ready to move out?"

"As ready as they can be without a few weeks in a shipyard. We'll be able to make some repairs on the way to Jupiter. That is where we're going, isn't it?"

"Damned straight. I expect to get the same response from the rest of the ships in the next few hours. As soon as we're done rearming, we'll leave for Io."

CHAPTER SIXTEEN

IT TOOK six days of wrangling and shouting between various parties in the Jovian system, with Governor Johnson playing referee, before they finally accepted the inevitable and agreed that they would allow him to come to Io and that they would meet to hear what he had to say.

That didn't mean they were happy about it. Or that they'd be easy to convince about joining forces with his fleet.

Sara Kernsky seemed to be having just about as much luck herding the Mercenary Guild director-level Factors into giving her a hearing, too. She didn't give Brad any details, but her fury couldn't be fully hidden at mealtimes.

Her anger boiled over at dinner that night. It was a semi-private affair with Brad, Michelle and Captain Alycia Nah in attendance.

"These people shouldn't be running a damned garbage scow, much less the damned Mercenary Guild," Kernsky growled into her wine. "It's like arguing with kindergarteners."

"Is it truly so bad?" Nah asked. "Surely, they can at least accept the need to discuss whether an overriding contract is needed in a civil manner."

Kernsky laughed without the slightest bit of humor. "You'd think, but it seems they like to fight just as much as some of our mercenaries.

Three are in favor of the idea, though one of them is wavering, one of them is completely against it, and the last one won't commit and keeps dodging the meetings."

"This is kind of a big deal," Michelle said in a soothing voice. "It's not supposed to be something that happens often or easily."

"But sticking one's fingers in one's ears and saying 'nah nah nah' when the end of the world is looming isn't rational," Kernsky retorted.

She then inclined her head toward Brad's flag captain. "No offense, Captain Nah."

"It's a quirk of language that I'm more than familiar with," the Fleet officer said in a wry tone. "Thankfully, I hear it less often as I get older, so I'll let it pass this once. Do you think the one no vote is in the OWA's pocket?"

"Damned right I do. I just have no way of proving it, and without clear evidence of his wrongdoing, we can't eject him from the board. That means we'll have to convince the last person, Gustave Kutschinski, to actually come to the meetings and approve the overriding contract."

"You might want to see if he needs protection," Brad said. "It's possible the OWA is threatening him or his family. The Cadre certainly liked that tactic."

She nodded. "The thought occurred to me and I've had some people looking around. As far as I can tell, his wife and twin daughters are safe and sound. We've seen them moving around in public, with a set of guards that we know to be mercenaries he uses for personal protection.

"They don't seem like they're being held against their will, but he's out much less often. He stays home and rarely appears in public. It's out of character and worries me."

That was a mystery, Brad conceded. "I suppose we'll have to sort that out once we get him into the Guild Hall to talk about the overriding contract.

"For my part, I think Governor Johnson has convinced the rest of the governmental leaders to be on Io for the meeting with me. I'm not sure which one of these competing gatherings needs to happen first."

"The politicians," Michelle said promptly. "They have bigger egos.

If you slight them by meeting the mercenaries first, they'll fight you harder."

"I have to agree," Kernsky said. "With so many political leaders at hand, the directors won't be able to take offense, even if they're miffed. I would, however, meet with the Guild the same day, if you can manage it. Time matters."

"I wish we could get there faster," Brad grumbled. "None of these problems is easy to deal with at a distance. And now that the Agency has reports that the damned *Lord Protector* is at Saturn and on board his stolen battleship, I think we can all safely assume that it won't be long before he has his attack force in order and makes his move."

"Wishing won't get us to Io faster," his wife said. "Or make dealing with recalcitrant mercenaries or politicians any easier. I know that you have to worry about what's going on there, but I'm tired of rehashing it over every meal. Let's talk about something else. Anything else."

Brad nodded and let his wife move the topic of discussion to something less depressing or apocalyptic. He'd have another week to fret over the meetings on Io. It wouldn't help him to develop an ulcer in the meantime.

———

"Approaching Io space," one of his staffers said. "All ships report battle readiness."

While Brad didn't expect anyone to ambush his forces there, and they couldn't detect any potential enemy formations, it paid to not take chances. He'd been attacked when he'd thought himself safe before.

His caution proved unnecessary. No stealthed vessels launched attacks. No enemy fleets appeared out of deep space. Weirdly, it disappointed him a little. He'd been spoiling for some kind of fight.

"Keep our picket ships out," he ordered. "Come down one level in alert status for all but the ready-response ships."

That would allow his crews to get food and still have the fleet ready for action in short order if the situation changed.

Besides, he expected the inevitable attack to come when he left his flagship. The gathering of politicians was the most likely ambush target, even with all the security precautions that were no doubt being taken. The Cadre had a long history of being able to get people into places no one thought possible, and then attacking.

He'd try to disappoint them this time, but his options were limited by geography. In this case, the fact that he was meeting the political leaders of the Jovian system on their territory. They'd already told him that he was limited in the size of his escort. There would be no over-powering show of force like had been the case back at Olympus Mons City.

Due to his rank, they'd allowed him a mixed guard of Marines and mercenaries from the Vikings. Far fewer people than he'd like, but more than he'd had on many hostile occasions. It would have to be enough.

He rose to his feet. "Inform Captain Nah that I'll be departing as soon as we hit closest approach with Io. The Commodores will make any changes needed to the standard orders, with Commodore Bailey in overall command."

With that delegation done, he left the flag bridge and headed for the landing bay. A heavily armed squad of Marines stood there, eyeing a similarly sized group of troopers with Colonel Saburo in charge. For his part, the mercenary ground commander was ignoring the Marines.

"Admiral," his friend said with a grin. "We were beginning to think that you wouldn't make it."

Brad shook the Colonel's hand. "You're just mad you were stuck here while *Oath of Protection* and *Oath of Vigilance* were completed. Trust me, you didn't miss much. There was almost no call for hand-to-hand."

"You wound me. My father released your new ships this morning. Commodore Hunt already has them in hand and they've joined the rest of the Vikings. We're ready for any trouble."

"That's good news, but they're not my ships. They're hers until all this is settled. We should all get aboard the pinnace and down to Io."

While he went to deal with the political situation, Sara Kernsky was taking a shuttle to a different city on Io to argue her case in front of the Mercenary Guild Board. She'd call him if she had anything he needed to know.

The two groups of armored men managed to get aboard the small craft without too much bumping into one another, and Brad sat down with Saburo on one side and Major Chitrangada Papadakis on the other. Moments later, the pinnace was detaching and they were off.

"Are you going to keep that rank when you come back to the Vikings?" Saburo asked. "We'll need more ships to support an Admiral."

"That assumes I'm allowed to come back," Brad said with sigh. "You have no idea how messed-up things are in Fleet command right now. They have their claws in me, and even if we manage to somehow take out the OWN ships, they don't know who they can really trust.

"Under circumstances like that, I'm not sure they'll let me go back to reserve status. My mercenary days might be over."

"You could always resign your commission," the Major, her voice almost ridiculously soft and feminine, completely at odds with her tough exterior and combat armor.

"Could I?" he asked. "I'm not so sure. Besides, until we settle the OWA, that's a moot point. What's the plan when we get down to the surface? Which one of you is going to be in overall command?"

"I am," the Major said firmly. "No offence to Colonel Saburo, but you're a Fleet Admiral—one of only *four*—and that makes me the woman on the ground making sure you stay safe."

"Her reputation precedes her," Saburo said. "I have no objections. This time."

"We're scheduled to land at one of the smaller spaceports near the capital," she continued as if Saburo hadn't spoken. "We'll get close and then completely screw up their landing pattern by switching to another one that the good Colonel's father recommended to him, and that he so helpfully informed me of.

"Once we're down, we'll meet some of his vehicles rather than the government-provided ones at the first port. They'll get us to the meeting site, though I'm sure there will be much gnashing of teeth and rending of clothes. It's hard to ambush you when they don't know precisely where you are."

Brad grinned and checked his weapons.

"That's going to make us all *very* popular. Let's make it happen."

———

As predicted, their sudden change in itinerary caused a lot of consternation and yelling. Thankfully, Brad wasn't the one who had to deal with it. The poor pilots were the ones being heaped with abuse and dire threats.

That didn't mean that he escaped completely unscathed, though. Once the pinnace had landed and the mixed guard contingent started him toward three ground cars waiting for them, a man in coveralls indicating that he worked for the spaceport authority came screeching up in on a little scooter. He leapt free and sent it clattering to the ground as he huffed over toward Brad.

Brad had never actually seen anyone huff with such intensity. The fury literally roiled off the short man.

"What the Everdark do you think you're doing, coming across the flight pattern like that, you damned madman? You could've killed someone!"

Saburo made to shove them man back, but Brad held out a hand. "I'm sorry, but it was necessary."

The man's eyes almost bugged out of his head. "Necessary? You high-handed Fleet buggers think you own the damned system? You and your kind—"

Major Papadakis, who was oddly the same height as the raging man, stepped into his personal space and forced him back without touching him. "Watch your mouth or you'll be picking up your teeth."

Her tone left no doubt as to her intent to personally knock them out.

They'd gathered quite a crowd of observers, and Brad could see that they were ready to back the man confronting him.

Brad held up his hands. "I'm not some Fleet flunky from the Inner System. I'm Brad Madrid and I own the Vikings mercenary company out of the Io Shipyard. I'm not here to tell you what to do, but you have to accept that the OWA might not want me to be alive to make that point.

"I'm sorry we had to come here with no warning, but I'm going to see your leaders right now. They'll tear a strip off me, I have no doubt. Let's not start a riot here."

That didn't fully mollify them. They were scared people spoiling for a fight, if his guess was correct. No matter that their government was declaring their neutrality, they'd heard what had happened at Mars and Saturn. They'd be worried and frightened, and people in that frame of mind might fight when it better suited them not to.

"You there," a voice bellowed. "Stand down."

Brad turned and found an imposing man in coveralls similar to the first man approaching, his eyes locked with Brad's. "You're stalling my incoming flights. Get your asses out of here and get that ship back where it's supposed to be before I fine you for that stunt."

When the first man started to say something, the larger one shook his head. "Control retroactively cleared the landing, Vic. Let it go."

Not wanting to chance the tide of opinion changing, he nodded to the larger man and headed for the vehicles. "Thank you."

"You can thank me by killing that Cadre scum," the man said coldly. "And give the damned government a backbone while you're at it."

"I'll do my best, but don't expect miracles."

The other man held the vehicle door open. "I've heard of you, Madrid. You've pulled people out of the fire before. Now shut up and do it again."

"Yes, sir," he said, not seeing any other answer that would satisfy them both.

The man slammed the door as soon as Brad was inside, and the vehicles took off for the designated meeting area. Brad really hoped he could perform the miracles needed to save the Commonwealth and the Jovian system. It was all on him now.

CHAPTER SEVENTEEN

BRAD EXPECTED the convoy to head for the Governor's office but was surprised when they instead went to the Mercenary Guild Hiring Hall.

Basing his company out of Io, Brad was intimately familiar with the building. The large building was where prospective patrons came to meet with officials and company leaders to discuss terms and measure one another up.

As Brad was exiting his vehicle, he noticed that the guards arrayed around the building weren't just the security details for the various officials he was expecting to meet. Oh, they were there, but there were more armed and armored mercenaries mixed among them than Brad had ever seen outside an actual raid.

The layers they occupied were interesting as well. The civilian security details were the outer shell, and the mercs protected the inner layer and the building itself. He wagered that he'd find more mercs inside.

That said a lot about how much trust the various Jovian leaders had at the moment. They had more confidence in the Mercenary Guild than in one another, at least when it came to their own precious skins.

They had picked the right man for the job, though. A large man with dark red hair—though now with some grey mixed in—dressed in combat armor stepped up to Brad with a grin.

"You've stepped up in the world, Madrid. Or down. The jury is still out on that."

Brad smiled warmly and shook Commander William Branson's hand. "How are Heimdall's Raiders treating you, Bill?"

"Pretty good. The Commodore retired last month, and I drew the short straw."

Brad's grin widened. "Congratulations, Commodore. Now all you have to do is make the final leap to Platinum."

The other man clapped his hand on Brad's shoulder. "That'll be easier than you bringing all these stuffed shirts around to your way of thinking."

"That bad?"

"That bad. Look, I know you've been out here with us for years, but I'm not sure you really understand how pissed-off people are. The idiots on Earth treat us as if they're doing us a favor by letting us bend over and grab our ankles. They don't just talk down their noses at us; they hire subordinates with longer noses for the express purpose of looking down on us.

"We're tired of being treated like we owe the Inner System just because we're alive. You're not going to find it easy to convince anyone in there to back you without a fight, even with the damned OWA breathing down our necks."

"Perfect," Brad said with a sigh. "As if this wasn't going to be hard enough already."

"Hey," the other man said with a firm squeeze of Brad's shoulder. "That's why you run a Platinum outfit. You solve tiny problems like this every day before breakfast.

"Seriously, though, good luck. We know how this is going to end and you've got to make them see the light. If you don't, those Cadre bastards—no matter what they call themselves—are going to see us all dead or enslaved."

"No pressure," Brad said with a shake of his head. "You just keep anyone from shooting us up while I do it."

"We're on that. Lock this down, Madrid, and do it fast."

With a nod to his guards, Brad headed into the Mercenary Guild Hiring Hall and got his next surprise. Rather than mercenaries keeping the inner watch, the open area was packed with men and women in matte-black clamshell armor and carrying stubby-barreled riot guns.

He'd seen something almost exactly like them before, but it took the slender woman stepping out to greet him to spark the memory. It had been a long time since they'd met. Even before he'd become a mercenary.

"Arbiter Blaze," Brad said, extending his hand. "They brought you all the way from Ganymede for this?"

Kenna Blaze, the arbiter who had awarded him ownership of *Heart of Vengeance* after he'd killed all the pirates on the small ship, smiled at him as she firmly shook his hand.

"They decided they needed someone of impeccable character to moderate the sure-to-be-tumultuous negotiations about to take place. Since nobody like that was available, they called me.

"For the duration of these talks, I'll be hosting the conversation and making sure that we stay on track as much as possible. Tempers are high, Admiral Madrid. I'm the bucket of ice water on hand to put out any unexpected fires."

She was more than that, he knew. If the Arbiter Guild was involved, the woman in front of him was going to have a hand in making the final decision. He'd need to convince her that his plans were the best course for survival if he hoped to come out on top.

His wrist-comp chimed with an incoming signal just after they started into the large building. "If you'll give me a moment, I should see what this is," Brad said.

"Of course," Arbiter Blaze said. "We'll wait just ahead."

The message ended up being a high-priority message from President Barnes. A small video of him appeared on the screen. It was straight and to the point.

"I hope I catch you before you're already caught off guard, but the Jovian systems have contracted the Arbiter Guild to come to a decision on how or if they will assist in their own defense.

"I don't know who will be there, but you're going to have to negotiate hard on the behalf of the Commonwealth. Let me stress that. The Commonwealth. Not the Inner System.

"No matter how much the outcome of this meeting might annoy the vested interests on Earth, Mars, and Venus, you need to do what it takes to get these people fighting the OWA."

His image held Brad's eyes for a few moments. "We've moved past the point where a reasonable man could hope the Commonwealth will emerge the same after the conflict is done. The goal isn't to save that entity. The goal now is to save us all from a brutal dictator and then let the pieces fall where they may.

"Good luck, Madrid. You speak now with my voice and on behalf of the Commonwealth. Do what needs doing, no matter the consequences to the current order. Barnes out."

Well, that was unexpected. He'd come to cajole the Jovian politicians as a Fleet officer, not to represent the entire Commonwealth. Since he had no idea what they'd say or do, much less what the Arbiter Guild would decide was the best course for all involved, this was anyone's game.

———

Arbiter Blaze led him to the largest meeting room in the hall and stopped at the well-guarded door. "Pick two people to come in with you, Admiral. The rest can join the other guards outside the building. We'll call them back in to pick you up once we're done."

He could see that Major Papadakis wanted to argue, so he held up his hand. "This isn't our call. You take the outside guard command, Major. I'll take Colonel Saburo in with me. Just him."

The woman wasn't happy, but she knew how to obey orders. "Yes, sir."

Brad followed Blaze inside with Saburo at his heels. This was the best choice, really. Saburo was an Io local, as well as a mercenary in good standing. Considering how Fleet had treated the Jovians over the years, he'd send a different message to the politicians than Major Papadakis.

People filled the conference room, some of whom he recognized but many he didn't. Someone had helpfully put placards in front of the seats. That was how Brad was able to find where he was supposed to sit.

Someone had thoughtfully placed him beside Ilene Johnson. The tall blonde governor of Io smiled somewhat wryly at him as he took his place.

"You certainly know how to get everyone stirred up, Admiral. Leading a Fleet here was a bold move that could end up backfiring on you."

"It's a gift. What am I looking at?"

"A fight," she said, her expression sobering. "I've already decided what I think the best course of action is. The only course of action, when you get right down to it. I'd rather you hadn't put me into the hot seat, but I agree with your basic analysis.

"Many of my compatriots are unconvinced and believe this is just another ploy to string us along to get what the Inner System wants, and then to let us deal with all the fallout. We'd do all the fighting and they'd reap the profits."

"I hope I can convince them otherwise. Who decided to let the Arbiter Guild make the final decision?"

"They were something of a default. No one here is going to let someone else dictate their actions, so we needed someone who could make a decision without all our drama and personalities. Not only is the Arbiter Guild trusted, they're unlikely to have any infiltration from the Cadre or, more recently, the OWA."

Brad nodded. That made sense.

"I was given authority to negotiate on behalf of the Commonwealth. Knowing how the Arbiter Guild works, I'll have to agree to be bound by their decision."

Johnson raised an elegantly sculpted eyebrow. "President Barnes is taking quite the risk there. A lot of powerful people won't be pleased that the Commonwealth isn't telling us how we need to behave. Or them being bound by someone else's decision."

Brad looked over at where Arbiter Blaze had been standing, but she wasn't there. In fact, she wasn't in the room at all.

"I trust Arbiter Blaze. Where did she go? Shouldn't we be getting this started?"

"She's bringing in the final party to the discussion."

At that moment, the door opened back up and Arbiter Blaze walked in with three men behind her, none of them known to Brad.

The rear two took up places with the other guards while the man sat at the table, just about as far from Brad as it was possible to get.

Brad focused on the man's placard and his blood went cold and then hot. It said *Jamal Youden, OWA Representative.*

Arbiter Blaze stepped up to her chair before Brad could decide how he should react. She picked up a small gavel and rapped it on a hard plate of the same material set in front of her. The negotiations were under way.

———

"As all are now present," Blaze said in a professional voice, "we should get started. I'll require the Commonwealth and OWA representatives to be bound by my final decision. Do you agree?"

"Yes," Brad said.

"Of course," the man representing the OWA said with something of a smirk.

"I believe everyone knows me and one another, with the exceptions of the Commonwealth and OWA representatives," Blaze said. "In the spirit of expediting things, I believe we should disallow any opening speeches stating everyone's positions.

"In the case of the Jovian system, I have received all your position papers and will take them into account in my decision. You will, of course, be allowed to ask questions and make statements as we proceed, but we don't have a week to allow everyone to repeat *at length* what they've already told me."

That caused a rumble of discontent in the crowd, and Johnson leaned over so that she could speak softly in his ear. "That's going to piss them off. Politicians love the sound of their own voices, me included. Still, that kind of posturing wastes valuable time, so I think I agree with her this time."

"Who is Youden? Is he from the Jovian system or is he here special for this meeting?"

The governor shrugged slightly. "I've never heard of him. Until I saw the sign, I didn't think the OWA was going to be represented at the meeting. Frankly, I'm not sure where Blaze found him. It's always possible he was planted here like Mader was back before he stuck a knife in my back."

Brad's never-too-damned brother had once served the woman beside him as a trusted aide and confidant. He'd almost certainly been the one to betray her son to the slavers that had tried to kidnap him.

No matter where Youden had come from, Brad had to deal with his presence. Frankly, it might be better to have him there to attribute the actions of the OWA on rather than speaking hypothetically.

Auditor Blaze turned to Brad. "Admiral Madrid is here to represent the Commonwealth and Fleet. I suggest we allow him to state his position, though I suspect we all know what he wants."

Youden stood before Brad could, obviously primed to act. "I object."

Blaze turned toward the other man, looking somewhat bemused. "People usually wait for someone to actually say something before they object to it, Mister Youden."

The OWA representative smiled, an expression that wouldn't be out of place on a shark. "I object to your introduction as it isn't accurate. These people deserve to know who they're listening to.

"Allow me to correct the record. The man in the uniform is Brad Mantruso, the Lord Protector's younger brother. His representation to you is thus already proven a lie and his position is little more than sibling jealousy."

Well, that certainly tore things.

CHAPTER EIGHTEEN

To say that Youden's announcement caused consternation among the gathered politicians was something of an understatement. At least two-thirds of the people gathered leapt to their feet and started shouting. It was so loud that no one could understand what they were saying, but the tone certainly indicated their negative reception to the news.

Arbiter Blaze's expression said that she wasn't pleased at the revelation or the interruption—possibly both—and she began slamming her gavel down and didn't stop until the noise level dropped to the point that she could shout over those who were undeterred by her attempts to regain control of the meeting.

"Order! Order!" she bellowed in a voice even Saburo nodded his approval of.

When several loudmouths kept demanding Brad answer the charges—at least he could now understand what they were saying—she gestured for several of her troops to grab the offenders.

They objected to the treatment, but she was unmoved. "You were warned that I would not tolerate disruption of these proceedings."

"He has to answer the charges," one of the men being held. "Release me at once! Do you know who I am?"

She frowned slightly. "Actually, I don't, but even if I did, the results will be the same. Admiral *Madrid* will have a chance to respond to the OWA declaration, but you won't be here to hear it. Escort these gentlemen out to their guards and then bar them from the building."

That sparked another round of swearing and threats, but she seemed unmoved and silence fell in the room as her guards removed the offenders.

Blaze looked around the still-crowded conference room. "Disruptions will not be tolerated. I don't care who you are; if you interrupt these proceedings, I'll throw you out. If you can't live with that, leave now."

When no one made to leave, Blaze rapped her gavel once and looked at Brad. "The gentleman from the Outer Worlds Alliance has called your identity into question, Admiral. As I've personally known you for quite some time, I feel there must be more to the story. How do you respond?"

Brad rose to his feet and smiled at her before looking around the room of suddenly hostile people. And the smirking Youden.

"I was born Brad Mantruso but took another name after the Terror killed the only family I had ever known. Anyone that knows me knows that I've devoted my life to getting some revenge on the Terror and the Cadre.

"What they don't know is that the Terror was my uncle by birth. I didn't know it either until very late in the game. And, in any case, I killed him for the crimes he committed against humanity."

He paused to let that sink in. "I felt changing my identity was the best way to keep word of my quest for revenge quiet. That worked out just fine.

"Since the representative from the OWA brought my relationship to their Lord Protector into this conversation, I'll address that, too. I had no idea who Jack Mader was, or that his name was actually Mantruso. It came as a great shock to me but changes nothing about him.

"He hid in the offices of the Governor of Io for decades, working for his uncle, the Terror, and the Cadre. When I killed the Terror, he stepped in to lead the Cadre as the Phoenix. I'll wager none of you knew that."

"Objection!" Youden said, leaping to his feet. "That's a lie! The Lord Protector has never been a pirate! He's a freedom fighter that wants the same thing as everyone else here in this room."

"Sit down, Mr. Youden," Arbiter Blaze said. "You opened this can of worms, so you get to see it dumped onto the table. Interrupt again and I'll make you eat them."

She turned her gaze back to Brad. "Keep it brief, but you're allowed to respond to that statement."

He nodded. "Thank you, Arbiter. The Commonwealth has plenty of indisputable evidence that the Phoenix is a pirate and the leader of the Cadre. I personally saw him working with the Terror and have no doubts.

"As for him being a pirate or a freedom fighter, I think his tactics speak for themselves. He was in league with the former President of the Commonwealth to overthrow it and has killed more innocent people than we can possibly comprehend. Actions speak louder than words. You've seen who I am by what I've done. Judge Jack Mantruso by his own actions."

He could see that his words had swayed some of the opinions in the room, but with them being quiet, it was hard to guess at how much. The only thing he could clearly see was the rage in Youden's eyes.

Good.

————

The Arbiter nodded. "Thank you for clarifying the matter, Admiral Madrid. Now, since we've all gathered to hear what you have to say, I think you should begin."

She turned her gaze to Youden. "If anyone has any objections or questions, that can wait until the Admiral completes his statement. Further interruptions will not be tolerated from anyone. That includes you, Mr. Youden."

With her control reasserted, Arbiter Blaze gestured for Brad to begin.

"Many of you are aware of the attacks at Saturn, Mars, and Earth," he said evenly. "What you might not realize is how badly the Cadre and the conspiracy they were part of changed the playing field.

"The Cadre, and when they changed their names, Outer World Intelligence and the Outer Worlds Navy, used everything from bribery to compulsion by holding families hostage to destroy or capture a lot of ships. Our fighting force is damaged right when Jack Mantruso is making his move, which is no coincidence. The bottom line is that Fleet can no longer protect you or the Commonwealth. Not alone."

He paused to once again look around the room. "Mutineers captured Task Group *Immortal*. It and all the ships Fleet contractors built for the Cadre are at Saturn, fueling to come in and conquer humanity.

"You've declared your neutrality, and I'll tell you that means nothing to pirates like these. They'll tell you it does until they're ready to deal with you. They want an empire with no one outside their control. My *brother* told me so himself to try and convince me to join him."

Brad could see that Youden was itching to break in, but Arbiter Blaze's warning was keeping him in his seat. Barely.

"I'll provide what data we have, but the bottom line is that First Fleet is going to fight for your freedom, and for the rest of humanity as well, but we cannot win alone. You're going to have to fight in your own defense or you'll become slaves to the likes of the Terror and the Phoenix.

"Those of you who don't know me personally have heard of me and know my reputation. If you hadn't before I came here with First Fleet, you certainly did so before this meeting.

"Am I the kind of man who wants to betray you into becoming serfs to the Commonwealth or slaves to the OWA? Compare me to the Phoenix and I'll win every single time. Thank you all, and thank you, Arbiter Blaze."

He sat and waited to hear what Youden had to say. This was going to be interesting, considering everyone out here knew what kind of bastards the Terror and the Phoenix had been.

"Mr. Youden," Blaze said. "I suspect you have a rather different point of view. State it succinctly, please."

Youden rose to his feet and smiled. "Admiral Mantruso misstates just about everything. What would one expect of a tool of the oligarchy of the Inner Worlds? We all know how they've used and abandoned us over the years. If anyone wants to hold you under its heel, it is them. And him.

"The Outer Worlds Alliance has come together to throw off the yoke of oppression. We're freedom fighters and I reject the label of *pirates*. The Lord Protector has been maligned. Many of the acts attributed to the Cadre have actually been carried out by the willing hands that support the oligarchs and want to keep us their slaves."

He turned his smiled on the crowd. "Have we called on freedom-loving members of Fleet to fight against the oppressors? Yes. Have we gathered a secret force to end the corrupt and tyrannical rule of the rich and powerful? Yes.

"But I remind you all that we have given our word that the Jovian system will remain under its own control. We respect and honor your neutrality. Don't be fooled by this embittered and deluded man. Eject the Commonwealth forces and be free."

To his shock, Brad heard murmurs of agreement in the crowd. How could they be so blind?

He had to hope that Arbiter Blaze was made of sturdier stuff. He thought she was, but only time would tell.

Arbiter Blaze nodded. "Thank you, Mr. Youden. Ladies and gentlemen, I will now open the floor to a few, select questions. If I feel any of the questions are repetitive, I'll shut you down. If I feel you're making a personal attack, I'll shut you down."

After a long look around the room, she made a gesture to begin. Almost every hand went up.

Blaze pointed at Ilene Johnson. "Governor Johnson."

The tall blonde woman rose. "I have a question for each, if I may."

"Proceed."

She turned to Brad. "I was unaware of your identity, but it doesn't really concern me one way or another. I knew Jack *Mader* for years, which means I've known you a far shorter time than the Lord Protector and trust you far more. I know both your characters and can tell the heroes and villains of the tale.

"Yet that doesn't excuse everything the Inner System have done to us. The Jovian system is done being the lapdogs for those who seek to control us. Those days are done. What say you to that?"

"I received a message from President Barnes before I came in, telling me to do what was best for humanity rather than the Inner System," Brad said. "No matter how this plays out, the military might of the Commonwealth is going to be spent for decades. Your forces here could assert their independence without a strong Commonwealth or the OWA breathing down your necks, if that's what you want.

"Do what you need to do—but keep a firm eye on the facts and the personalities. You've known President Barnes for a long time. Will he try to keep you in the Commonwealth if you're determined to forge your own path?"

Governor Johnson nodded. "You've chosen a wise course in how you phrased that question. I don't believe that President Barnes would try to keep the Jovian system in the Commonwealth if we decide to leave it. He might wish things were different, but he's a good man."

She turned her attention to Youden. "I've known your Lord Protector for over twenty years. He betrayed my son to slavers and worked for the Cadre to bring piracy into the Jovian system and across the Solar System. Those aren't anything more than facts.

"Why should I believe your words when I've seen his actions? In other words, was he lying about who he was then or is he lying now?"

Youden spread his hands. "I can't control what you've been told, but I can say with absolute certainty that the Lord Protector has only the best of intentions toward the Jovian system. If you maintain your neutrality, this drama will play itself out and you will keep your freedom."

His expression hardened. "If you decide to fight with the oppressors of humanity, though, all that changes. The Outer Worlds Alliance will stamp out the corrupt oligarchy and free humanity. If you attempt to impede us, then we'll be forced to free your citizens as well.

"We'd see that you get fair representation in the Outer Worlds

Alliance, but no one would ever trust any of you in leadership positions again. I'd also be afraid of what they might find when the OWA started auditing the finances of those opposed to freedom, if I were you."

Governor Johnson's expression became cold. "They say a leopard can't change its spots, and I say a bully can't change either. The Commonwealth and Admiral Madrid aren't threatening us, but you are."

She looked out over the crowd. "I've heard enough. We know what each of them wants and we've already chosen in our own hearts who we will individually support. Everything else is posturing. I say we ask them both to leave and get down to shouting at one another."

That earned a surprisingly agreeable rumble from the crowd.

"I also agree," Arbiter Blaze said. "If we have any other questions of merit, we can call them back in. If you agree with this course of action, raise your hands."

Slightly more than half agreed to end the questioning. Brad wasn't sure if that was a good sign or not, but he rose gratefully when he was asked to leave.

Youden also walked out of the conference room. He smiled at Brad as he and his guards made their way toward the front of the hall.

"No matter how this plays out, you're going to die," Youden said smugly. "You really should've stayed on Earth."

"Everyone dies, Mr. Youden," Brad said as he stopped to let the man leave without him. "What matters is how we live and what hill we chose to die upon. If I can take my brother down with me while saving humanity from the 'Lord Protector', I'll die a happy man."

CHAPTER NINETEEN

MAJOR PAPADAKIS WAS WAITING for Brad when he came out of the hall. "Factor Kernsky sent someone for you. The mercenaries here confirmed this was someone they knew, but I'm still suspicious."

"Considering how well the Cadre and OWA have everyone penetrated, I'm not going to call that paranoia," Brad conceded. "Where are they?"

She gestured for two of her Marines to escort a short man up. He looked vaguely familiar.

"Admiral Madrid," the man said. "You don't know me, but I'm Samuel Juras. We met briefly, but I'm sure you don't remember me. I was Factor Kernsky's receptionist back in those days."

That jarred Brad's memory enough and he did remember the man. They'd barely exchanged a dozen words, but he'd met him the second time he'd gone to Kernsky's office.

"I do remember you, Mr. Juras, though only just," Brad said as he extended his hand. "What can I do for you?"

"She's currently meeting with the directors and sent a recording for you. I'm not privy to the contents, but she wanted me to make sure that you knew it really comes from her."

"As I said, I barely know you," Brad countered. "How can I be sure of that?"

The man smiled. "She told me to tell you something that she said would mean something to you. It was something you talked about when you first met. She said, 'Tell him that midsummer may once again take wing.'"

Brad immediately nodded. Sara Kernsky had commanded the frigate *Midsummer* for the Red Wings Mercenary Company when the Mercenary Guild issued the last overriding contract and took out the Cadre cruiser *Black Skull*. The ship had never flown again, and the Red Wings had died as a mercenary company that day.

The message in and of itself proved nothing, but along with his knowledge of the man, he was provisionally willing to grant this was a genuine message from Kernsky.

"I'll take the recording, then. Why didn't she just send something over the com?"

"Because she has her doubts that it would remain solely between the two of you," the man said as he pulled out a small slate and extended it. "She said the password was your darkest secret, Admiral. One word."

That hardly took much guessing. He entered *Mantruso* and the lock screen went away. At the time she'd recorded that message, his identity had been a closely guarded secret. Now? Not so much.

Her image appeared on the screen. "Admiral Madrid, you need to hear this in relative privacy. Please pause this recording and send Samuel on his way."

The man obviously heard that. He bowed slightly and took his leave.

Once he was gone, Brad moved himself and his guards to where no one would be able to overhear the recording. Then he started it playing again.

"As we discussed," she said, "I'm meeting with the directors. Four of them, anyway. The fifth is refusing to attend. At this point, we need him. The OWA has gotten to him somehow. If you could bring him with you to the Mercenary Guild offices—not the ones at the Hiring

Hall but the ones at the city center—then we at least have a chance to get that contract.

"We'll probably be here arguing all day, but if you could make something happen a little sooner, that would be better than hearing these people expel hot air. I'm attaching a pass to get into his gated community; otherwise, the guards won't let you in. Don't dawdle."

The recording concluded with an address for the missing director and for the offices.

"Major, verify both addresses," Brad said. "I doubt this is manufactured, but I want to be sure. Saburo, I want you to take point and scout the director's home. If we need to rescue him, I want to be sure that we have a good exit strategy."

Time was wasting and he needed to get the politicians from both the Jovian system and the Mercenary Guild on his side before the sky fell on them all.

———

Director Gustave Kutschinski lived in an exclusive neighborhood, just as one might expect of someone with wealth and influence. Brad, having been raised in space, couldn't see the attraction, but he supposed others might feel the same way about how he lived.

When he arrived at the gate, Brad presented the pass Kernsky had given him. That seemed acceptable, though they gave the size of his escort an unfavorable look and demanded to see IDs.

"I'm here on Mercenary Guild business," Brad said, presenting his wrist-comp. "That's why my escort is mixed."

The two guards had a brief discussion and opened the gates. "You're free to go in, Admiral. Please check in on your way out."

Saburo took one vehicle ahead once they were inside. Five minutes later, he called Brad and told him to come ahead. The Colonel had set up just around the corner from the address they'd been given.

"How do we want to handle this, Admiral?" Major Papadakis asked briskly. "If he's under compulsion, he won't open the door."

"If he sees the size of your escort, he won't open the door, either," Saburo added.

"You two are with me," Brad decided. "We'll go right up and keep buzzing until he lets us in."

That said, he marched up to the director's home and pressed the buzzer. Rather to his shock, the door opened almost immediately. A tall, fit woman dressed in casual clothes sporting bright colors smiled at him.

"Yes?" she asked.

"My name is Brad Madrid and I'm looking for Director Kutschinski. It's urgent."

Her face took on a sad expression. "I thought he already told the office he was sick today. I'm afraid that—"

"Is that someone from the Guild, honey? Let them in."

The woman's expression took on a disproving air. "You're sick, baby," she called over her shoulder. "They can come back later."

"It will only take a moment," Brad lied, sticking his foot in the door.

From the look she gave the offending appendage, she was considering slamming the door on it. He hoped Fleet uniform shoes were half as tough as the boots his Vikings wore.

A large man came up behind her and put his hands on her shoulders. "It's okay."

The woman—his wife, Brad assumed—sighed and stepped back. "Keep it short, Gus. I want them gone before I take the kids out to the park. I'll make tea. The hot liquid will do you good."

He led the three of them back into a luxurious living room. An open counter allowed Brad to see the man's wife bustling around the kitchen and setting up to make tea.

Rather than taking a seat in the most comfortable-looking chair, Director Kutschinski gestured for Brad to take it and sat in the one set away from it. Saburo stepped over to the fireplace with its cheery false flames, and Major Papadakis remained near the hall leading back to the front door.

"Director Kutschinski," Brad started, "we need you to come in for the meeting of the directors. It's extremely important."

"So Factor Kernsky said," he rumbled. "She has a quorum, so they can do business without me. As my wife said, I'm not feeling at all well."

Brad started to respond but hesitated when Kutschinski started blinking at him strangely. While he did so, he continued speaking.

"I understand that she's seeking something very important to her, but if she can't convince the other four directors, I doubt she can convince me. I tried to be polite when she called, but I really must insist that she stop."

He'd almost finished speaking when Brad realized what he was seeing. Morse code. SOS. An old Earth code that Saburo had insisted he learn. This repeating code meant someone was in distress.

He almost said something but realized the other man believed he was under observation. Brad's gaze flicked over the wife, but she didn't seem like a threat. There could be someone else in the house.

The man had small children. Were they being used as a lever against him? Kernsky said that the wife and kids had been seen out and about, and the wife had just indicated they were going to the park soon. It didn't make sense.

"This is an all-hands-on-deck sort of thing, Director," Brad said. "They need to have your vote, even if you end up saying no."

As he spoke, Brad tapped his knee in response to the man's silent message. "What threat? Kids?" his code asked.

Kutschinski's eyes caught the exchange and he inclined his head slightly.

"I don't understand why you people can't get it through your heads. I'm not going in to vote today."

The man's eyes said, "My wife and nanny are Cadre."

His wife came into the room with a tray holding a tea pot and three cups. "Here we go. Why aren't you in your chair, dear?"

As she stepped up beside them and set the tray onto a side table, Brad punched her hard in the solar plexus, hoping to Everlit he wasn't making a terrible mistake.

———

Brad's strike sent the woman staggering back, clutching at her middle, but all her husband did was steady the teapot so that nothing fell and broke. Saburo and Papadakis were slow to react, but he could hardly blame them. No one could've expected him to abruptly attack a woman they didn't know was an enemy.

The unexpected nature of the attack didn't stop the woman for groping at her back, probably for a weapon.

Surging to his feet, Brad swept her legs out from under her and pinned her with a knee as he searched for the weapon. He found a pistol in a concealed holster and tossed it away.

"Secure her," he ordered quietly, a hand clamped over the woman's mouth. "Where are the kids?"

"In their bedroom," Kutschinski said. "The 'nanny' has a submachinegun. Her orders are to kill the kids if things go sour. Please save them."

"Saburo, you have the prisoner. Major, you're with me."

They'd made some noise but not enough to alert the other bad guy, he hoped. Brad started to lead the way, drawing his sidearm, but Papadakis got in front of him and had her weapon out. She moved surprisingly softly for someone in armor.

Not completely quietly, though. A woman with mousy brown hair stuck her head out into the hall, her eyes widening as she saw the two of them sneaking up.

She yanked her head back just as Papadakis snapped off a shot that splintered the doorframe where the woman's head had been a second earlier.

The shockingly loud noise made the kids in the room scream as Brad and Papadakis barreled through the door. The kids were in a large crib to the side of the room, a pair of girls about two years old with bright ribbons in their hair.

The woman had yanked open a drawer and retrieved a submachinegun, and was already turning toward the intruders. That was good. Brad would much rather have someone shooting at him instead of at kids.

Papadakis dodged left, so he went right. The woman had to pick one of them.

She went for Papadakis, opening fire on full automatic. The heavy slugs slammed into the Marine officer and she went down, her return fire going wide.

Brad shot the woman in the chest until she dropped, dead before she hit the floor. Then he ran to Papadakis. She was still alive.

Everlit, she wasn't even badly hurt. Her armor had taken the brunt of the attack, with only one slug grazing the exposed flesh of her left hand across the back.

"I'm okay," she said, climbing stiffly to her feet. "We need to secure the children and withdraw. There might be others in the house or a team nearby."

Kutschinski came running into the room and grabbed his kids up.

"It's okay," he said, stroking their hair. "Daddy's here."

"Director Kutschinski, is there anyone else in the house?" Brad asked.

"No, but I'm sure there are more of these bastards around here somewhere."

Brad licked his lips. "How…ah, did your wife get involved in this and why would she kill her own children?"

"Because she's a stone-cold bitch," Kutschinski said sadly. "She fooled me when we met three years ago, and I never had a clue until the vote for the overriding contract came up for discussion. We have to get to the offices but quietly. I'm sure they have the headquarters under observation, and they'll do literally anything to keep the Mercenary Guild from coming after them."

"Bring the kids," Brad said. "We'll take your wife with us and leave the other woman here. We can't waste a single second now. If they take out the directors, it will keep the Mercenary Guild out of the fight until they get here in force, and that would be the end of us."

CHAPTER TWENTY

BRAD HALFWAY EXPECTED someone to stop them on the way out of Director Kutschinski's neighborhood, but the guards just waved them through the main gate. That didn't mean someone hadn't heard all the shooting and called the authorities. Their time was short.

Yet the director had been right when he'd said that they needed to stay low, because the OWA certainly had the Mercenary Guild offices under observation. If they were spotted going in, they'd almost certainly be attacked.

"Is there a less-obtrusive way into the offices, Director?" Brad asked as the two vans moved into heavier traffic. He really hoped they could avoid an ambush on the road. Vehicular gun battles had the proven potential to kill a lot of innocent people.

The man nodded. "We can use the freight entrance. I suppose they might have that under surveillance, too, but unless we plan to get in through the utility tunnels, that's the best way."

Brad pursed his lips. "Are the utility tunnels large enough to let us in?"

Kutschinski blinked in surprise. "I honestly don't know. That was more of a nudge to the action vids I watched as a kid. I know the service tunnels enter in the basement and that we have them secured against intrusion."

Brad started to suggest it might be a good idea to look there for a way in, but another thought floated up to his awareness. The Cadre had always been excellent at slipping through the cracks of whatever defenses they needed to penetrate a target. Could they have people in place to use something like the utility tunnels to get into the Mercenary Guild offices?

If so, the building might rapidly become a trap. If they were stuck on the upper floors of the building, then a force coming from below could grind them down. Or they could just blow up the building. They'd done that before, too.

"It might be better if we can get Factor Kernsky and the rest out of the building rather than going in to meet them," Brad said slowly.

He looked at his wrist-comp. It was close to when normal folks would be breaking for lunch.

"Right now, the OWA is still confident they have you under control, Director. They probably won't jump in any sooner than they have to. It would be much better from their point of view if they could keep things nonviolent. They want us divided, so shooting at people will be a last resort."

Kutschinski shrugged, holding his daughters tighter. "So, what do we do?"

"Saburo, look up a map of the area around the offices. If we can get the other directors out, we'll want a fast getaway from the reaction team they'll have around here somewhere. That's in addition to the troops they'll have positioned to rush the building.

"You can bet the directors have mercenary guards inside, so the OWA will need a lot of people to overcome that when they hit. They'll have teams in vehicles around here somewhere, too."

Brad looked pointedly at the director's children. "We'll want to get you and your kids clear before we try this. It could end very badly."

"We can put my kids off," Kutschinski agreed. "And my bitch of a soon-to-be-ex-wife. I definitely want her alive to answer some extremely pointed questions later. As for me, I'm staying. If we can get the three directors that aren't in the OWA's pocket with us, we can authorize the overriding contract before they kill us."

"I hope we can prevent any of us dying," Brad said dryly. "Still, I take your point. Where can we drop your kids and your…um, former wife safely?"

"One of the satellite mercenary offices," he said promptly. "The Pythons have a place they use as a headquarters nearby. I know them well enough that I think I can get them to help us out."

"Make sure you tell them to keep their mouths shut when you go in. Leave the woman out here and go in with your kids. That won't stand out like hauling a prisoner around."

"I can call them to send someone to the curb, if you'll share a com. She didn't allow me one, for obvious reasons."

One of the Vikings handed over his com to the director and the man was soon speaking with someone.

"Hey, it's Gus. I need a personal favor. A discreet one. Meet me at the curb in ten minutes and bring some trusted friends. Parents, if possible. My kids are with me."

He hung up after an inaudible response and handed the com back to the mercenary. "Thanks. They'll be there. Just pull right up into the loading zone."

It took them slightly more than ten minutes to work their way to the street outside the Python's offices. Four mercenaries, all female, lounged against the wall, watching traffic with warriors' eyes.

When Saburo stopped the van in the loading zone, one of the mercenaries straightened, walked casually over to the van, and opened the sliding door. She stared at the packed group of mercenaries and Fleet Marines.

"Well, it looks like someone's having a party and forgot to send me an invitation. I'm hurt."

Director Kutschinski grinned. "I think I can make it up to you. Admiral Brad Madrid, meet Captain Erika Dunham, one of the senior policymakers for the Pythons."

"Captain," Brad said, inclining his head.

"I've heard of you, Admiral. The Vikings are a stand-up bunch and we've worked together in the past, though not me personally. What's the situation and how can the Pythons be of service, Director?"

Kutschinski gestured toward his bound and gagged wife struggling in the back of the van. "My wife turns out to have been Cadre all along. I need you to hold on to her and my kids while we go extract the rest of the directors from what I suspect is going to be a trap."

"Done," the woman said instantly, motioning for her friends to come up and take the children.

She eyed the prisoner with distaste. "We'll get her inside and lock her down. Are you going to need armed support for this run? I can probably get a team ready in ten minutes, though we won't be heavily armed and armored."

"How long would it take to get a heavy team or two ready?" Brad asked.

"Half an hour or I'll have some asses," she assured him.

"Then I think I have a better plan," he said with a nasty grin.

———

Once the mercenaries had the kids and the prisoner out of the van and into the building, they took off. The women had been clever in moving the bound prisoner through the curious crowd of passersby.

They'd laughed and joked, loudly proclaiming that the prisoner had gotten drunk and let her friends tie her up. That now she'd have to explain her awkward situation to her commanding officer.

Brad had to admit that was clever. It was plausible enough that none of the people walking by could dismiss it out of hand. If the authorities came calling to ask questions, the Pythons could produce a different woman with a similar appearance to verify the story.

Of course, all that would be moot if Brad's suspicions were confirmed and they had a running gun battle down the streets of the city.

The next step in the plan was to get the directors—at least the three that were probably not in the OWA's pocket—to come out so that he could rescue them without springing the trap he suspected was set up in the basement.

He used his com to call Factor Kernsky. She answered after a few moments.

"How did the meeting with the political representatives go, Admiral?" she asked in a low voice. "I hope better than things here are going."

"That all depends on who you ask, I suppose. They're still talking and told me they'd call me back in if they needed anything from me. My reading on the crowd was that it could go either way, though I'm given to understand that Arbiter Blaze is going to make the final decision."

"I wish we could let her make a ruling here," Kernsky muttered darkly. "We're still missing a director, and the four we have seem more inclined to argue than look for compromise. I wish someone would go to Kutschinski's house and drag his ass up here. We need him badly."

The director in question snorted a little and shook his head at that.

"Well, you can't tell the boss to do anything, if you know what I mean," Brad said nonchalantly. "Why don't we do lunch? We can go over everything and see if we can figure something out."

"Sure," she said. "Come on up."

"I'd rather not," he said firmly. "I've seen far too many conference rooms and offices over the last few months. I need fresh air and I'm sure you and your friends do, too. Bring them along and you can get back to arguing after a good meal. And maybe some alcohol."

She chuckled. "I could use a drink. Everdark knows that might help loosen them up. What do you have in mind?"

"We've got room in our vehicle for four people, so bring three friends along and meet us out front. We'll go to a place that someone recommended, and that'll give people time to cool off and come back at the problem from a fresh angle."

"Okay. How long until you get here?"

This was the tricky part. Brad had to assume that someone was listening in and that he might start the clock ticking on a hostile response.

"We're a bit out, so you have plenty of time. I made a reservation at Midsummer for us, and they said they'd split the red wine four ways for us. Say we'll be there in an hour."

"One hour is perfect," Kernsky said without missing a beat. "We'll be in the lobby. When I see you pull up, we'll come out and meet you."

"Excellent," he said. "See you then."

Brad ended the call and looked over at Kutschinski. "We'll pick her up in fifteen minutes."

"Exactly how did you work that in there?" the man asked. "I gather *midsummer* is a code of some kind, as was the wine, but I don't get it."

"Let's hope the OWA misses the significance, too. Factor Kernsky captained the frigate *Midsummer* for the Red Wings on the last over-riding contract. She was the junior-most of four captains."

Comprehension dawned on the man's face. "So, she knew to divide the time by four. Interesting and creative. Something you discussed ahead of time?"

"I had to work it out on the fly," Brad said with a shake of his head. "We're lucky that she's quick on the uptake."

He leaned forward and addressed Saburo in the front passenger seat. "Tell me you have the course worked out, Saburo."

The Colonel nodded. "We'll be there on time. The other van is going to be behind us to slow down any pursuit. The most important part of the plan is getting the critical people out of the trap. Since she's back there, Major Papadakis will have to be the delaying force."

And a damned dangerous job that would be if they accidentally sprung the trap. He'd have to hope they slipped in and got the directors and Kernsky before the shit hit the fan.

That hope collapsed as soon as they turned onto the street where the offices were and saw the fighting already spilling out of the building. A cluster of people was exiting under fire and shooting back into the building in return.

"Take us in fast," Brad ordered, pulling his pistol and preparing to shoot out the sliding door, over the heads of anyone coming in.

He had enough time to recognize Factor Kernsky with a thin man over her shoulder, charging for the van as it came to a screeching halt. Kutschinski opened the door to let her, her charge, and the men right behind her in.

Brad started firing over her head as she came in low, targeting the armored men firing at her and the mercenaries trying to buy them time for the directors to escape.

The attackers looked like Cadre—OWI now, he supposed—commandos. Well, except for the woman in a suit that was screaming for them to kill everyone in Brad's van.

She wasn't shooting the little pistol in her hand, but she was technically armed, so he shot her down, figuring that anything he could do to delay the direct attack on the van was a win.

She went down just as the last of the people making a run for the van piled inside and Kutschinski slammed the sliding door closed.

That was when every bad guy in sight opened fire on the van.

CHAPTER TWENTY-ONE

A HAIL of bullets smashed into the side of the van moments after Director Kutschinski had slammed the door shut. Brad fully expected the barrier to fail catastrophically, but to his surprise, it stood up to the abuse. It had to have been armored. Score one for Major Papadakis.

The impacts still managed to fracture the clear plate that acted as a window, but none of the bullets penetrated. Brad wasn't certain how long it would last.

Even as the van accelerated away from the ambush, Papadakis and the guards with her opened fire on the attackers. As much as he wanted to order his van to stop so that the troops on board could assist her, he knew that his duty lay in getting the directors clear.

Factor Kernsky almost fell over in the face of the vehicle's acceleration but managed to deposit the wounded man on her shoulder safely into the laps of two Marines, who started assessing his injuries.

"Did you get the bitch?" she demanded.

"You mean the one that was directing the attack?" Brad asked. "Yes."

"Good," she spat. "I knew that she was dirty, but I never expected her to be ready to have us executed at a moment's notice. I hope you killed her."

"Me, too. Who was she?"

"Director Evelyn Richards," Kutschinski said. "It seems we have an opening on the board. I suppose we'll have to have a meeting to talk about that."

The injured man chuckled and then sucked in a sharp breath when one of the Marines finished opening his shirt and cleaning the wound. "We've got a quorum right now. Not sure how much longer that's going to last. I feel like I might pass out."

He looked at Brad. "The board requires four directors to be present to act as a quorum."

"We need to vote as quickly as possible on the overriding contract, then," Kutschinski said. "I move that we open this meeting of the board and dispense with the reading of the minutes from the last meeting. Do I have a second?"

"Seconded," the wounded man said.

"I hereby move that we approve an overriding contract against the Outer Worlds Alliance. Do I have a second?"

"Seconded," one of the other men said.

"All in favor?"

All four of the directors present raised their hands.

Brad had no idea which of the three other directors had been hesitant, but the attack seemed to have firmly cemented their vote.

"The board of the Mercenary Guild hereby approves an overriding contract against the Outer Worlds Alliance," Kutschinski said. "I hereby direct that all mercenary units, whether they be engaged in other contracts or not, be summoned to Io as quickly as possible. A preference is given to units with ships, but ground troops will also be needed. This is an all-hands-on-deck mission."

"I have other business for the board," the wounded man said, his eyes seeming a little less focused than a minute before.

"Proceed," Kutschinski said.

"It appears that the board has a vacancy. An extremely recent and welcome vacancy. So that the board may continue to perform its function if I pass out or worse, I nominate Factor Sara Kernsky to fill the opening. Do I have a second?"

"Seconded," Kutschinski said immediately. "All in favor?"

All four directors' hands went up.

He smiled at Factor—Director—Kernsky. "I wish that your elevation had occurred under less-arduous circumstances, but welcome to the board of the Mercenary Guild, Director Kernsky."

"If you don't mind," she said, "I'll send the overriding contract now. I took the liberty of having something prepared so everything is already in order, and the sooner we can begin getting it executed, the better."

"I concur," Kutschinski said. "Do it."

The van took a corner at a speed that threatened to send it into the other lane of traffic before it managed to straighten out. Just ahead of them, Brad could see a vehicle approaching at a high rate of speed with a man holding a rocket launcher leaning out the window.

"I'd get that sent and adjourn your meeting, because we've got company," Brad said grimly.

————

Rather than dodge the vehicle, Brad's driver swerved into oncoming traffic and forced the other vehicle to abruptly change course. That could have resulted in a head-on collision, but that probably would've been more survivable than a direct hit from the anti-vehicle weapon.

It turned out that the other driver had no desire to run headlong into the van he was trying to catch. He swerved to the left and was promptly struck by a vehicle in the other lane, causing both of them to lose control and slam into the building nearby. Thankfully, there were no pedestrians in that particular section of sidewalk.

Saburo turned in his seat to face Brad. "Major Papadakis is reporting that she can see several vehicles taking off in pursuit of us. She said that she's got the attack squad on the run, but they disabled her van. She's not going to be able to provide us any backup."

"Then we'd best hope that the Pythons are ready to receive incoming fire," he said. "You keep working with the driver to get us to a place where they can intercept the pursuit we picked up."

Brad turned his attention to the Marines and Vikings in the van. "We'll be stopping as soon as we get to the designated defensive area.

We'll pile out and look for whatever the Pythons have arranged as a barricade. We've got to stop the Cadre from overrunning us."

With that said, he turned his attention to Sara Kernsky. She was focusing on the injured director, who'd lost consciousness since Brad had last looked at him. The wound looked bad.

It was entirely conceivable that the Mercenary Guild would be looking for another new director before this fight was over. The two Marines were providing what care they could, but they had no way to deal with internal injuries or bleeding.

"Director Kutschinski, you might want to give your contact another call and ask her to have some medics standing by," he said. "I suspect that seconds are going to count once we arrive."

The man nodded, took the com he'd borrowed earlier back from the Viking that owned it, and made the call.

"They just came out of nowhere," Kernsky said bitterly. "We'd just gotten to the lobby when they came pouring out of the stairs. We thought we were ready, but they were shooting by the time we'd hit the door. He never had a chance."

Brad put a hand on her shoulder, steadying her as the van took another corner at an excessive rate of speed. "The OWA had this set up in advance. They were waiting for the right moment to decapitate the Mercenary Guild. I tried to be subtle, but I suspect calling you triggered them to move early."

She lifted her eyes to meet his gaze. "I think you were pretty damn subtle. While it's possible that your call could've started the ball rolling, they had to have been on a hair trigger already. Let's just save the blame for the bastards that deserve it."

"If they're taking a shot at us, it makes me wonder if they have a bigger force in position to go after Arbiter Blaze and the politicians at the hiring hall," Brad said. "In just a couple of minutes, we're going to be fighting this particular group of pirates, but they had to have had a plan to deal with the leadership here in the Jovian system if it came down to shooting."

Kernsky paled and started tapping on her wrist-comp. "I'm sending her a message right now, but you're probably right. Worse, they knew that building was going to be under heavy guard. They either have a force big enough to kill all of those mercenaries and private guards, or they have something worse in mind."

At that moment, the ground seemed to buck under them, and the driver lost control of the van. It slammed into the vehicle in front of them and flipped over it before coming back down on the roadway, rolling, and finally smashed the building beside the road. Brad's vision went dark.

———

Brad woke abruptly and realized that not much time had passed since the explosion and crash. Everyone had been tossed around inside the van, and those that had not been secured had suffered the worst.

The director who'd been shot was now in the front of the van and, based on the angle of his neck, had been prescient about the board needing to have four live members in case he died.

The other directors that Brad didn't know had managed to secure themselves and, other than being shaken, seemed to be in good shape. That just left Sara Kernsky.

She'd flown forward with the impact, but Saburo's seat had blocked her from being thrown into the front of the van. Based on the blood running down her face from her scalp, she'd struck the roof, but she was conscious and already stirring.

A quick check of the rest of his people showed that they were all alive, though some had obviously been injured in the accident. He supposed they were lucky that they'd only suffered one casualty.

The van had ended up on its roof, so Brad carefully undid his restraints and lowered himself. Once he was oriented, he tried to open the sliding door and found that it was jammed. As it was bulletproof, he resisted the urge to try and kick the window out.

"Saburo, can you get your door open?" he asked.

His voice sounded steady. Good.

The Colonel wrestled with his door for a moment and then it popped loose. He staggered out of the vehicle and bent down to find his pistol where it had fallen during the crash. He then turned to face the direction they'd come, obviously looking for the pursuit that Major Papadakis had said was coming.

Brad gestured for the driver to help him get the deceased director out of the van. Then he helped Kernsky and the other directors out and saw that they were safely protected by a ring of his Vikings and Marines.

She stared down at the dead man and shook her head. "I'd hoped to never see anything like this again, once I retired from being an active mercenary. Will the killing ever end?"

"I certainly hope so," Brad said. "But the only way we're going to make that happen is to stop the OWA. Did you get your message out? If that explosion was at the hiring hall, there's no way that any of them got clear before the blast."

He oriented himself and verified that the smoke rising in the distance was in the direction of the hiring hall. Based solely on the distance and the relative lack of damage around him, he didn't think they'd used a nuke. Or if they had, it had been a small one. A full-size nuclear device would have obliterated the city.

Kernsky checked her wrist-comp. "My message went out, but I haven't received a reply yet. I'm not sure that I'm going to at this point."

There was a fair bit of panic in the crowd around them. People were running around in terror—which was completely understandable —and there was a lot of screaming and shouting. The smell of something burning was starting to sting his nostrils, too.

What there wasn't was shooting. Where had the OWI commandos gone? They should've been here by now.

"Saburo, do you still have a signal? Call Papadakis and get a status from her. Is she still engaged?"

The mercenary brought his wrist-comp closer to his mouth and began speaking into it. Moments later, he nodded and said something else. Then he turned toward Brad.

"She says that the hostiles withdrew just before the explosion. They went back into the building, and she was about to have to make a decision on following them or trying to meet up with us when everything went boom.

"If I were a betting man, which I am, it sounds like someone gave the order to break contact. If they knew that the overriding contract had already been executed, there was no longer any need to kill the Board of Directors. That may mean that our pursuit won't be coming."

Brad shook his head. "We can't count on that. We need to get under cover and find a way to the spaceport so we can get back to the fleet. It's too dangerous down here. If they managed to decapitate every government in the Jovian system, one Everdarkened storm is going to break loose."

Sara Kernsky's wrist-comp signaled. She answered the call and her eyes went wide. As the other person spoke, she sagged with obvious relief in her expression.

"It's for you, Madrid," she said. "I think you'd better take it."

Unsure of what to expect, Brad took her wrist-comp and looked at the screen. Now that he was facing it, the privacy function didn't prevent him from hearing or seeing the other person on the call clearly.

It was Arbiter Blaze.

He felt himself sagging a little in relief of his own. "I have to confess that I wasn't expecting to ever see you again, Arbiter Blaze. You're looking unexpectedly well for a woman that just survived an explosion."

"Ironically, we'd broken for lunch and I was a good distance away from the hiring hall. At this point, I have no way of confirming who might have died in the explosion, but I'm hopeful that the majority of the participants had decided to get out and get some fresh air.

"Governor Johnson was with me, so she is the only one of them I can say with absolute certainty survived. The initial reports are that it was a conventional explosion and that the hiring hall is completely gone.

"The buildings around it absorbed the majority of the blast and funneled it upward. I'm certain that everyone is scrambling to make sure it didn't compromise the integrity of the dome, but if you're not in a safe place, you might want to get to one soon."

"We're just getting organized to head toward the spaceport where our shuttle can pick us up," Brad said. "We managed to rescue most of the directors of the Mercenary Guild. Unless they object, we'll take them with us at least as far as there, and then they can make their own way to somewhere safe.

"They've issued an overriding contract, so I'd expect a lot of mercenaries to be headed back this way in the very near future. How will the explosion affect the Jovian system, if it took out most of the leadership?"

"Badly," she said bluntly. "One thing that it will not affect is whether the Jovian system will support your actions against the OWA. That choice rests with me and I've made my decision. Jupiter will fight beside the Commonwealth fleet and Mercenary Guild.

"The only thing I insist on is that you personally are in command. Together with whatever mercenary companies you can gather, we'll do our very best to stop the OWA under your banner.

"Those bastards made very clear that they were no different from the Cadre and they vindicated everything you said earlier. Sometimes people just can't stop themselves from doing the very thing that's going to get them in trouble. Let's hope it kills them this time.

"Call me back when you're back on your flagship and I'll have a better report on the casualties here. Good luck, Admiral. And good hunting."

With that, she disconnected the call and he handed the wrist-comp back to Kernsky.

That news was a relief, but Brad knew it was only a start. What happened with the Jovian system after the fighting was over, even if they won, would be a separate matter. For now, though, it would have to be enough.

It was time for him to go on the offensive. And that meant he had to kick the OWA where it hurt and do it fast.

CHAPTER TWENTY-TWO

As soon as he made it back aboard *Incredible*, Brad summoned his senior officers for a planning meeting. For the moment, it was only the Fleet side, because Michelle was going to be helping organize the mercenary companies as they came in.

She wasn't experienced enough to command them, unfortunately. They wouldn't hold enough respect for her to act as her subordinates. Thankfully, the board of the Mercenary Guild had thought of that and selected someone they could be sure would be able to give orders that the various mercenary companies would follow: Director Sara Kernsky.

It had been a long time since she'd commanded a ship in battle, but her reputation was solid and her authority unquestioned. In this case, she wouldn't be leading any specific ship but would be acting as the flag officer directing the mercenary contingent under Brad's command.

To do that, she first had to get all mercenary ships gathered at Io. Many of them were already in the Jovian system, but some were coming from the asteroid belt and various other locations scattered around the Solar System.

While she was doing that, Brad was in his office with Commodores Bailey, Nuremberg, and Jahoda. All of them looked grim.

"What a damned mess," Bailey said straight off. "How did the OWA get all of these people in here? How did they plant explosives inside the mercenary hiring hall? Do they have every single organization out here penetrated six ways to Sunday?"

"Pretty much," Brad said without much emphasis. "The Cadre has had a long time to put people in positions of power out here. The Jovian system is their playground. Jack Mader—long before anyone knew he was Jack Mantruso—was a senior political operative on Io for almost two decades.

"Every time they've made a move in this area, it's caught us by surprise because they have forces and observers that we just can't guess at in reserve. Everdark, they had an entire chemical weapon research facility buried in the Trojans."

Commodore Nuremberg leaned forward and scowled. "I know that you don't mean it like it sounds, but you act as if you're already defeated. We don't need to sit here, going over how screwed we are. We need to find solutions to take their strength and break it.

"They have to be just about finished with their fueling operations at Saturn. Once they start for the Jovian system, we're going to have to meet them. As it stands right now, that's going to be a tough fight. How can we improve our odds?"

"Fuel," Jahoda said. "Even though they're going to top off their tanks at Saturn, if they hope to strike Mars and then still make their way to Earth for the final fight, they're going to have to refuel again.

"They can't risk running out before they get to Earth or, worse yet, in the middle of the fight to conquer the planet. That means interdicting all sources for refueling here is critical."

Brad had to agree. While he knew that the OWA had several small prototype refining systems that could work on ice bodies, for that many ships, they'd need something a lot bigger. He knew that the easiest way for them to refuel would be using the refineries serving Jupiter itself, but he had to know that Brad, or whoever had ended up in command of the Commonwealth forces around Jupiter, would destroy those before he allowed them to fall into enemy hands.

So, that meant there would be another fuel depot hidden somewhere in the Jovian system, like the one he'd found in the Belt, though undoubtedly a lot larger. They'd had to have used it to fuel the ships that attacked Mars, since they hadn't controlled Saturn at that point. The trick was going to be finding it in time to make a difference.

Brad was about to say that when his wrist-comp signaled. Since he'd set it not to disturb him, someone on his staff had overridden that to allow the call to go through. That probably meant it was bad news.

He brought the screen up and answered. "Madrid."

Arbiter Blaze appeared on the screen, her expression even grimmer than the last time Brad had spoken with her. "I'm glad to see that you got back into orbit, Admiral. My hopes that the majority of the political leaders of the Jovian system had escaped the hiring hall seem to have been in vain.

"We're still looking for anyone that might have been out of the building at the time, but all indications are that the blast killed a minimum of sixty percent of the political leadership out here. A minimum. Worst case, that number goes up to seventy percent."

Brad felt his stomach do a slow roll.

"That's awful," he eventually said. "Do we have any idea how they got the explosives inside the building?"

Blaze shook her head. "And with the destruction of all the security systems, we'll probably never know, unless we capture whoever planted them. Our friendly local OWA representative seems to have disappeared, so he's very high on my list of suspects.

"I wish I could say that I'm confident that we'll catch him before he escapes from Io, but I'm not. Frankly, if he isn't already in space, I'd be astonished."

The disarray that the various political entities would be going through from having their leadership killed was almost unimaginable. The only thing that kept it from being an utter disaster was the fact that they had decided to allow Arbiter Blaze to make the final decision before they'd been killed and that she'd survived. The OWA had missed the one person that they'd absolutely needed to kill.

"I appreciate the update, Arbiter," he said formally. "If you don't mind, I'm going to continue to funnel the communication between the civilian authorities and my command through you. Honestly, during this crisis, I think that the Arbiter Guild is going to play a key role in maintaining the stability we need while the new leadership gets on their feet."

She smiled slightly. "I think you're doing them a disservice, Admiral. Each government has a clear line of succession. Even as we speak, the highest-ranking survivors are taking the helms of their various governments. Things are a mess, but you can rest assured that they're going to do everything they can to help you win the fight that's coming.

"But your point is a good one. The Arbiter Guild will continue to work with everyone involved to smooth the process and assist in any way that we can."

"Good," Brad said. "Then if you could start getting me the names and basic information for each government's space vessels, we can start putting together the grand force we're going to need to defend the Jovian system."

————

Brad immediately dispatched some of his smaller ships to scout the likely line of advance that the force that had attacked Mars had used. He knew he was taking a risk, because the refueling depot would be guarded. Unfortunately, they didn't find anything.

In the few days that it'd taken them to search, Director Kernsky had gotten the majority of the mercenary ships and companies sorted out. They didn't have anything larger than destroyers, but what ships they did have were powerfully armed and crewed by experienced personnel.

The various armed forces of the different political entities that made up the Jovian system were slower to gather, but they were beginning to show up in force as well. Even though Arbiter Blaze had insisted that he was in overall command, he felt it would be best if he focused his attention through a single person to convey his orders to those ships.

As the combined force was gathering around Io, he turned his attention to the commanding officer of Io's own militia space forces,

Commodore Giles Buckley. He was the most likely candidate for the job.

Even though Brad had more than enough on his plate, he knew that he had to take the time to meet with the man face to face. Buckley was waiting to meet Brad when he docked at the Io shipyards.

The man's appearance wasn't anything like what Brad had guessed based simply on his name. Rather than a tall, thin white man with blond hair like he'd imagined, Buckley was a short, rotund man with deep black hair and a dark reddish-brown tint to his skin.

It took Brad a moment or two to figure out the man had to have an American Indian genetic background.

Buckley smiled knowingly as he extended his hand. "It surprises everyone the first time," he said with a hint of humor in his voice. "I obviously took after my mother. Welcome back to the Io shipyards, Admiral.

"While we've never officially met, I have seen you around and about the shipyard on occasion, back when you were a simple mercenary. Though I'm given to understand that *simple* may not be the appropriate descriptive term. Your reputation precedes you and I'm looking forward to working with you."

"I hope you still think so once we're done talking," Brad said with a slight grin while he shook the man's hand. "I'm afraid that I'm about to make your life significantly more complicated than it was just a minute ago."

Buckley shook his head. "If you're going to ruin my day, let's at least do so over a decent meal. I took the liberty of having something brought to my office so that we could eat in peace and discuss whatever you needed to speak about without distractions."

With that, the man led Brad and his escort to the offices of the Io space force.

Brad left all but two of his Marines in the outer office, with the intention of posting the remaining two outside the door while the two officers ate and talked.

Before he opened the door to his office, Buckley gave Brad a grin of his own. "I understand that you've come to give me a surprise, so I don't feel badly by having a surprise of my own for you."

Before Brad could respond, Buckley opened the door and he saw what Buckley had meant. Seated at a small table near the desk, eating something out of a cup with chopsticks, was Agent Kate Falcone.

———

"Don't you just turn up in the oddest places," he said as he stepped into the room and extended his hand. "It's good to see you again, Kate."

She set her cup and utensils down, rose to her feet, and pulled him into a hug instead. "You saved my ass from a black-site prison. That deserves more than a handshake."

Once that was done, she stepped back and looked at him with her hands still on his shoulders. "You're developing a bruise on the left side of your face. I'm assuming that means you've been in the thick of it."

The corners of his mouth twitched upward. "Not intentionally. That's just how things worked out this time. What brings you to Io? Please tell me you've got some good information on where the OWA is coming to refuel. We could really use it."

Her expression turned a bit sour and she shook her head. "I wish I did, but the Agency is in the dark just as much as you are. They have to have a facility here somewhere, but none of the operatives we have looking for it have found any evidence that tells us where to look.

"That probably means they have it fiendishly well hidden and are using some kind of civilian facility to camouflage it. We'll keep looking, but it's going to be difficult to find it and deal with it before they leave Saturn."

At Buckley's gesture, Brad sat next to Falcone and started searching the bag of takeout Chinese for something that would suit him. His skill with chopsticks was limited, so he availed himself of the fork.

"I don't suppose you happened to bring any good news to go with that?" he asked with a lopsided grin. "I could sure use some right now."

"How would a drone carrier and its escorts of your own sound?" she asked. "I realize that's not exactly a battleship, but used in an intelligent way, it could provide quite the boost to your offensive capabilities."

Brad certainly wasn't going to turn down additional ships. Like she said, a drone carrier could be a real asset if someone used it well.

"This is one of the Fleet units that I heard about? I'd wondered why they hadn't been included in First Fleet."

She shook her head with a grimace. "Sadly, the OWA managed the same sort of trick they pulled with their new battleship. There was a mutiny on board the drone carriers and their escorts, and then heavy fighting between the loyal and mutinous units. At least one drone carrier got away intact, but we think a second one escaped with moderate to heavy damage."

"Perfect," Brad muttered. "One more club in their hands to beat me with."

He smiled sourly and gestured for her to continue. "So, where does the drone carrier I'm getting come from? The Agency?"

Kate nodded. "We've been testing one for our own use, not as a weapons platform but for scouting large areas of space looking for the Cadre, now the OWA. Don't worry; we can replace the stealthed reconnaissance drones with weapons easily enough, though the intelligence you could get from the eyes in the sky might be very useful."

"The extra ships will help. Thank you. And I'll consider how the recon drones might prove helpful."

He looked over at Buckley, who was eating fried rice and listening intently. "As fun as this reunion is, I came here to see you, Commodore. We've got to work out the specifics of how the Jovian security forces are going to operate with my Fleet units and the mercenaries. And now the Agency units.

"You're the man on the scene, so I think you should be in tactical command of the Jovian units. Just like my other Commodores, I'll pass along the strategic directions and you'll work with the people you know to make the magic happen."

Buckley nodded. "That's basically what I expected to hear. I'm ready and my people will make sure that everything works as smoothly as it can. We're only going to get one shot at this, and we've got to make it work the first time."

"And the Agency is going to be able to provide more than just fire-power," Kate said. "I've got a lot of information about the Jovian system that we can go over to help try to narrow down where there refueling base is located.

"Taking it out won't make the fight for Jupiter any easier, but it will cripple their advance on Mars and Earth. Given enough time, the forces around Earth can get their act together and participate in the defense of the Inner System. To do that, it falls to us to stop them here."

Brad knew that was a tall order, but he had to play the cards he'd been dealt or fold. He wasn't the kind to just give up, so he'd find some way to stop the Cadre and save humanity. Somehow.

CHAPTER TWENTY-THREE

BRAD ARRIVED BACK at *Incredible* a few hours later, still without a concrete plan to find the refueling station the OWA had to have in the area but feeling a little better about his chances of finding it before the hammer fell.

It turned out that it was his day for visitors. Captain Alycia Nah was waiting for him in the docking bay. She wasn't alone. Standing beside her was an attractive auburn-haired woman that Brad knew well but hadn't expected to see anytime soon: Dr. Gina Duvall of Serenade Station.

He smiled. "It's good to see you, Doctor, though something of a surprise. I'm a little bit busy, but is there something I can do for the Doctors' Guild?"

"Think of this as something like a house call. If you've got just a few minutes, I'd like to inspect the replacement we grew for your hand. It won't take very long."

Now very certain that something odd was going on, Brad nodded. "Of course. Nah, I picked up some new information while I was away talking to Commodore Buckley. Once I'm done speaking with the doctor and letting her poke around as much as she likes, I'd like to have my core flag officers available for a conference call. Can you set that up for me?"

His flag captain nodded. "Of course, sir. We'll be set up in the wardroom when you're ready. I also have some new information to add to our tally, but it's not very important in the grand scheme of things."

With that out of the way, Brad led Dr. Duvall back to his office. Once they were safely behind the guarded door, he turned to the woman and smiled a bit lopsidedly.

"Not that I'm unhappy to see you, Doctor, but what is this really about?" he asked as he sat on the edge of his desk.

"The Cadre, or whatever they're calling themselves these days. I have information that they're active in the Trojans. Unfortunately, it wasn't the kind of information that I could just send to you. It had to be delivered in person and in a way that didn't raise suspicion beyond a certain threshold."

Without asking, she stepped over to the bar built in his office and poured herself a little of something with a red tinge of color to the liquid. She sipped it and nodded approvingly.

"You're familiar with how the Doctors' Guild works, so I don't need to explain how we try to maintain our neutrality in things that are going on. You were present when the Guild decided that the Cadre had violated our rules and would no longer receive any medical treatment.

"What you might not realize is that we also decided to begin gathering information about Cadre operations in case it became necessary to share that with Fleet or perhaps even the Mercenary Guild."

Following her lead, he poured himself a very small glass of whiskey and sipped at the fiery liquid. "And it's now time to share that information? I hope this doesn't mean that the OWA is active in the leading Trojan cluster."

"The opposite, actually. We have a number of general physicians that visit the various stations and settlements in the *trailing* Trojan cluster to take care of their general health needs. Over the last several months, we've become aware of a change in behavior there."

Brad frowned, concerned with what she'd just said. "That is troubling. What type of altered behavior are we talking about?"

"The people have become more afraid. They're jumpy. Some of the folks that the doctors doing the visits know well have vanished and no one will tell them where they are. In fact, all of our usual sources of information have simply dried up.

"It's as if they were warned not to talk to the doctors about anything at all. Even the number of visits by people that need care has dropped precipitously. Statistically, that's impossible. What that tells me is that the OWA is doing something in the area."

That certainly did sound suspicious. "If that were all you had to say, you could've still gotten me the information without coming in person. There something you haven't told me yet."

Her expression grim, she nodded. "While we never told any of our personnel to try and gather more information, I'm very much afraid that one of our physicians may have asked the wrong question of the wrong person.

"A small ship with a medical team and supplies—a mobile clinic, if you will—has gone missing. I'm very concerned that the OWA now has my people."

That was about what Brad had expected. "We're going to be searching the entire Jovian system over the next several days, so we'll be happy to keep an eye out for your ship and people, but I just can't devote a specific group of ships to search for them. I'm sorry."

"I think you misunderstand," she said tossing back the last of her drink. "I'm not asking that you help me find them, though I want that. I'm saying that they are an opportunity for you to find where the OWA is hiding.

"Most people don't know it, but all Doctors' Guild ships carry locator beacons. Their use is meant to be for indicating a ship that's been infected with some plague and should be avoided. Something like a quarantine light. A warning to stay clear.

"An even-less-known fact is that it can be made to transmit remotely and on frequencies that aren't normally monitored. If one of your ships comes within range of where our missing ship is being held, you can trigger a response that might very well go unnoticed, and then turn the beacon off again."

Brad had to admit that the news did open up some possibilities. Combined with the arrival of Falcone and her secret carrier, that might just give them the edge they needed to find the secret OWA refueling depot. If, of course, they could be subtle enough.

"I think I might have a plan that helps us both," Brad said with a smile. "You realize that, technically, you're not violating any of your oaths. You're not telling us where the OWA is hiding anything. You're not divulging any secrets that your patients may have passed along.

"All you're doing is asking us to locate a missing vessel and giving us the key to find it. If the OWA just happens to be holding your ship in a location that sensitive to them, that's hardly your fault, is it? And if we rescue your people and smash the OWA facility, well, those kinds of things happen."

She smiled coldly at Brad. "That's exactly what the board said. I wish I could give you more information, Admiral, but at this point, I'm not sure that you need it. On behalf of the Doctors' Guild, we thank you for your assistance in this matter.

"I realize that you're a very busy man, so I'll let you get back to what you need to be doing. I did bring along a number of physicians in case something untoward happens during the search. It might be helpful to have a lot of medical personnel on hand if things go…badly for someone. We have a lot of friends in the trailing Trojans. We'll want to save as many of them as we can."

———

Captain Nah was waiting for him in his office when he finished with his meeting with Duvall. She stood as Brad walked in and took his seat, and before resuming her own.

"What have you got for me?" he asked. "I hope it's good news."

She nodded. "It's good news though, in the scheme of things, probably not extremely helpful. Still, everything helps. Dr. Duval arrived with a fleet contingent that had been stationed in the leading Trojan cluster at the request of the Doctors' Guild.

"No big ships, but I doubt you'll turn away six destroyers and a dozen smaller ships. The destroyers are half-and-half *Warrior*-class and *Bound*-class."

"I certainly won't turn my nose up at that," Brad said with a smile. "I'm sure Commodore Bailey will be thrilled to have additional *Bound*-class ships. I remember being told that these ships were out here, but I'd forgotten in all the excitement. Is that it?"

"That's it," she confirmed. "I have the others standing by for a videoconference with you. If you have no further need of me, I'll get back to my bridge and get to a few other tasks that have been awaiting my attention."

He checked his desk comp and found the communications link already set up, just waiting for him to join. Once he did so, video images of Commodores Bailey, Nuremberg, Jahoda, and Buckley appeared. Also joining them was Director Kernsky.

"Thank you very much for joining me," he said. "Since we've last spoken, I've come into possession of a couple of bits of information. Please check to make absolutely certain this channel is encrypted on your end while I do the same."

He double-checked the status of the communications link and confirmed that it was encrypted at the highest level. That didn't necessarily mean that the OWA hadn't penetrated it, but this was the best he could do to make sure what he said next didn't get out.

Once each of the others had verified that their links were similarly encrypted, he continued. "Actually, I suppose the first thing that I should do is address one bit of housekeeping. Director Kernsky, I'm afraid your title really isn't conducive to commanding units in space. It's more of an administrative title than a command one, so I believe that it's best you assume the rank of Rear Admiral so that it's absolutely clear to the mercenaries who is in command of their operations."

The woman blinked. "Do you really think that's necessary?"

Brad nodded. "Yes, I do. Chain of command is extremely important when the torpedoes are flying. Someone might be inclined to argue with Director Kernsky, but they'll be less inclined to fight Admiral Kernsky. You're not going to be sitting in an office or board room now.

You're going to be on the command deck of a ship, just like the last time you fought the Cadre."

"Why Rear Admiral? Why not just Commodore like everyone else under your command?"

He laughed. "Have you seen how many mercenary companies are commanded by Commodores? You can't throw a rock without hitting one. No, if you're going to be in charge of units commanded by Commodores, you need to be an Admiral."

She shrugged slightly. "Whatever works, let's just do it."

"Make sure you dig up something that will work as uniform, Admiral. You'll also want to get the board to agree that overall command needs to be in the hands of someone with that temporary rank just to make everything legal."

After she nodded, Brad turned his attention to the other officers awaiting his attention. "Information has come into my possession that indicates the OWA refueling facility is in the trailing Trojans. In addition, we may have a way to locate the base more precisely without looking like we're doing so.

"It's going to require a little trust on your parts because I'm not ready to reveal the details of precisely how were going to locate the facility, due to the classified nature of the source of the data. You'll just have to take my word that it comes from someone I trust. Two someones, actually."

"So, with all this secrecy, what exactly can you tell us about your plan?" Bailey asked, her voice mildly sarcastic.

"That we're going to send a group into the trailing Trojans to await a signal. Scouting forces that you don't know about will nose about, and when they find where the base is located, they're going to summon us.

"The problem is that we can't seem as if we're focusing our attention there. The OWA can't realize that were on to them or they're going to bring in whatever defenses they have in the area. If they think we're searching and won't locate them, they'll stay quiet and we'll have the opportunity to smash them."

Commodore Nuremberg's eyes narrowed. "You keep saying *we* as if you're going to be there. You're not planning on going along on this mission, are you, Admiral?"

He nodded. "I understand that I'm responsible for the entire fleet, but if we don't destroy the OWA refueling station, the Inner System is going to fall. I've got to oversee this operation and make certain that it's successful, or everything else we do is for nothing.

"I'll directly command this particular group of ships while the majority of the fleet remains here at Io. Just to keep from announcing our interest in the trailing Trojans, we'll send a small group of ships to search the leading Trojans. That's probably a good idea in any case, simply because we don't know if they have something there as well."

"Which ships are you planning on taking?" Commodore Jahoda asked.

"We'll start with your ships, Commodore. We'll add in half of Commodore Bailey's units, commanded directly by her. Those numbers shouldn't stand out too greatly."

"And exactly how are you going to prevent people from realizing that you're no longer here at Io?" Nuremberg asked.

"Sleight-of-hand," Brad said with a grin. "I'm going to swap transponder codes with Commodore Jahoda's cruiser. For all intents and purposes, anyone that looks at what ships are still here will see me parked in orbit.

"I understand that this is not what you want to see your commanding Admiral do, but this is what's happening. We're going to have one chance to find the OWA's secret refueling base and destroy it. I don't intend to waste it."

CHAPTER TWENTY-FOUR

THE EXTRACTION from Io went off without a hitch. Brad had been worried for the first twenty-four hours that someone might have spotted the switch between the two cruisers' identities, but no one seemed to notice.

Standard traffic between the forces headed for the trailing Trojans, and the fleet gave him the opportunity to handle basic communications with the people that needed to hear from him, though at some delay. He of course never participated in real-time communications so as not to reveal his absence.

Falcone had told Commodore Buckley that she would lead the way with her forces to begin the scouting mission and contact Brad only when she had something to report. The woman seemed pleased that she would have a way of detecting the location of the missing Doctors' Guild ship but was rightfully worried that the responding signal would be detected.

Brad hoped that she was overthinking it, but past events had proven that they couldn't count on luck alone. The chances of the OWA forces' detecting the signals existed, and if they did spot them, no one knew precisely how they would respond or with what.

As the signals would be coming in on an unknown frequency, and in a band that was normally not monitored, a single pulse would likely not make them too suspicious. If they detected the response from the doctors' ship, all that changed.

The settlements and stations in the trailing Trojans were spread out over a fairly wide area, so his forces could not be in a position to respond to all locations. He also needed to present the appearance of searching the area for himself.

To do that, he'd decided to keep his main force together and send out the smaller ships to look at the most remote areas. That meant that he could take the larger strength of his task force through the more central area of the Trojans.

The first two days of the search proceeded without incident or breakthrough. Then, just after breakfast on the third day, his flagship received a tightbeam communication with codes belonging to the Agency.

Once Brad decoded the information, Kate Falcone's image appeared on his desktop screen. She was grinning.

"We found them. A mid-sized out-of-the-way station called Warren's Folly. It's listed in the database as a mining facility owned by a collective of miners.

"One of my drones passed by at a fairly high rate of speed and sent the signal when it was on its way past the small body that they are supposedly mining. The responding signal from the doctors' ship was unmistakable. As per the plan, the drone immediately sent the signal to turn the transponder off and circled around to see if there was any reaction.

"It appears that the bastards didn't notice the signal, or they decided it wasn't intended for them. They certainly didn't hear the beacon, or that would have set them off. My professional opinion is that we managed to get a clean hit on them without them noticing us in return."

Brad smiled. That was excellent news. Still, it was only half of the problem.

As if she were reading his mind, Falcone continued. "I've called back most of the recon drones I had out and I've retasked them with searching the general area around this mining station. I haven't had any hits yet, but I'm certain we're going to find that the OWA has ships in the area to defend their base.

"The trick is going to be finding them without them spotting the drones. Admittedly, they're not going to be using active sensors and the recon drones are damned stealthy, so I think we're going to manage to get the jump on them. The only question is going to be how large their guard force is.

"This base is critical to their mission of attacking the Inner System. If it gets taken out before they refuel their fleet, it puts everything they want to accomplish in jeopardy. That means they're going to have a force to be reckoned with.

"Once I get more information, I'll send it to you. You can send a return signal via tight beam on the course that this transmission came from and I'll get it. Falcone out."

Her final words tempered Brad's enthusiasm with a little realism. This was not going to be an operation where he could just attack the base by surprise and take it out. No. He'd have to take the ships that would respond into account as well.

That meant there would be two simultaneous operations in progress. Once he was in position to attack the base, he'd send his ground forces with as little warning as possible. That gave the best chance to recover any prisoners they might have and to take the facility in as good a condition as possible.

While that assault was happening, he was going to have to use his ships to come down hard on the OWA guard force. His attack would also have to happen from stealth.

The timing was going to be tricky, and if either group discovered his presence before he was ready to carry out the dual attacks, it could turn the entire affair into a bloodbath.

Sometimes, one just had to trust in the process. His people knew what they were doing. If anyone could execute their attacks in such a way that it took out both enemies, they could. Now all he had to do was wait for Falcone to tell him how ugly the odds were going to be.

———

The odds turned out to be tilted in the enemy's favor more than Brad had hoped. It took Falcone twelve hours to locate where the OWA forces were hiding, and then another twelve to fully scout their positions and gauge their strength.

While it was difficult to determine the precise makeup of the enemy ships hiding in the darkness, they had as many cruisers as he'd brought with him and almost five times as many smaller ships, though fewer destroyers than he'd feared.

That would make a stand-up fight a chancy affair. If he was able to ambush them, he could probably take them out without too much damage to his ships. If they became aware of his presence, they could potentially beat the ships that he brought with him.

No matter what he decided to do, he was going to have to execute his plans carefully. Timing was going to be critical.

There were also a steady stream of ships coming from all over the trailing Trojan cluster, probably delivering things to the refueling station that was still under construction. Once the stealth drones had gotten a good look at the mining facility, they'd been able to determine where the hidden tanks were being placed and just how large they were going to be.

The size of the operation brought home to him that the OWA might just be bringing even more ships than he'd been preparing for. What had looked like it was going to be a difficult fight against the OWA might end up being a last stand against overwhelming odds before his inevitable death. Jupiter might just become his Thermopylae.

He summoned more of his fleet units to join him. They'd come in small groups so as not to be noticed by the enemy. With any luck, he'd be ready to strike in forty-eight hours. If he could hold out until then, he might be able to bring the hammer down without undue risk to his forces.

They now needed to capture the refueling station intact. Someone down there knew exactly what forces were going to be needing fuel.

For that matter, why just fuel? That base was probably loaded with munitions to rearm the OWA after the fight in the Jovian system. Its loss could be very painful for the enemy, but with the forces it implied, that might not stop them from conquering the Commonwealth. He had to know for sure.

Once he had his ships in motion, he sent a message to Falcone expressing his concerns and asking if they could meet. A few hours later, she told him to expect her shortly.

She arrived just after dinner in a small fleet shuttle that just coasted in out of the darkness, giving them the agreed-upon passcode. He waited for her in the landing bay after having shooed everyone else out. There was no need to blow her cover unnecessarily.

Falcone stepped out of the shuttle, dressed in the fleet uniform of a Lieutenant Commander, and saluted him sharply. "Reporting as ordered, sir!"

He chuckled at her antics and gestured for her to proceed him into the ship's corridor. "I've already taken the precaution of clearing a direct route to my office, so there's no need to worry that someone's going to spot you, Kate."

"I'm not exactly worried about anyone figuring out who I am," she said after she stepped up beside him. "It's more habit at this point. All the bad guys know who I am, since they had the Agency penetrated so deeply. It's almost like I'm playacting at being a spy rather than being one."

They made it to his office without any interruptions and he soon had her seated at the small table off to the side of his desk. Once she'd made her selection, he poured them both drinks and then sat across from her.

"This is going to be delicate," he said after taking a sip of the excellent whiskey. "I've got more ships coming in to help us take care of the guard force, but the timing is going to be a royal pain. We're going to have to hit the base after we get into position to ambush the OWA ships.

"If we don't position everything just the way we need, the assault forces going to be in danger or the ships we hope to take out from stealth are going to bring their defenses online and give us a lot more of a fight than we'd counted on."

She nodded and set her glass on the table after taking a sip of her own. "It's more complicated than that. We need to get the assault forces down to the mining station and into position as quickly as possible while still keeping the enemy unaware that we're doing so.

"Just looking at the size of the refueling installation, I suspect that your brother has a few more ships than he's admitted to possessing. Somewhere down there, someone knows the exact force mix that he's bringing into play. Having that information is absolutely critical to the survival of the Commonwealth."

"It would be nice to have," he admitted, "but at this point, I'm not certain that knowing it makes that much of a difference. I'm not certain that the fight is survivable, so victory in this case just means stopping them from obliterating Mars and Earth.

"*Immortal* and her battle group alone can very likely destroy the majority of our forces. All of the other ships that they'll be bringing with them just guarantee their success in seizing the Jovian system."

"Maybe, maybe not," Falcone said. "I have some information that you're not aware of that might possibly give us a small chance at taking *Immortal* out of the fight."

"If it involves bringing *Amaranthine* out from Earth, I don't think that's going to make any real difference. Yes, she's a battleship, but she's so far out of date that she's not going to move the needle very far. We might have had a chance with *Eternal*, but that's why they smuggled nukes aboard her."

Falcone shook her head. "I understand that. No, I'm talking about a system on board *Immortal* herself. Specifically, an anti-mutiny override. That would basically take the entire battleship off-line."

"It sure would've been nice if they'd managed to activate it when the mutiny *actually* happened," Brad grumbled. "I'm not sure how it can help us now. Is it something that can be activated remotely?"

"No. It's going to require physical access to either the Admiral's office or the flag bridge. Based on what we know about Vice Admiral Wu, we don't think he went over to the other side. That means they killed him quickly enough that he had no time to activate the anti-mutiny override.

"Based on his ego, it's our assessment that Jack Mantruso has registered himself with the battleship's computer as its new flag officer. That puts the override under his control."

"That's still not very helpful," Brad said. "I doubt we can trick him into activating it."

She smiled. "Probably not. That doesn't mean that we haven't found a way to trigger the override. All we have to do is get it on board *Immortal*, into the admiral's office or flag bridge, and activate it. That would take the biggest piece off the board."

"Is that all?" Brad asked with a tad more sarcasm than he probably should've used. "I'm sorry, Kate. That's just crazy. If we try to get anywhere near that battleship to land troops, they'll blow us out of space."

"I never said it would be easy. I just said it would be possible. We believe that we've worked out a method to get a small boarding party over to *Immortal* without being seen. Getting them back out again would mean winning the fight, though."

"That's a suicide mission," Brad said grimly.

"Perhaps. There's also another little twist. This mission is going to require your personal touch. Quite literally."

He raised an eyebrow but said nothing.

"The override is genetically coded," Falcone said. "It's designed to detect the appropriate flag officer before activating. That means that Jack Mantruso is the only one that can activate it under normal circumstances.

"We believe that we have a method that will allow someone with a close genetic link to activate it as well. Since the only other person that has the all-important genome sequences is you, that means you're going to have to lead this 'suicide mission.'"

CHAPTER TWENTY-FIVE

BRAD LISTENED to Falcone's crazy plan and tried to see how it could be anything other than a long, convoluted way to commit suicide, but he just wasn't able to do it. What she'd proposed was an act of pure desperation. He'd do it if he had to, but it would have to be his absolute last option before he'd agree to do it.

In the meantime, he had to deal with more realistic problems. Knowing exactly where the OWA forces were located at least made an ambush possible, but that didn't make it *easy*. He'd have to maneuver his forces very carefully to avoid being detected on approach.

If the enemy spotted him coming in, the fight would be on. With their strength, he couldn't afford to do this the hard way. He had to avoid giving them any warning at all if he wanted this to work, and that meant dealing with a problem that he knew existed, even though none of his people had spotted it yet.

He hadn't been subtle when moving his ships into the trailing Trojans to look around. The OWA had had to know exactly where he was to give Falcone an opportunity to search without being detected. He had been the decoy. That meant they had someone watching his ships.

Unfortunately, space was big. If there were only a couple of small ships parked a good distance away from his current location, they'd have an idea of his task force's disposition. If Brad suddenly moved every ship he possessed, they'd know that he'd found something interesting. Someone would go running back to the OWA fleet and let them know.

He could deal with them, but only if he knew exactly where they were and how many of them were watching.

Brad escorted Falcone back to her shuttle but stopped her at the hatch. "We've undoubtedly got a couple of OWA ships monitoring us right now. I'd like you to bring some of your drones around us and locate them. Since we know where the main enemy force is at, it's time to make sure that we don't give him a warning when we move."

She nodded. "And once we have them located, how do you plan on dealing with them?"

"I'll break off a couple of the smaller units from the group that's coming to join forces with us. If I bring them in from behind where our observers are located, I can trap them against the fleet and crush them."

Her eyes narrowed and she slowly shook her head. "That's too chancy. Why not let me take care of it? I can send some standard drones in once the recon versions have located the bad guys. I can take them out before they get even a single peep of warning to their masters."

He had to admit that he liked her idea, but he wasn't sure how it would work. "I understand that your recon drones are heavily stealthed, but what about the combat drones? Every time I've been involved with fighting them, they haven't exactly been the most difficult things to see, even when they had been trying."

"That's because the people that have been using them have been idiots," she said bluntly. "They trust that you're not looking to see them rather than using the hardware to its best advantage. It's all fine and good to just cruise in from deep space and hope no one notices you, but there are a number of things you can do to decrease the chances of being spotted at all, even without having drones that are more heavily stealthed than normal.

"Which, by the way, my drones are more heavily stealthed than the ones Fleet had provided to the regular units. The whole goal of having an Agency drone carrier was to make sure that no one saw us before we used it. And that included making sure that no witnesses were left behind when we'd finished attacking them."

"So, how does it work?" he asked. "What kind of maneuvers can you execute to reduce the chances of being spotted?"

She grinned. "The way that they're going to see any drones coming at them is either through heat signature or the drone blocking a light source. In this case, a star. We'll come in slow and steady. If the drones are moving directly toward their targets, then they won't be blocking out stars in an arc of space as they move. Just the ones directly behind them.

"That's going to take someone very observant to spot them under these circumstances. Also, if you can do something to get their attention at the right moment, they'll definitely not be looking for what's about to happen to them"

He nodded. "I think I can work something out."

————

"Exactly what are we doing again, Admiral?" Captain Nah asked over the link between the flag bridge and the cruiser's regular bridge. "It looks as if we're playing shuffle-the-fleet."

"Is that a real thing?" Brad asked, raising one eyebrow.

"It can be," she admitted. "It's not usually so blatant, however."

He grinned. "We've got some OWA ships monitoring our position. We're going to take them out before we move to the refueling facility."

"Don't you think you should tell me where they are so that we can get ships into position? Or are you planning on using the reinforcements that will be here in a few hours?"

"Neither. We've got an unseen ally who's going to take care of them for us.

"I'm not exactly happy to have an unseen ally at all," the Fleet captain said. "Don't you think I should know who all the players are? Or is this something that only the flag officers know?"

He shook his head. "Thus far, I haven't told anyone. The flag officers *do* know that we have an ally working behind the scenes, but I haven't mentioned any specific details to them at this point.

"I'll be doing so as soon as we start laying out the plan to attack the OWA ships, though. As soon as I do, you'll be the very next person I tell."

That didn't seem to satisfy the Fleet officer, but she apparently knew the futility of arguing with an Admiral. "As you say, sir. When will the attack take place?"

He checked the time. "Everything should go to pieces for the bad guys in just a few more minutes."

Captain Nah grunted slightly. "Shouldn't we be seeing something, then? The sensors are still not showing any forces moving to engage the hostile ships you've identified. Everdark, we can't even see *them* on our sensors."

"That's kind of the point. By the time they realize that they're being stalked, they'll be dead. We can't afford to let them get off a warning, or a lot of this starts coming apart."

His flag captain started to say something, but her attention swiveled to the screen just to the side of her video pickup. "We're detecting explosions at the points indicated, Admiral. A lot of explosions. Multiple torpedoes seem to have impacted the observers."

"Dispatch some of the smaller ships to verify the destruction of the enemy ships and pick up any survivors," he ordered.

"Sir, how can you be so sure that those three ships belonged to the OWA?"

"It's remotely possible that one of them didn't," he admitted. "That said, the odds of that are extremely small.

"If they didn't belong to the OWA, then they were the stupidest people I've met in recent memory. I couldn't take that chance."

Nah nodded. "I think you're right and I'm not going to lose any sleep over them; I just wanted to ask. I'll see that we get the area searched, but I can already tell you that no one is transmitting from those locations unless they're *very* good. Whoever they were, our secret ally took them out before they had a chance to warn the OWA force."

"Excellent. I'll get on the line with Commodore Bailey and we'll start planning what happens when Commodore Nuremberg arrives."

———

Once Nuremberg arrived, Brad had the ships of his fleet move away from the area they'd been supposedly searching while the Agency carrier had done the real work of locating the enemy forces.

The final attack plan was relatively straightforward when it came to the OWA ships. Commodore Nuremberg would be the hammer and his ships would be the anvil. The drones from the carrier would be the shiv he stuck in the OWA's back during the first confused moments of the fight.

Before any of his ships could get into place, he had to pre-position the Marines for their assault. Brad had no idea what kind of defenses the refueling operation had, but if they caught the Marines on their inbound leg, it would get ugly fast.

That meant Brad stopped his forces a bit farther out from the OWA ships than he might have otherwise done. Every Marine they had boarded their assault shuttles and left the fleet on a low-energy course that would see them approach the asteroid from the least active side.

Since the small craft were taking their time, Brad just had to hope that nothing came along to disrupt everything before they arrived. If the OWA ships detected any of his own vessels, the resultant squawking would leave the Marines hanging there in the middle of nowhere.

So, of course, the Marines were about three-quarters of the way to making their final attack run when Brad received a tightbeam message from Falcone. As her carrier was participating in the fight, at least this message was in real time.

"We've got a problem," she said grimly.

"Why did I know you were going to say that?" Brad said with a sigh. "What's wrong?"

"One of my outermost recon drones has picked up a group of incoming ships. They don't look like combatants. In fact, I know they're not. Some of my people have been nosing around the settlements, and we finally got word about what all the ships that are coming and going from the refueling facility are for.

"The OWA is using skilled locals as slave labor to build and expand the refueling facility. By now, it has to be mostly done, but none of the people they've kidnapped have returned home. They're still down there."

That made a sick kind of sense. The Cadre had never shied away from keeping their prisoners in a handy location where they could execute them when they were finished using them. Why should he expect that the OWA was any different?

What he wasn't sure of was how that changed his options.

"Did your people get any idea of how many prisoners they're holding?" he asked.

"That's the ugly part. My best guess is that they've probably got somewhere between seven hundred and a thousand people down there, not counting the ones that are coming in on these ships.

"Most of them aren't construction people; they're friends, relatives, and children to use as hostages against the skilled prisoners. If they don't do their very best, someone gets spaced as an example."

Brad rubbed his face. This was *exactly* the kind of complication that he didn't need right now.

The tactically smart move would be to continue exactly as they'd planned. That, however, would be a strategic disaster, even if it wasn't morally reprehensible.

If he threw thousands of innocent people into the meat grinder without even trying to save them, public sentiment about the Commonwealth would go from negative to outright hatred in a single heartbeat.

"Understood," he said tiredly. "I think I have just enough time to get some amended orders to the Marines. They're going to have to divert part of their forces to locate and protect the civilians.

"Once the fighting starts, we're going to have to finish the enemy ships as rapidly as possible and then get down there to help. There's no way that the forces we sent can successfully execute both missions. They're going to have to have us backing them up and fast."

That meant he'd have to take out the OWA ships in the alpha strike or he'd never be able to get the unarmed shuttles down to reinforce the Marines. If that happened, he might lose them all.

He couldn't fail. He wouldn't fail.

CHAPTER TWENTY-SIX

For once, things worked out almost exactly as he'd planned, at least as far as the space attack went. Brad had gotten his ships into position just in time. Commodore Nuremberg struck from the dark space beyond the refueling facility with no warning, her ships laying down heavy fire right on schedule.

Commodore Bailey had her *Bound*-class destroyers firing so that their mass-driver rounds would arrive immediately after the attacking force revealed itself. No need to give them early warning or fire after the enemy ships had already started moving.

The OWA ships turned to fire at Commodore Nuremberg's cruisers only to receive Brad's torpedoes straight from behind. Caught between the opposing forces, they had no easy way to defend themselves.

That difficulty became much more severe when Falcone's drones opened fire, completing the surrounding globe of attack. With torpedoes coming from every direction, the enemy coordination disintegrated, and they tried to flee in every direction.

They were unsuccessful.

In fact, their lack of supporting fire for one another resulted in the destruction of each and every enemy ship, and they managed to inflict only slight damage on his ships.

Brad was elated. He'd had to slog through every single fight against the Cadre and the OWA. All too often, they got the edge and he got the shaft. He couldn't expect this type of good luck every single fight, but with the toughest battle of his life looming in his future, he'd take it this time.

As soon as he was certain that the fighting was over, he got the other flag officers and Falcone on the com. "Commodore Bailey, you're in charge of search and rescue. If we can find survivors to give us any information about what the OWA has planned, that would be helpful. Commodore Nuremberg, you're in charge of overwatch. If somebody else comes in looking for a fight, I want you to give it to them."

Nuremberg nodded. "What about Agent Falcone's carrier?"

He'd explained exactly who Falcone was as they'd planned this attack. Neither of the Fleet officers had seemed shocked by her appearance, though the carrier had been a welcome surprise.

"She'll spread her recon drones out beyond where you're looking to provide an early warning in case someone tries something fancy.

"I'm particularly worried about additional ships carrying prisoners. If they come along, we're going to have to seize them and liberate the civilians."

"And the ground assault?" Commodore Bailey asked.

"We've gotten word that the Marines landed safely and have launched their attack," Brad said. "I'd like you to send a few smaller ships toward the facility, Commodore Bailey. The shuttles with our non-Marine fighters will come in behind your shield, and you'll provide covering fire to make sure they land safely. If anything shoots at them, take it out."

"You bet your ass I will," Bailey said. "Agent Falcone already identified the heaviest weapons clusters, so we'll take them out first. Anything smaller than that, we can handle on the fly."

"Then let's get busy," Brad said. "We don't want to give them any more time than we must to kill prisoners or destroy information."

With that, he dropped the Commodores from the feed and turned his attention to Falcone. "At a guess, the Marines have maybe a sixty percent chance of carrying out both of their mission objectives. Maybe a ninety percent chance of winning one of their two fights if they devoted their full force to the objective.

"In any case, that battle is going to be over soon. We have to plan for what happens after we take the refueling facility."

She nodded. "The next step is freeing the rest of the trailing Trojans. It's obvious from what Dr. Duvall told us that the OWA has people everywhere to make sure that no one that comes visiting sees something they shouldn't. We've got to dig them out."

Brad rubbed the bridge of his nose tiredly. "We'll start that as soon as we suppress them here. One way or the other, the fighting here is going to be over too quickly for them to really dig in. That's not going to be true with the rest of the settlements. They have to know that no matter what they called themselves, we'll treat them like pirates. They'll fight to the death."

"Of course they will," she said. "Nothing is ever is easy as we'd like, but we've got tens of thousands of people to save in the trailing Trojans. A cold-blooded man would say that he had more important things to focus his attention on, with the attack that's bound to come at Jupiter before much longer. That's not you, Brad. You care about these people and you're going to see them freed."

He didn't even pretend that that wasn't true. "You know me too well. I just can't stand by and watch scum like this hurt innocent people."

"Well, we'd best get you down to the refueling facility so you can take charge of protecting the people there," she said. "You know that's the angle you're best suited for."

He smiled at that. "Bailey and Nuremberg aren't going to be happy about that."

"Tell them to complain to management. You're the man in charge, so you get to call the shots. My shuttles should land about the same time as yours, so I'll see you there. Let's go kill some Cadre scum."

———

As soon as Brad's shuttle launched, he saw that his hopes of slipping away to fight unnoticed were doomed. His shuttle was immediately bracketed by a pair of frigates. They fell in on either side of him and made no bones about their intent to shield his shuttle all the way in.

The ride in wasn't nearly as exciting as some of his landings under fire, but that didn't mean it went without issue. Commodore Bailey's ships had taken out the large weapons platforms before any of the second wave made it close to the refuelling facility.

Even though the defenders had to know they were coming, the OWA had never planned to stand off a major attack without support ships. Concealment had been their best defense and now it was gone.

Once the primary defensive clusters were destroyed, it was simply a matter of taking out each launcher that revealed itself after that. The defenses fell silent fast, either from destruction or learning the age-old lesson that the nail that stood up was struck down.

The Marines had breached a major ore-loading bay and that was where Brad's shuttles landed. It was a good thing that the bay was huge, because the assault shuttles took up a lot of the space even before his shuttles landed.

He saw a platoon of heavily armed and armored Marines waiting for his shuttle. They'd known exactly where he was.

Major Papadakis's voice came over the command circuit as soon as the hatch opened, and the armed Fleet personnel started flowing out under the shouted orders of various Chief Petty Officers.

They all wore unpowered Fleet Marine armor. He had his mercenary armor on but kept his helmet off so that he could see more clearly. Falcone trotted over even as he gave in to the inevitable.

"Don't think I don't know where you're hiding, Admiral," Papadakis said dryly. "You might as well come out."

"I'll have you know that I'm not hiding," he huffed as he came out, his eyes already taking in the forces in the bay and planning how to get them where they needed to be most effectively. "Who ratted me out? Captain Nah?"

"I'm sure I wouldn't know," the Marine officer said virtuously. "And before you get set on leading a charge into the teeth of the enemy, let me assure you that I'll take a court-martial before I let that happen. You might be here to fight, but you'd best have some realistic expectations. Sir."

He chuckled in spite of her insubordination. "I never plan on going hand to hand. That's just my usual luck. You were hit on Io, weren't you? How are you feeling?"

She waved his concern away and pulled off her helmet. Her face had a bandage that covered her right cheekbone.

"It's a damned scratch. Only took six stiches and doesn't impede my combat effectiveness. I'm good. Besides, I hear the ladies like a Marine with scars." The last was said with a grin.

"It looks like your ragtag group of Fleet brawlers are ready to move out," she continued. "The prisoners are isolated in the mines. Two separate areas so they can keep the workers separated from the hostages.

"The Marines struck hard and fast, separating them from the OWA troops meant to slaughter them. Sadly, that isn't to say that the few guards actually in with them didn't try. There are some casualties, but Senior Lieutenant Gockel said they only lost a few dozen out of roughly fifteen hundred people, counting the new arrivals on the freighters that they'd just processed.

"Monique is a damned good Marine. She and her people took some casualties of their own getting into a blocking position, but the prisoners turned the trick. They killed most of the guards with their bare hands as soon as the Marines attacked."

Brad never liked hearing about losses, but as a mercenary commander, he understood that there were no bloodless victories. Light casualties were a lot better than heavy, and in these circumstances, he'd been ready for a serious butcher's bill.

"We need to hit the guard force rather than trying to swap places with Lieutenant Gockel," he said decisively. "The fastest way to get her freed up to help the rest of the Marines is to break the guards' will. Do you have a map?"

A gesture from her brought one of the Marines a step forward with a slate already out. It showed part of the facility. A green dot was the standard indicator of his current location.

There were a fair number of other tunnels shown, but hardly enough to be the entire base. This must be all that his people had seen with their own eyes. Even as he watched, another tunnel appeared as the map updated.

There were three yellow areas, two of them close together. He pointed at them. "These are the prisoners?"

"Yes, sir," she confirmed. "The larger group is the hostages. The red splotch off to the side of them is our best guess at the central location of the guard forces. As you can see, they have Gockel blocked from getting reinforcements."

"Then let's go fix that," he said as he fitted his helmet on. It was time to kill pirates.

———

The next half hour was sadly lacking in killing pirates for him. The Marines refused his order to move forward and assist in breaking into the guard post. It looked as if the Major hadn't been kidding about being willing to take a court-martial. Not that he'd push it.

Most of that time was spent working around the unexplored area to get into position to hit the guards from an unexpected direction. The lack of accurate and complete maps was a pain and could potentially hurt them if they missed a heavily occupied area.

They'd just have to make do and adjust if needed.

Some of the Fleet damage control specialists came up with a way to get them where they needed to go by using maintenance tubes to slip into the area behind the guard post. There were undoubtedly easier ways to get there, if one knew the base layout, but he'd take it.

Once he had everyone into the storage areas behind the guards, he sent scouting parties out to find what was around them. As he knew roughly the direction where the guards were, he sent the majority of his forces right behind that set of scouts.

It was a good thing, too. The scouts in that direction took only took a few minutes to find the rear of the guard force, and even though they'd been careful, the pirates spotted them and turned some of their number around to attack.

"Hit them hard," Brad ordered. "Break them now while they're facing the wrong direction. Signal Lieutenant Gockel to attack with everything she has."

From the sound of the explosions that almost instantly started going off, the Marine officer had been waiting for just that order. They had the guards between a rock and a hard place, so he sent his people forward as fast as they could move. Falcone and her people went with them.

Which was exactly when his other scouts started screaming about incoming troops from the unexplored areas just behind Brad. Screaming that was almost immediately followed by a lack of response that told him he was now the one in the pincer.

CHAPTER TWENTY-SEVEN

BRAD BARELY HAD time to get his forces turned before the first of the OWA commandos barreled around the corner behind them, rifles already firing. Their speed indicated that they were trying to overrun and break the forces attacking their comrades as quickly as possible.

Unfortunately for them, they weren't facing the Fleet personnel they'd already crushed. At least, not completely. Major Papadakis and her heavily armed Marines were the rock that their wave broke upon.

The Marines formed the core of the makeshift defensive formation and used their heavy weapons to blow large holes through both the attackers and their lines. Even so, that didn't stop the bastards. Say what you would about their morals, the commandos had courage.

They continued forward, a seemingly unending flood of killers out for blood. In seconds, they were among the defenders, attacking with rifles, pistols, assorted metal swords, and mono-blades.

Brad had already emptied his rifle into the charging pirates, managed to reload it, and got off half of another magazine before a mono-blade that wasn't even aimed for him took off the barrel of his weapon, missing the fingers of his left hand by just a hairsbreadth.

With the ease of many hours of practice, he managed to get both his pistol and mono-blade in hand. Using each as required by circumstances took all the hard-won experience he'd acquired as a mercenary in far too many life-and-death fights.

He shot one of the attackers in the face and then used his glowing blue blade to take off the arm of the man attacking Major Papadakis. She shot the wounded man in the head before he could stagger away. The two of them ended up back to back, fighting the sea of bad guys around them.

"Those blades are interesting," she said over the command channel as she continued to shoot at the OWA fighters surging around them. "I wonder why the Marines never picked up using them. They look handy."

He pushed them both back to avoid a regular sword that whistled through the air in front of him, and then bisected the attacker from shoulder to hip in a bloody strike. He fired the last two shots in his pistol, taking down a woman that seemed to be an officer or senior noncom, and holstered it so he could reload it later.

"They're hard to defend against," he agreed. "But they take a lot of practice to master. You can't just pick one up and expect to survive a fight with a skilled user."

He exchanged several swings with a snarling pirate before he cut the man's hand and mono-blade in two. A well-practiced backswing took the man's head off, spraying him and Papadakis with arterial blood.

"Push forward," he ordered over the general com frequency. "Take the offensive and make them retreat."

That was easier said than done. Even back on their heels, the commandos were far better trained than most of Brad's people. Now that almost no one had a loaded firearm, the fight was close and bloody.

He started to wonder if his people could actually force them back at all. If not, they were in deep trouble.

A commando with a blood-red sash that was actually spattered with real blood waved his arm and pointed back toward Brad and his people. Yep. Here they came again.

Then something bright flashed over Brad's shoulder and impacted the pirate squarely in the chest, blowing him into gobbets of flesh and blood. Just as suddenly, new fighters in Marine armor flowed into Brad's formation and brought their heavy weapons to bear on the pirates.

Lieutenant Gockel and her people had arrived.

His trained shock troops broke the attackers' wills and drove them back, but the Marines didn't pursue them far. Brad approved. It was far too easy to run into an ambush that way.

Once the field was cleared of active enemies, Brad ordered his people to make sure all the living got what medical care they could. Many would still die, both pirate and Fleet, but he'd try.

"Admiral, Major," a tall figure in Marine armor said. "Thanks for the assist. We've broken the guards behind us, and the prisoners are secure. I recommend we bring these tunnels down to keep those bastards from making another rush at us as we pull out."

"Get it rigged," Papadakis said, not even pretending to wait for Brad to have an opinion. "We'll withdraw to the prisoners and follow you out of the mines. That'll get us to the shuttles with you still supporting us most of the way. You can break off to support Bravo Force then."

"Copy that," Gockel said. "Pull back with the wounded while we rig the charges."

Brad put the arm of one of the walking wounded over his shoulder and helped the man toward the prison area of the mines. He shot Papadakis a look.

"I wouldn't keep pushing the whole ignoring-my-rank too much further," he cautioned her over the command channel. "I'm not a pampered civilian. I know what I can and what I can't do."

"Then you know that you have to make it out of here alive," she responded promptly, unabashed at the dressing-down. Compared to the best chewing-out the Marines could manage, he was probably a piker.

"The Jovians won't work with Fleet unless you're in change," she continued. "You're the one indispensable person on this mission. If I don't get you back to the fleet alive, the OWA is going to crush the Jovian system.

"So, knowing that, you're not going to bitch to me about making sure you make it and save the goddamn Commonwealth, are you?"

He snorted, amused at her audacity and more than a bit nonplussed at her blunt response. "I suppose not."

"Then let's get the Everlit out of here, sir, before they manage to flank us again."

Honestly, she was right, no matter how much being shepherded along annoyed him. He had bigger fish to fry, so he needed to get what information he could there and then make certain that the OWA fleet had no refueling options once they finally showed up. That meant he needed to get a move on.

———

As they headed back to their appropriated loading bay, Brad listened in to the combat channels. Even with the reinforcements they'd freed up, the Marines were still meeting stiff resistance. The OWA had a lot more combatants on this rock than anyone had expected.

He had the people under his command briefly quiz each of the prisoners, and they were able to confirm there were a high number of trained troops there, as well as a lot of tankage for fuel. Tanks that were built and mostly full.

The loss of this facility was going to hurt his rat bastard of a brother, and Brad was damned pleased about that. He still needed prisoners to know what he was going to be hit with, though.

They started loading the prisoners into the shuttles as soon as they made it to the bay. It was going to take multiple trips to get them away from the fighting completely, but the bay was defensible enough.

He found Papadakis directing the hardening of the bay. It looked as if she had her people digging in for a sharp and protracted fight. Good.

"How mad are you going to be if I don't head back to my ship right now?" he casually asked.

"Pretty mad," she said, shooting him a narrow-eyed look. "Are you yanking my chain? If so, this isn't the time, sir."

"I'm actually serious. The Marines are hitting a lot more resistance than I like, and I want to throw our people into the fight to change the odds."

He held up his hand before she could argue. "This is happening, so spend your time figuring out the best way to make it work. There are a lot of OWA fighters. How can we best screw up their defense and take this facility?"

With a not-so-muffled curse, she retrieved a slate and started looking over the maps. She flipped through the pages as if she was looking for something in specific. After a minute, she stopped flipping and zoomed in on something.

"We don't have complete maps of the facility, but the tanks are somewhat isolated," she said. "The control area has to be somewhere near them. It wouldn't make sense to have it separated by very much. None of our people found a way to get in, though. The fighting is taking up a lot of our attention, but someone should've spotted it. If we take the control center, we can do some serious distracting."

Brad thought back to how the Cadre had hidden the tunnels servicing the fuel tanks in the base they'd planned to use for the attack on Ceres. "I might be able to figure that one out. Do we know where the closest approach to the tanks will be?"

The major nodded. "I can get us there, but it won't be without some risk. The fighting is in an adjacent section of the base."

"Let's get the first tranche of civilians on the way to our ships. We'll leave half our people to guard the bay, including most of your Marines."

He could almost hear the sound of her teeth grinding at the last part.

"They're supposed to be guarding you, sir," she managed to get out without screaming, which seemed almost miraculous.

"Take one squad," he offered. "Our best chance of making this work is by avoiding drawing attention to ourselves anyway."

"Yes, sir," she said with a sigh. She then started yelling at her people and sorting out the defense of the bay.

He watched her work with sympathy. It was always a mess when your boss was intent on sticking his head into a rock grinder. Still, that was the only way he saw to capture this base intact enough to get the answers he desperately needed. He'd have to take the risk and hope for the best.

———

Twenty minutes later, they were slipping through what was obviously a hastily abandoned section of the underground tunnels. Brad could hear the sound of fighting somewhere nearby, but the strange echoes made determining the direction they came from impossible.

Major Papadakis stopped and gestured around them. The chamber they were in looked like any one of the ones they'd just passed through.

"We're about as close as we can get to the tanks," she said. "Now what?"

"Stand clear and have someone with a heavy gun shoot the walls closest to the tanks," he said. "If this is like the last time, we'll find a hidden tunnel."

"And so might the slugs we fire," she countered. "How thick are the doors, do you think?"

"Not that thick," he admitted. "What's plan B?"

She motioned for one of the Marines to step up. "This is Sergeant Chavez. He's my go-to guy with charges. Can you crack that wall without endangering the tanks, *mi amigo*?"

"Sure, Major. Give me a minute."

The man set about placing a number of small charges along the indicated wall and then the Marines cleared the general area. As soon as they were away, Chavez set off the charges with a muffled *thump* that threw dust up into the air. In the low gravity, it would be there a while.

One look at the wall showed Brad that the gambit had been successful. The hidden door was down and the tunnel beyond showed only minor damage.

"Well done," he said. "Now we need to clear the tunnel and look for the control room."

Without responding directly, Papadakis sent her people into the tunnel, conspicuously standing between Brad and the opening. He took the hint and stayed where he was.

Two minutes later, a call came back over the general channel. "The tunnel is clear, but we have an armored hatch down here, as well as a number of monitoring points for the tanks."

"Do we have a way of looking past the hatch?" Brad asked. "You know, like tapping into the video in the control room or something?"

"I'm sure that's possible," Papadakis said in response, "but not with the people and equipment we have here."

"Then let's go get ready to breach it."

The two of them joined her men down the tunnel and he examined the hatch. It was thick and seemed well mounted. Any charge capable of blowing it open was going to take out the rock around them and expose the entire area to space.

Worse, it might set off one of the tanks, which would set off the rest. That wouldn't be survivable. He was in the position of having a hammer and needing a scalpel.

Well, he supposed he'd have to come back to it later. They'd go relieve the Marines and deal with the control area last, hoping they'd manage to get the data they needed.

"We have incoming," one of the Marines near the rear said. "Hostiles entering the tunnel."

The sound of rifles firing made him duck, but there was no cover. They were trapped.

CHAPTER TWENTY-EIGHT

IF THE ATTACKERS expected their sporadic fire to pin his Marines down, they were sadly mistaken. Papadakis had her people on their feet and charging almost as soon as the shooting started.

"Push them back and secure the entrance," she snapped. "Chavez, put a charge on the wall and prepare to breach it. We'll bypass the armored hatch and hope for the best."

She fixed Brad with a hard stare through her armored visor. "You stay here, Admiral. I don't have the spare time to keep an eye on you."

With that, she was off, and the fighting up the tunnel intensified. Brad was left with Sergeant Chavez and a pair of Marines no doubt tasked to keep him from doing anything hasty.

Rather than focus on the fighting, Brad kept his attention on the demolitions expert. "Do you think the wall will be vulnerable?"

"Probably," the man said as he started affixing a larger charge to the rock near the hatch. "This wasn't built as a stand-up armored facility. The tunnelling looks at least a few years old, so this is probably a converted chamber. There, it's armed. One flick of a switch and *boom*! It won't be enough to cause the tanks to rupture. I hope."

"You're filling me with confidence. Let's get as far back as we can and wait for the Major."

He was about to say more when the metal hatch beside them started opening. The people inside had decided they were going to come out and play. Perfect.

Rather than draw his weapons, Brad grabbed the charge Chavez had just affixed to the wall and tossed it through the hatch, between the feet of the first armed man coming out.

"Blow it," Brad ordered, throwing himself back and shielding his head.

The concussive wave slammed him into the rock wall and stunned him. The world seemed to be moving in slow motion and sounds were oddly muted as his ears rang. Someone was shouting over the com, but he couldn't make out the words or meanings.

He staggered to his feet, swaying badly before he caught himself, and hefted his rifle. The three Marines seemed to be in much better shape. Their armor must've been better at keeping their brains from being scrambled in the concussion.

Rather than trying to give orders he wasn't even sure they'd understand, he headed through the open hatch and into chaos and devastation.

The control room wasn't all that big, and the blast had ruptured several control consoles and the people that had been operating them. That said, the devastation was far more contained than he'd have expected. The charge must've been shaped and expended most of its force down a certain line of attack.

Which meant that the rest of the room was in better shape, and so were the men climbing to their feet and pulling weapons from their belts.

Brad wasted no time trying to count them but took cover behind a shattered and smoking console, opening fire on the cluster of pirates in front of him while the three Marines dropped down beside him. He really hoped they'd called for backup.

Unlike the fighters in the rest of the base, the people here weren't in armor, except for the half-dozen that the bomb had taken out at the hatch. Worse for them, they were only armed with pistols. This was going to be a very short and brutal fight for them.

One of the pirates broke cover and dashed for a console along the far wall. Figuring that allowing him to get there could be bad in any number of ways, Brad shot him in the back three times, killing him well short of the controls.

Two other pirates leapt up and headed for the same console as soon as the first man went down. Brad emptied his rifle into the two runners and dropped them just before the magazine emptied.

"Cover me," Brad shouted, hoping his companion's ears worked better than his, dropped his rifle, drew his pistol and mono-blade, and raced for the console himself.

His timing was good, and he took the head off another pirate as she rose to make the dash herself. The spray of blood from her neck blinded the man who'd been following her, making him easy prey for Brad's backhand slash.

There wasn't much cover near the target console, so Brad just crouched low and used his pistol to shoot at anyone that seemed to be thinking about making a run for him.

His new position had the survivors caught in a crossfire and one of them threw down his weapon. That just prompted the man beside him to shoot him in the head, earning a pair of shots from Brad.

The remaining three threw down their weapons together and raised their hands.

Brad scanned the rest of the room but didn't see any more active fighters. He rose slowly to his feet, keeping the prisoners under a watchful eye while the Marines secured them.

"Two of you keep an eye on the hatch," he said. "Chavez, make sure the rest of these bastards are either dead or secured."

That done, he looked over the console that everyone had been excited about. As he'd expected, it looked like it had a self-destruct timer on it. Thankfully, no one had managed to activate it.

It also had an undamaged and unlocked computer interface. That might prove to be helpful, too. He rarely got his hands on Cadre data before they'd manage to purge it. If he could hold this room, he might get everything he needed.

A loud explosion outside the room sent dust back into the air and reminded him that he needed to hope Major Papadakis beat the attackers back or he'd be playing defender all too soon.

———

His hearing improved enough over the next few minutes to get a report from Papadakis and an ass-chewing for getting into a fight without her. She mentioned something about tying him up and shipping him back into space, but he thought she was joking. Probably.

She sent those least able to fight back to help defend the control room while she did her work, which presented Brad an opportunity to take advantage of the OWA controllers leaving the console logged in. He could have done it himself in theory, but he knew he needed to keep his eyes on the big picture right now—and even commanding a mercenary company had left his computer skills rusty, let alone running a *fleet*.

He didn't have the combat hackers he'd hired for his Vikings, but two of the crewmen had extensive experience in computer systems, and he quickly had them digging for the information he needed as well as anything else they could find.

A lot of the data was still going to be encrypted, but there was a good chance his people back on the Fleet vessels could crack that. They couldn't get data out of an erased drive.

While his people worked, Brad looked over the surviving consoles. He found one that captured his interest when he saw the rotating video feeds from other locations inside the base. This must be the security controls.

He sat down and started running through everything, trying to get an appreciation of how the fighting was going. Unsurprisingly, it seemed his people were slowly gaining the upper hand. Papadakis was pushing the group that had attacked her and the control room area back and had already cleared the area immediately outside the control room.

The prisoners they'd been evacuating in the bay were loading their second wave and would be gone in less than five minutes. The other Marine forces were still going head to head with a large force deeper into the mines. Resistance was fierce, but the OWA troops had nowhere to go.

Or did they?

The bastards always seemed to have a rathole to slip out from and escape, at least the ones in charge. If they went true to form, the leadership was down there and had a way to get off this asteroid.

Getting past the fleet guarding it wasn't going to be easy, but Brad wouldn't say it was impossible, if the stars lined up just right. The best place to stop them was down here.

Video feeds were scarce down in the mines, but he finally found one that showed a number of men and women rushing toward the far side of the asteroid.

Two things immediately stood out about them. First, they were pushing crates on grav repulsors. Those were like the panels that generated gravity, but these were made to aid in moving heavy cargo. Even so, the task was probably causing a lot of cursing. The people doing the moving were obviously not used to maneuvering anything that bulky.

Secondly, the man in the lead was someone Brad recognized and deeply wanted to have a long conversation with: Jamal Youden, the OWA representative who had almost certainly been behind the mass murder of the majority of the Jovian system's political leadership.

That made stopping them that much more important. No matter how much this was going to piss off Major Papadakis, he was going to have to capture the man and his secret cargo before he slipped away, and that meant he'd be operating solo. Relatively speaking.

He snorted in amusement when he realized she might just truss him up and send him off to his flagship after all.

"Get a move on, people," he ordered. "We've got some bad guys to catch."

———

Saying that proved a lot easier than making it happen, as it turned out. His maps of the facility were nonexistent, so he was forced to have one of the computer people divert to finding them for him. That ate up five minutes but allowed him to share the layout of the base with all the people under his command, including the Marines doing the fighting elsewhere.

Once he had the complete map, he quickly figured out where the OWA leadership was going. There were a few isolated domes on the far side of the asteroid, and one of them was the likely goal. It was labeled as storage, but that had to be crap. There was a ship hidden in there.

The heroic thing to do would be to rush down some of the alternate passages and block them from escape at the last minute.

Brad chose the less adventurous but far more effective path of calling on one of Commodore Bailey's ships to put a lot of mass-driver slugs into the dome in question while he moved his forces to cut off the group's options to retreat.

The mass of the asteroid was too high to feel the individual impacts, but he imagined he felt a vibration anyway.

His force had two missions: to trap the escapees and to attack the rear of the holdouts the original Marine force had pinned down in the mines. If they could do both those things, the fighting there would be over.

Keeping in mind how upset Papadakis was going to be, he stayed back from the leading edge of the group and simply directed their movements. Two-thirds of his forces went to attack the OWA holdouts fighting the Marines, while the smaller group focused on trapping the high-value targets.

As things turned out, the trapping part was the easiest. He and his forces plugged them into a single tunnel segment with him on one end and the destroyed dome on the other. Based on the reports from the corvette that had done the firing, the ship in the dome was in just as bad a shape as the structure. The OWA leadership had nowhere to go.

Based on the lack of real shooting, they didn't have much in the way of armaments, either. He bet they were regretting leaving all their commandos behind.

That didn't mean they were unarmed, of course. No, they had some pistols and a few rifles. Nothing that could hold off a determined push on his part. He only needed to make them see that clearly.

"You're trapped," he yelled around the corner toward the enemy. The two Marines acting as his guards made sure they were between him and the corner, like they didn't trust him not to race around it and start swinging his mono-blade.

"You'll never take us alive," Youden shouted back. Brad couldn't tell if the man recognized his voice or not. Honestly, it didn't matter.

"That remains to be seen. We know you were behind the attack on Io, Youden. Perhaps some of your compatriots were as well. If so, I can't help them. If anyone wasn't involved in that attack though, I *will* promise them that Fleet will keep possession of them and not allow for lethal punishment for their crimes. This is a one-time offer and expires in ten seconds."

A loud, undignified squawk sounded less than two seconds later, and the noise of a scuffle made its way to Brad's ears. Someone wasn't allowing the grass to grow under their feet.

"We've got him down," a different male voice said. "We accept your deal and surrender."

Brad gestured for the Marines and some of the Fleet personnel to go secure their new prisoners. In just a minute, the all clear was given and Brad came around the corner to look them over.

Youden's eyes widened at the sight of him and he snarled. "You!"

"Me," Brad confirmed. "I have to say that I'm looking forward to chatting with you, Mr. Youden. It'll be interesting to see what you have to tell me."

"You'll get *nothing* from me!"

"We'll see," Brad said, feeling content. "No matter how this plays out, I wager that I'll enjoy the outcome more than you will."

Youden grinned savagely. "We'll see if you still feel the same way when your brother comes along and chops your head off."

"If Jack comes calling, I'd be more worried about my own head, if I were you. In any case, I'll take my chances. You and your mistakes here have given us a fighting chance."

CHAPTER TWENTY-NINE

THE FIGHTING TOOK hours more to wrap up, not counting the time spent searching the mines for OWA fighters who had gotten away, but the end result was never in question. Major Papadakis finally caught up with him but managed to stop herself from ripping his head off for his shenanigans, for which he was grateful.

The computer experts had managed to copy the data off the base computers while he'd taken care of the OWA leadership, but as he'd expected, the majority of it was encrypted. The prisoners were likely to be helpful in this, if they could be properly motivated.

The crates were interesting. They held the prototypes the OWA had stolen from Blackhawk Station that allowed for the refining of fuel from ice. They'd copied them, of course, and there were larger examples of them in use here at the refueling facility, but Youden had expected his people to destroy those. These were meant to seed another facility somewhere.

Brad made arrangements for the crates to be sent to his flagship, but they were little more than a curiosity at this point. No, the more interesting haul was in senior prisoners. Captain Nah arranged to have them all put together, and Kate Falcone observed them for a few hours while Brad coordinated things from his flag bridge.

Once they had the facility fully locked down, he made his way down to join her before holding a videoconference with his flag officers.

"What can you tell me?" he asked when he stepped into the compartment she was using as an observation room.

She pointed out five of the prisoners. "The others treat these five with subconscious deference. They've obviously been told not to, but their body language gives them away. I'd stake my life that those are Youden's lieutenants."

"Are any of them in the Agency databases?"

She shook her head. "I'm still waiting for word, but I'm sure they're Cadre. It makes me sad that you promised them their lives, but Mercury still sucks. They'll wish they were dead in a few years. If, of course, we win this war."

He nodded. "Do you think you can induce them to give us the codes to unlock the encrypted data?"

She grinned. "I'll get what we need. Especially if I can get a few positive IDs on them. What are our plans going forward? Do we return to Io or do we clean out the trailing Trojans?"

"I want to clean them out of here. We'll have time before the OWA forces arrive, and I don't want to leave this kind of scum at our backs. It's not going to be pretty, but the Marines can dig them out."

"You know that they won't die easily," she said a bit sadly. "They'll use the civilians as human shields and other atrocities."

"I know," he said, leaning back against the wall. "I don't get how so many people can be monsters."

"Did you ever hear that old saw about everyone being the hero of their own story?" she asked. "It's bull. Some people are nothing but wolves and see everyone else as sheep. They'll do whatever they can to see themselves in a better place, no matter how much misery they leave in their wake.

"Are some people going to die when you clear the Trojans? Yes. Here's a truth. The Cadre or OWA, whichever you prefer, would kill them anyway. You can't save everyone, Brad. Make a statement in how you try to save as many as you can."

"I'm not sure that's going to help me sleep at night, but thanks. I'll go settle on a plan with the Commodores while you find someone to tell us what we need to know. They either know the force mix Mader is going to lead here, or they know the encryption key, or both. I'm counting on you to get everything you can."

"I'll make it happen," she assured him. "Better yet, I'll even do it without spacing anyone."

"I'm not convinced that makes me feel any better, but I did make a promise. Do the best you can."

"What about Youden?" she asked. "He has no immunity. Can I lean on him?"

He smiled coldly. "Do whatever you need to in regards with him but keep him alive. I'll be needing him soon, if I don't miss my guess."

Brad turned toward the door but paused. "Thanks, Kate."

"It's what partners are for," she said, already turning back to face the observation screen.

He left the room still mulling over how he was going to clear the Trojans. Like she'd said, it was going to be bloody, heartbreaking work, but he needed to make it happen as fast as he could, no matter the blood and pain that it was going to cause.

————

Brad made his way to the wardroom and found everyone already gathered. Commodores Bailey and Nuremburg were on one side of the table, Commodore Jahoda and Captain Nah were on the other, and Major Papadakis sat at the far end of the table from his seat. All rose as he entered.

"As you were," he said, shocked at how easily that response had rolled off his tongue and how accepting he'd become of the gesture of respect.

Once everyone was seated, he joined them, taking a moment to look at each. "Let's start with Major Papadakis. Is the refueling facility secure?"

"Yes, Admiral," she said. "I have a casualty list for your perusal, but all things considered, it's lighter than I'd have guessed going into the fight. It came down to the triarii in the end, but the OWA goons paid the heavier price.

"The facility was rigged to blow, but we short-circuited that plan when we captured the control room. Rather, you did. I should file a protest at your reckless actions, but I doubt it will change your nature any, so I'll save myself for a better opportunity."

Brad chuckled. "No, I don't suppose I'll change much at this late date—I'm still more comfortable with a blade in my hand than my feet on a flag deck.

"What about the space around the refueling base?"

"All clear," Bailey said. "We took out every ship that was in the area and captured the civilian ships as well. We're still looking at the crews, but I'm going to bet they're Cadre or in the pay of them. We have pickets out to catch anyone else in the area that comes looking."

"Good," he said with a nod. "That leads to the next topic. What do we do about the Trojans? The OWA has people everywhere. As soon as we start cleaning them out, things will get very ugly."

"Can't be helped," Nuremburg said with a frown. "We can't leave them where they are. The deaths in battle will be bad, but at least the civilians left will be free. If we leave the OWA alone, they'll just keep committing atrocities and more people will die in the end, probably in more terrible ways, too."

"I'm afraid Commodore Nuremburg is correct," Jahoda said. "We have to strike now before they have a chance to dig in. The longer we wait, the harder and bloodier this is going to be."

Brad nodded in response, grudgingly accepting the inevitable. "We need to finish cleaning out the refueling facility—and we may as well restock our own ships. I'll contact tankers in the rest of the Jovian system to come take what they can, too. We'll destroy the base and any fuel left once that happens. At the very least, we'll blow it when we head back for Io.

"We'll need transports to take the OWA prisoners as well. As far as the high-value captives, Agent Falcone is trying to get a lever on them to decrypt the computer data we recovered. Keep your fingers crossed on that and we might be able to plan for exactly the odds we're going to face."

"What about the civilian prisoners and the hostages?" Captain Nah asked. "We need transports for them, too. We can't just take them to the nearest settlement. The OWA is still in control there."

"I'll ask for something along that line as well," Brad assured her. "They can go to Io for now."

A low chime on Captain Nah's wrist-comp indicated an incoming signal. She excused herself and had a short exchange with whoever was on the other end before disconnecting.

"We have a large number of ships inbound," the officer said grimly. "Bet's they're friendly?"

Brad rose to his feet. "No bets. Everyone to your ships and go to battle stations."

———

To his utter surprise, the ships *were* friendly. He didn't find out until he had the entire task force arrayed for battle, but the incoming signal was from *Oath of Vengeance* and he was looking at an image of Michelle moments later. Flanking her were Sara Kernsky and Saburo.

"Brad," she said in the recording, still too far away for a two-way conversation, "This is Michelle aboard *Oath of Vengeance*. We're leading a mercenary force out to help you clear the trailing Trojans. We got word that you found the refueling facility and we're bringing tankers to clear off what we can and some transports for the prisoners."

His reaction was a mixture of relief and gratitude that his wife had been on top of this, especially when the clock was ticking down. And, honestly, the mercenary ground forces would be a more welcome sight in the settlements than the Fleet Marines, given public sentiments.

He sent a brief response but waited for the incoming ships to get close enough to respond in real time before he called Michelle back.

"You're a lifesaver," he said as soon as she came on the channel. "You're just in the nick of time."

"Of course I am," she said smugly. "I can't claim all the credit, though. Director—excuse me, Admiral—Kernsky has been paying very close attention to what you were doing. As soon as we were sure you were committed to the attack on the refueling facility, we set out.

You're not set up to deal with lots of civilian prisoners and Cadre scum.

"We brought a variety of ships to take them all back to Io for sorting out. We also have tankers to get what fuel we can. Waste not, want not."

"Perfect," he said. "We're going to send ships to break the OWA hold on the other settlements, but the mercenaries will be welcomed more readily than Marines. That isn't to say we won't provide the muscle we can. Who is going to command the troops?"

Michelle grinned. "General Saburo. His promotion is under Admiral Kernsky's banner and the rank is only temporary, unless of course I want to see him keep squirming for a while longer once the fighting is finally over."

He noted that neither Saburo nor Kernsky was on the bridge of his former flagship now. "Excellent. Where are they?"

"On their way to your flagship. This is the kind of planning that needs to happen face to face. I estimate they'll dock with you in about twenty minutes."

"I'll be sure to be there to greet them. Love, this is going to be an ugly fight."

"No uglier than life under the OWA," she said with a shake of her head. "Don't let this drag you down, Brad. We're with you. You didn't cause this tragedy, but you will end it."

She looked down at one of the repeater screens at her knee. "I have to go. Looks like it's time to get our ships into position, and I wouldn't want to embarrass you."

"Nothing you can do will ever embarrass me," he assured her. "I'll try to find time to come see you during the next few days. I really, *really* need to feel you beside me."

"I'll make sure and get the wine ready," she said in a sultry voice. "Now go kick some ass, lover."

As soon as he broke the com connection, one of his aides started fanning her face and grinning. He felt himself reddening but said nothing about her antics.

"I'll be in the docking bay if anyone needs me," he said, clearing his throat.

The blush had almost gone away by the time he'd walked down to the bay. The shuttle from *Oath of Vengeance* was on final approach and Major Papadakis was there with an honor guard. He briefly wondered who had tipped her off.

"Temperature too high?" she asked after taking a look at his face. "I can call Engineering and have them kick the cooling up."

Now he knew who'd called her. Everyone thought they were comedians, including him on occasion.

"I'm good," he assured her. "Thanks so much for asking."

They stood in silence as the shuttle came to a halt and the passengers started debarking. The first out the hatch was Admiral Kernsky, followed closely by General Saburo.

The third person was a surprise until he thought about it for a moment. Then he realized that Arbiter Blaze's grim presence was inevitable.

It was really going to suck to be Youden.

CHAPTER THIRTY

BRAD EMBRACED SABURO QUICKLY, then shook hands with the two women.

"It's good to see you, Arbiter Blaze," he greeted the woman who'd thrown Jupiter's support behind him. "I did think we were keeping my presence here at least a little under wraps."

"If you're keeping secrets from your allies, you're doing reconciliation wrong," Blaze pointed out. "Commodore Bailey understood that much, at least. You left a clever woman in charge."

"I did," Brad agreed. He looked past the landed shuttles to survey the refueling station beneath them. "Not a bad place for her, either. The space battle was the easy part of this."

"And the hard part has barely begun," Saburo said grimly, Brad's friend looking on edge. "No one has done the kind of urban warfare I'm expecting here in the cluster. The mercenaries we've brought have seen the closest thing to it, but not on this scale."

"I'll have Falcone and Papadakis prep a briefing," Brad promised. "You won't be going in blind or alone."

The Asian Jovian native nodded.

"I have four thousand mercenaries under my direct command," he told Brad. "What did you get me into, Brad?"

"Much the same mess I'm in," Brad replied.

"Only not as bad," Kernsky added. "Madrid has a *lot* more than four thousand people under his command."

Brad shivered. It was easy to forget that aspect of it behind the calm numbers of ships. Easy to forget that even a corvette or frigate had a crew of between twelve and thirty. Destroyers were easily sixty or seventy—and his cruisers were over three hundred.

And at that, he wasn't even sure how many ships were going to make up First Fleet for the final clash. It depended on if they lost anyone else there in the trailing Trojans.

"We've probably got about two thousand Marines ready to go as well," he told Brad. "I'll have Papadakis follow your lead. We want merc boots on the ground, not Marines, as much as we can."

"Nobody out here likes the Commonwealth," Blaze agreed. "But from what we've heard about OWA operations out here, they almost certainly like the Alliance *less*."

"That's what I'm relying on," Brad confirmed. "In other news, Arbiter, I have a present for you."

"What kind of present?" she asked. "Should I be hoping for battle-ships or planning to hide from your wife?"

Brad glared at Saburo to muffle the other man's chuckle.

"How about Jamal Youden in chains?" he asked.

The humor vanished and Blaze's eyes went cold and hard.

"You have him?"

"He was trying to coordinate something here," Brad confirmed. "We haven't had time to interrogate him or the other senior OWA officers yet, but once the Agency is done with Youden, he's yours.

"His sins are against Jupiter, and the Commonwealth will surrender him to Jovian justice." He raised a warning hand.

"*After* he's told us everything he knows."

"He doesn't get promises of life, Admiral," Blaze told him coldly. "Jovian law is clear: the Arbiter Guild must confirm any sentence of death under the Governors' authorities.

"With Youden, I think we'll just skip the middleman."

———

Falcone met them outside the brig with a broad grin on her face.

"That looks positive," Brad told her.

"Jamal Youden might be convinced that the Lord Protector will rule all humanity, but he's *less* convinced that he'll survive to see it," the Agent said as she nodded to Brad's companions. "The moment he accepted we were actually about to start removing pieces, he pissed himself."

"The Arbiter Guild cannot condone torture, Agent Falcone," Blaze said quietly. "Youden's fate is set in stone, but that's still a bridge too far."

Brad carefully made sure that Blaze couldn't see his face. He wasn't *proud* of some of his past actions, but he'd definitely used torture a time or two himself. He trusted Falcone not to have crossed that line, but he wasn't *certain*…and he wouldn't blame her if she had.

"Arbiter, the entire star system is at war and we are only a few bad calls away from risking the end of human civilization," Falcone pointed out. "That said, torture is crap for getting accurate information and is a line I'd rather not cross myself. We have all of the tools, though, and that was enough to get Youden whimpering."

"Did we get anything useful?" Brad asked.

"He didn't know shit about their operations here in the Trojans," the Agent admitted. "I've got a few more lieutenants to sweat before I put together a briefing for Saburo here.

"The grander scheme, though? He gave us a lot. The refining gear was heading for a meteor swarm that is expected to pass near Jupiter in a month. They were going to use it as an anchor for a surprise flanking attack with the cruisers here."

"That fits the Phoenix's profile," Brad admitted. "Biggest fucking hammer in human history, and he still wants to come at things sideways. We've short-circuited it, then?"

"We've short-circuited the fleet part of it, but it sounds like there may be more going on that Youden didn't know about," Falcone told them. "He's a troubleshooter, a roving operative, but he's not in the inner circle, from what I can tell."

She smirked.

"From the way he talks, *he* thinks he's in the inner circle."

"Do you still need him, then?" Blaze asked, her voice chilly.

"I think he's given me everything he can. I'm going to finish the interrogations, then I'm going to take *Hades* out to the meteor swarm and check in on what else was going on there."

"Keep me informed," Brad ordered. "I can spare a few escorts if you need them."

So far as he could tell, the Agency's carrier had done a good job of using drones without losing them, but he doubted a couple of destroyers would go amiss if *Hades* was going hunting a long way from home.

"We'll be in touch before I leave," Falcone promised. "I'm done with Youden, but I have other customers."

Brad nodded, then turned to Blaze.

"Arbiter?"

"If you're done with him, he owes the people of Jupiter some answers," she replied. "I want him."

"Pass on anything you learn about the attack," Brad told her. "But the attack he led was on Jovian soil. He's yours."

"Thank you, Admiral."

Blaze stepped ahead. Brad couldn't resist following along, making sure he could hear what she was saying as she stepped past the Marine guards.

"Jamal Youden?" she asked. "You know who I am."

He couldn't hear Youden's response.

"I have a long list of questions to ask you, Mr. Youden, but let's get started with the very simplest thing, the one that will make very sure you understand where you sit."

Youden said something else. Brad was close enough to hear the tone, a wavery forced defiance.

"Jamal Youden, by the authority vested in me by the contracts between the Jovian governments and the Arbiter Guild, I hereby sentence you to death."

———

Leaving the prisoners to the tender graces of Falcone and Blaze, Brad led Kernsky and Saburo back to his office and poured them all drinks with a shake of his head.

"Interrogation was never my strong suit," Brad said quietly. "Ship command or sword fighting, those I'm comfortable with. Getting answers from people? I'm glad to have Kate."

"And the Mercury mines," Kernsky said with a snort. "Falcone has a reputation."

"She does," Brad agreed. "How's the situation back at Jupiter?"

"The new Governors are arguing and trying to run rings around each other," the Guild Admiral told him. "About the only thing they *do* agree on is that their militias are at your command."

She shook her head.

"I'm not sure half of the vice-governors and so forth that have fallen into control of their worlds even know how many ships they have," she pointed out. "None of them are going to be spectacular, you're going to get mostly frigates and corvettes, but it's fifty or so of those."

"Plus the Guild; that evens the odds in a lot of the lighter classes," Brad concluded. He was pretty sure he still had the edge in cruisers, but *Immortal* was still the biggest problem.

"Doesn't help much against a battleship," Saburo grumped, echoing Brad's thoughts. "We have a plan for that big bastard yet?"

"Shoot it until it dies?" Brad suggested, then shook his head. "Falcone has a crazy moonshot she's run by me. It's a damn suicide mission, though, so I'm leaving it in my back pocket."

He didn't need to tell them that it was a suicide mission for *him*.

"I hope we get some useful intel on the OWA positions here, too," Saburo said grimly. "There are half a million people and fourteen major settlements in the cluster. If we're going through them blind, we're going to lose a lot of people."

Brad nodded.

"We're going to lose a lot of people anyway, Saburo," he warned his friend. "We need to make it clear that we'll treat surrendering garrisons as combatants—and anyone who kills civilians as a terrorist."

"That's the kind of fine line that's going to come back to bite us," Saburo Kawa warned. "So long as we decide *we* get to pick who's a legitimate combatant and who isn't, the OWA can argue they get to do the same.

"I don't want my people getting shot out of hand—and if they're going to flag anyone as pirates or terrorists, it's going to be the mercs."

Brad sighed. Saburo wasn't wrong.

"You're right. But we need to keep in mind that these people *are* guilty of terrorism and piracy."

"Then we try them for that after the war with the evidence we have then," Kernsky told him. "Blaze will help you put together neutral tribunals. But you *have* to respect the laws of war, or, well…"

She shrugged.

"As Falcone said, we're only a few bad calls away from risking the end of human civilization, Brad," she echoed. "I think that playing games with who gets to be called a uniformed soldier is one of those calls."

CHAPTER THIRTY-ONE

"ALL RIGHT EVERYBODY. Have a seat, grab a drink, and get ready for the damn home video," Kate Falcone said sharply. "The data we have sucks. Not in quality, but in what it tells us."

Brad was one of the handful of people in the room with Falcone, along with Saburo, Kernsky, and Blaze. Everyone else, including every mercenary officer and Marine officer in his fleet in the trailing Trojans, was getting the briefing by video.

In most cases, with the Agency woman blurred out and her voice adjusted by a computer. The OWA knew who she was, but the less they made it obvious who and where she was, the better.

"This is the trailing Trojan cluster of Jupiter," she continued, an image of the mess of asteroids following Jupiter in its twelve-year-long orbit. "Like the leading Trojans, it's a cluster of ice and rock that has proven damn useful over the years.

"Our best guess is that the Cadre moved in shortly after we removed the Raeburn Research Laboratory," she explained. "That, for those who haven't been briefed, was a covert facility used for the manufacture of illegal chemical weapons used in a number of bloody-handed Cadre operations.

"By the time the Outer Worlds Alliance officially came into existence, the Cadre had taken control of every station in the cluster and had already begun construction of the refueling station.

"Their control of the region was built on four pillars. The first was hostages, the same workers they needed to build Warren's Folly into the station we just took control of. Those hostages are now free and will be acting as our ambassadors to their home stations.

"The second pillar was fear of the squadrons anchored at the Folly," she continued. "Even a corvette is capable of wrecking most colonies and stations with a solid torpedo salvo. At a minimum, it looks like first the Independence Militia and then the OWN maintained multiple destroyers to cover the Folly.

"They're gone. No one is going to be bombarding those colonies from space now."

Falcone waved her hand, and red icons lit up every one of the major colonies and most of the minor ones.

"The red dots mark the third pillar of control, the one that's still in play. Those are Outer Worlds Alliance regulars. Combat troops, not necessarily equal to the commandos that defended the Folly, but still trained soldiers. Each of those dots marks between a squad and a company of soldiers.

"The biggest problem, however, is their fourth pillar: every damn station and colony in the cluster has been wired with explosives.

"Attached to this report is as much information as we have on the OWA deployment strengths and the location of the explosives. We're looking at about three thousand troops scattered throughout the cluster."

"Then it's a good thing we've got about six thousand to send against them," Saburo said as he rose to take over the briefing.

"The good news to all of this mess is that our Agency friends have confirmed that there is no central control for the explosives. Each station's bombs are under the control of the senior OWA officers present—and at this point, most of these guys are neither commandos nor Cadre.

"We have a reasonable chance of demanding surrenders and getting them. The *problem* is that if we demand those surrenders and we misjudge the officer with the button, a lot of people die."

Saburo paused, letting that sink in.

"So, what's the plan, General?" Brad asked. "The Fleet is ready to support in any way possible, but this is a ground show—and it's a Mercenary Guild show."

"It has to be."

"The biggest thing I need from the Fleet is the mother of all jamming fields," Saburo told him. "If we can concentrate our forces on a minimum number of targets, this job gets a lot easier. If they can talk to each other, though, then we need to hit them all simultaneously."

"I think we can manage that," Brad promised. "If nothing else, we have a small stockpile of OWA gear we can repurpose for just about anything."

"That helps a lot," Saburo replied. "If we can keep them cut off, we'll start with the largest settlements and work our way down. This won't be fast, people. Station by station. Corridor by corridor. We accept surrenders, we treat them as enemy combatants, but we clear these platforms.

"We have to." Saburo shook his head. "We can't trust that the OWA *doesn't* have fanatics willing to start pushing buttons."

———

Brad had about enough time to order his people to get starting on the jamming field before Falcone arrived in his office.

"Do we have enough repeaters?" he asked Captain Nah, gesturing the Agency operative to a seat.

"We probably would have on our own, but the OWA supplies contained a stash of com buoys," Nah told him. "We'll repurpose those as jammers before we dig into our own stockpiles. That's the advantage of capturing an enemy logistics base, Admiral: no shortages!"

"Well, let's get on using the OWA's gear against them. Let me know if you need an Admiral-sized hammer for anything," Brad said.

"Will do, sir."

The channel closed and Brad turned his attention on Falcone.

"You're heading out, Kate?" he asked.

"We are," she confirmed. "My crew is just finishing up cramming spare drones into every open space aboard *Hades*."

He arched an eyebrow at her.

"*Folly* had two full carrier loads of Javelins," she explained. "Since the only supply source I know of for those is a factory floating off the Ivory Coast on Earth, I'm not turning down a spare hundred or so fighters."

"Can you fit them aboard?" Brad asked.

"With difficulty," she conceded. "Last estimate I saw was that we were going to be able to fit an extra fifty drones, though we're still going to be limited to deploying thirty at a time."

"That's not a bad supply of backups, though. Do you need anything else from me?"

"I'll take you up on that escort if you've got any *Invictus*es or *Warrior*s to spare," she admitted. "I want to sneak up on that meteor swarm, so I need modern ships with modern stealth, but something about the situation is making me twitchy."

Brad pulled up his current fleet order to confirm his initial instinct.

"I only have three *Warrior*s with me, and I need their scanners and weapons for the landing ops," he told her. "I *do* have a pair of *Invictus*es: *Defiant* and *Invaincu*. I'll have orders cut for Commanders Johnson and Naumov to second themselves to your command."

He paused and considered. He didn't even know who *Hades*'s captain *was*.

"Or should I second them to the carrier CO?" he asked.

"I'll handle them," Falcone replied. "The fewer Agency names we admit to, the better."

"Even if the OWA knows them all already?" Brad said.

"Outer Worlds *Intelligence* knows most of our key operatives," she agreed. "But we don't know which ones and we don't know how much of that they've passed on to the OWN. There is a point to continuing the secrecy, Brad."

"I know."

"Speaking of secrecy, I assume your office is secure?" she asked.

"If it's not, heads will roll, but..." Brad smiled. He'd been a mercenary before he'd been a fleet commander, and for all that he appeared to have given the Commonwealth his life now, he still didn't fully trust the Fleet.

He pulled a combined jammer and white-noise generator out of his desk. It was hidden inside a nondescript bag that just *happened* to have enough copper and lead in its design to frustrate sensors.

He checked the telltales, then turned the device on.

"Now *nobody* knows what's going on in here," he concluded.

"Including your own security." Falcone sighed. "Promise me that you won't use that for anything else? The more often you use it, whether it's for meetings with me or *meetings* with Michelle, the less likely your people are to question your office disappearing off the air.

"That makes you vulnerable."

Brad nodded his understanding.

"What did you need, Kate?" he asked, his voice serious. If she wanted this completely off the record, he'd take it completely off the record.

"*Immortal* is still the key to all of this," she told him. "The mutiny override may be our only hope."

"And trying to get to it is a suicide mission," he countered.

"You want to tell me that taking *your* First Fleet against your brother's First Fleet won't be?" Falcone said bluntly. "You both are going to have about a hundred and fifty escorts. You've got ten cruisers; best guess is he'll have five. He's got at least three carriers; you have two—and that's assuming *Hades* gets back in time.

"Most of his escorts and cruisers are more up to date than yours. Everything shakes out slightly in your favor...except that *Immortal* could obliterate your entire fleet. You need a plan."

"I need a better plan than trying to infiltrate the Fleet CO and a boarding force onto the enemy flagship in the middle of an open space battle," Brad pointed out.

"I have an answer for that, at least," she said. "As everyone keeps reminding you, we can't risk you. You're the only thing holding this tentative alliance against the Lord Protector together.

"*And* you're the only tool we have here, so we need to make sure you manage to get there."

"I'm feeling so much more confident," he replied. "What have you got?"

"*Hades* has a long-range stealth insertion ship," Falcone told him. "It's a glorified boarding torpedo, and once its heat sinks are used up, they're gone...but it *should* suffice to get you and an elite team to *Immortal*.

"She's a battleship, Kate," Brad pointed out. "A 'team' isn't going to cut it. She'll have a couple hundred Marines aboard."

"A *Fleet* battleship would," she replied. "Our intel says that your brother is being a paranoid bastard. *Immortal*'s armories are either empty or in hard lockdown. He's brought a contingent of his elite Praetorians with him, but they're the only armed troops aboard the ship."

"Praetorians?" Brad asked. "*Really?*"

"He picked the name himself," Falcone confirmed. "I thought he was enough of a history buff to see the problem, but apparently not. Sadly, *these* Praetorians are pretty resistant to bribery."

"Let me guess, you tried?"

"The Agency did, at least." She shrugged. "No dice. The good news, though, is that while there are somewhere between thirty and sixty of Jack Mantruso's most loyal troops aboard *Immortal*, they're it. And there's *only* thirty to sixty of them."

"This is still a damn suicide mission," Brad replied, but he sighed. "Transfer your boarding torpedo to *Incredible*. If nothing else, I'm pretty sure we're carrying the only sets of power armor off of Earth."

"Yeah, because those suits need a bigger logistics train than *tanks*," Falcone pointed out. "Thirty-minute operating life, Brad."

"That will get us *to* my brother," he said. "I'm looking for other plans, Kate, but I'm not ruling yours out. Find out what's going on at that asteroid cluster and fill me in.

"After that, this is a waiting game. I'm more likely to get reinforcements now than my brother."

There were ships still being repaired in Mars orbit and new crews being assembled for ships in Earth orbit. Plus, the yards were working overtime to recommission mothballed cruisers and destroyers.

He wasn't going to see a lot of reinforcements anytime soon, but time was *his* friend, not the Lord Protector's.

"Are you sure of that?" Falcone said quietly. "He knew this war was coming. We didn't. So far, we think all of his ships came from the Inner System yards, but...do we really want to bet the future of the human race on the OWA *not* having shipyards?"

"Don't you have a meteor swarm to be investigating?" Brad asked plaintively.

CHAPTER THIRTY-TWO

IT HAD BEEN MADE VERY clear to Brad that there was no way in Everdark he was going to be participating in *these* landing actions. Instead, he sat on *Incredible*'s flag deck and watched thousands of soldiers go into battle on his command…and did nothing.

Four major operations went into action simultaneously, hitting the largest concentrations of OWA troops. Saburo led one op, Papadakis led another. Commodore William Branson of Heimdall's Raiders led the third operation, and Major Rashmi Boyce of the Commonwealth Marines was in charge of the last.

All were about half-and-half mercenaries and Marines, with the mercs leading the way.

Brad's own ship was backing up Papadakis, and he watched in silence as two of *Incredible*'s secondary mass drivers opened fire. The cruiser's big guns could have ripped Bordeaux Station into tiny pieces, but that was *not* their goal.

The target for those two guns was an innocuous-looking hydroponics facility near the center of the gangly conglomerate of girders, cargo containers, old ships, and small asteroids that made up the trailing Trojans' second-largest settlement.

An innocent-enough facility—except for the not-quite-well-enough-concealed radiation signatures that told Brad's people it contained enough plutonium for at least three fission bombs.

Fission bombs, however, needed to ignite properly—and being scattered across open space by high-velocity solid slugs was nothing of the sort.

"Nukes disabled," Nah reported. "You are go!"

"Hit them!" Papadakis barked, and new icons lit up on Brad's screens.

The cruiser had approached under stealth, her systems more than sufficient to hide them from a civilian station's scanners, and sent the assault shuttles ahead via a ballistic course.

Now that the bombs were *supposed* to be disabled, the shuttles' engines were coming to life at maximum power. The small craft were adjusting course to impact the station and slowing down to hit at velocities less than cataclysmic.

"Team Alpha is in," Papadakis reported. "They're heading right for the secondary bombs. No resi—"

Gunfire on one of the secondary channels cut her off.

"Team Alpha has hit resistance," the Marine Major concluded. "Reports are saying the bombs are guarded by commandos, *not* regulars. Other teams are in; we are deploying through the station."

There was nothing Brad could do from *Incredible*'s flag deck. The cruiser's involvement in this fight was over. He had a thousand people on that station…and if he even *twitched* towards a shuttle, he was going to end up tied to his chair.

Command sucked.

―――――

"Bastille is under our control," Saburo reported. His message was being relayed through the *Warrior*-class destroyer *Kitchener* and then sent by laser directly to *Incredible*. The other colony was close enough that they could have had a real-time conversation, but a recording was the best option for avoiding confusion and saving time.

"The explosives were under guard by commandos, but once we'd taken them out and secured control of the main life-support facilities, the regulars surrendered in good order." He shook his head. "The fighting was ugly before that. We're still assembling our casualty reports. Their regulars might not be fanatics like the commandos, but they're still frustratingly well trained and equipped."

With that, Saburo saluted and the recording ended. It seemed that Brad's Vikings were having better luck than his Marines.

"Papadakis, what's your status?" he asked over the channel to the Marine commander.

"Half of Team Alpha is dead and most of the rest are wounded," she told him grimly. "But they pulled it off. I just got confirmation the bombs are disabled. We're pushing the regulars back across the station, but they're dug-in and well equipped."

She paused.

"About the only good news I can see is that they seem to have evacuated civilians before they dug in. This is ugly, urban fighting inside a space station, and they don't seem inclined to surrender, but they're at least fighting like soldiers."

"What about the life support?" Brad asked.

"They control it and they're trying to fuck with us with it," she admitted. "I equipped my people for vacuum and it's saving our butts. I think that might be why they evacuated the civilians. Cadre might have been willing to massacre innocents to hurt us, but these guys are playing by the rules."

That was the first time since the OWA had been announced that Brad had heard one of his people draw that distinction and *really* mean it. That was, he supposed, the upside of the Phoenix building a nation and using its resources to fight a war:

Most of the people fighting for that nation *weren't* the monsters the Cadre had recruited as a matter of habit.

"Do you need reinforcements?" he asked. "Saburo has secured Bastille; we should be able to—"

"Sir! Scan data from Istantinople."

Brad turned to catch the main display. The sensor tech that had been shouting for his attention had already loaded the information onto the display, and his heart sank.

He'd known from the moment someone had said *scan data* instead of *message*, but it still hurt to watch the bombs go off.

Istantinople had been Branson's target, and like everywhere else, they'd intended to disable the nukes with fire from the starships. It looked like there had been a second set of nukes they hadn't known about, instead of the more conventional explosives used as backups elsewhere.

The third-largest settlement in the trailing Trojan cluster was now an expanding gas cloud, along with a thousand mercenaries and Marines.

"We have the situation here under control," Papadakis said grimly. "I'm guessing that wasn't good news."

"Istantinople is gone," he told her. "Fifty thousand people..."

"That's why they have damned commandos here, Admiral," the Marine told him. "I don't think most of the regulars would blow the stations...but the commandos are Cadre to the core. Fanatics with nukes."

"Secure that station, Major," Brad ordered. "*Incredible* will move to perform search and rescue at Istantinople. We'll leave *Axiom* and *Reliant* to back you up."

Those were older destroyers, more than enough to provide space fire support.

"Send me recordings," Papadakis requested. "If I run *that* through the station's emergency alert system, I bet I can get a few surrenders."

"Done." Brad shook his head as *Incredible* started to move. He hadn't even given Nah orders yet.

The Fleet simply knew that they couldn't stand by.

By the time they made it to the wreckage of Istantinople, the other primary strikes were over. As Papadakis had suggested, the image of an entire station of fifty thousand people vanishing in a ball of nuclear fire had a salutary effect on the OWA regulars.

Three stations and two hundred thousand people were now in Commonwealth hands. That left two hundred and fifty thousand people spread across ten major and twenty minor platforms—but the vast majority of the remaining troops were regulars.

They'd already met more commandos than Brad had expected. The bombs had been supposed to be under the control of the COs...but it appeared that the commando squads had as much faith in those officers' willingness to blow the stations as Brad did.

"Papadakis, Saburo, Boyce, I need you to get on questioning your prisoners ASAP," he told the three ground commanders. "At this point, I'm guessing we can get the regulars to surrender once it's clear we control the space around the stations and can board them at will, so I need to know where every damn commando in the cluster is."

"On that note, I have someone you need to talk to," Saburo replied. "Can we get a private channel?"

Even using laser relays, communication across the cluster was getting problematic. They'd need to drop the jamming field sooner rather than later.

Brad tapped a few commands on his wrist-comp, slicing the channel down to just him and Saburo. He was alone in his office already, so at least he didn't need to remove anyone on his end.

"We're secure," he told Saburo.

"Good. Brad Madrid, meet General Nadya Abreu," Saburo replied as he expanded his view and gestured for another person to enter the camera feed.

From the way the handcuffed woman shuffled over to him, she'd only just been escorted into the room. At some point in the fighting the woman had been shot in the shoulder, the wound clearly expertly treated and bandaged—but her eyes were cold and fierce.

"Admiral Madrid, I am the senior commanding officer of the Outer Worlds Army forces deployed to this cluster," she said formally. "This fight has already been a nightmare that has cost far more of my soldiers and officers than I prefer."

She shook her head.

"What little information I have suggests that the...other facility in this region has already fallen," she said calmly.

"You mean the Warren's Folly refueling and logistics base?" Brad asked.

Abreu slumped a bit. She'd clearly assumed that, but dancing around the name had been the bone she'd thrown out in case she'd been wrong.

"Yes. If Warren's Folly has fallen, then our presence in this cluster has failed," she said bluntly. "My minder is dead, but I have facilities and personnel scattered across this cluster."

"If you wish to minimize losses, I can drop the jamming so you can order them to surrender," Brad offered.

"That won't work," she replied sadly. "Some of the smaller contingents will obey, but the senior officers have their minders. Their… commissars, let's call them. They don't have a title, but we know their role.

"Any of my officers who attempts to obey a surrender order will be shot," Abreu said flatly. "Only the fact that you are jamming everything would stop those commissars from ordering their families murdered.

"If you're prepared to trust anything I say, I can give you a list of the positions that are held solely by commandos and the positions that I believe do *not* have commissars. The latter should surrender on my command…and the former will never surrender."

"The ones in between we're going to have to dig out," Brad said grimly.

"Yes." Abreu sighed. "I can tell you where the command facilities are. If you hit those first and remove the commissars and senior command, my regulars should then follow my orders to surrender."

"Why should we trust you?" Brad demanded.

"You don't have a single Everdarkened reason to," she snapped. "And I have *nothing* I can say to convince you to trust me, either. I have a wife and two kids on Triton, Admiral, and I never signed up to have them held hostage against my good behavior!"

Brad studied her face. He had no way to confirm or deny anything she said—except, possibly, by testing some of the "should surrenders" on her list.

Something in her eyes told him she was telling the truth, though, and he forced a smile.

"If your family is at risk, General, then I think the *official* record is going to show you as KIA," he told her gently. "Until things have calmed down enough that *someone* is in control of Triton that we can trust not to hurt your kids, at least.

"Send us your information, General. We'll do everything we can."

CHAPTER THIRTY-THREE

"SO FAR, the General's assessment has come out perfectly," Saburo reported. "Seven minor settlements have surrendered without a fight, and the three we assaulted based on her intel were guarded by commandos."

He shook his head.

"Those were bad, Brad," he noted. "We lost good people, but from what Abreu said, we're basically done with the commandos here."

"I'll be happy when we're done with them completely," Brad said grimly. "I'm guessing it was a commando—or one of these 'commissars'—who pulled the trigger on Istantinople. We're still looking for survivors, but..."

"Those stations are designed to break up and protect some people when hit by a meteor or something," Saburo told him. "They're not designed to survive a nuclear bomb."

"I know. But we have to try."

"It's been thirty-six hours. How likely are you to find anyone?"

"Not very," Brad admitted. "But there were fifty-two thousand people on that station."

"And the OWA killed them. Not you." Saburo's voice was hard.

"My brother," the Admiral replied.

"If you want to paint yourself in the blood of your brother's crimes, you're going to need a bigger brush," the mercenary snapped. "Now, I'm not an expert on Fleet deployments, but I can tell you that we're not going to need anything heavier than a corvette to deal with what's left of the cluster. So long as the jamming is up, we have the upper hand."

"Are you suggesting I should get moving?" Brad asked.

"Yes," his old friend told him. "We don't need you here, and we might well need you at Jupiter."

Brad sighed and looked at the screen pretending to be a window. Somewhere out in the debris field *Incredible* was orbiting was whatever was left of Commodore Branson, a man who'd done him more than one favor over the years. Getting the man vaporized seemed like a poor repayment.

"Evidence suggests that I might be best off well away from *anything*," he replied. "This whole operation was a wreck, and the responsibility for that stops here."

He stabbed his thumb into his chest.

"A wreck," Saburo repeated back to him. "You took out an equivalent OWN force without a single ship lost or even significantly damaged. You captured multiple OWA senior officers *yourself* to stop them escaping. We may have lost Istantinople, but we've already liberated a quarter million people.

"That's...a fucking glorious victory by most people's standards, boss. If you want to kick yourself over that, you're not going to find many people to help provide the boot."

Brad snorted.

"Doesn't feel like it from this chair," he pointed out. "We've lost, what, two thousand Marines and mercenaries in the ops so far?"

"Yeah. And that fucking sucks," Saburo agreed. "But that's war. Even we'd never really seen *war* before, Brad, and it fucking sucks."

"I'll move *Incredible* out of the jamming field and get an update from Jupiter," Brad promised. "There are ships out there that knew to come in and find me if anything critical came up, but you're right. I need to be back in the loop, not obsessing over one lost battle."

"Branson was a good man, and we'll mourn him," his friend said gently. "But right now, *Admiral*, you have a war to win. We'll send the *Oaths* with you. They're overkill for this job now, and someone's got to watch your back.

"Isn't that Michelle's job?" Brad asked.

"Yup. And the moment I tell her you need her more than I do, she'll be gone so fast, we'll think she invented FTL!" Saburo replied.

Brad chuckled. It was a sad, halfhearted thing, but it was real at least.

"Thank you," he said quietly, then considered for a long moment.

"I'm going to need you, too," he decided sharply. "Transfer command to Papadakis and get your ass on one of the *Oaths*. We have the beginnings of a plan to deal with the Phoenix, and I'm going to need the best fighters I've got for it."

———

The response from his subordinates at Jupiter arrived in astonishing time. Just the round-trip time for a radio message was the better part of half an hour, but he had a response from Bailey in roughly forty-five minutes.

"It's good to know the man technically in charge of this shitshow is still alive," she opened without preamble. "I've got a handle on the Fleet side of things, but the Jovian militias are getting *real* grumpy taking orders from even a Martian Squadron vet. Anybody from inside the asteroid belt is running uphill here, Madrid.

"We need you. It's not critical yet, things are trucking along so far, but we're getting pretty close to the point where you're going to need to smack some heads together."

She shook her own head.

"And the intel we're getting out of Saturn is ugly. I don't think we've got more than two weeks, maybe three, before the OWN makes their move. We're going to need those cruisers you ran away with before they get here.

"So, yeah. You needed to go, I get that…but we need you here. Not right this second, if there's still crap you need to clean up behind that jamming field of yours, but sooner rather than later."

The recording ended and Brad couldn't help smiling at the usual abrasiveness of his senior Fleet subordinate.

He checked the last set of reports from inside the jamming and found himself nodding. Abreu's intel had been the final piece of the puzzle and everything was falling into place. He couldn't pretend the rest of the operation in the cluster was going to be easy or clean—and certainly not bloodless!—but it didn't need him or the heavy warships anymore.

"Captain Nah." He opened a channel to the bridge. "I'm guessing that tagging our main concentrations in the cluster with lasers is still a sucker's game?"

"I can probably get the other two cruisers," she told him. "That's all I can promise you."

"Let's not risk it. Courier drones," Brad concluded. "Cruisers, destroyers, and every second corvette are to report to *Incredible*'s current location inside twenty-four hours.

"The Lord Protector is making noises towards Jupiter, which means it's time for us to go back to the main war and show him why he should never have started this fight!"

———

Brad had barely finished giving those orders when the admittance chime on his office sounded.

"Enter."

He wasn't expecting Michelle to step into the room. The *Oaths* had already met *Incredible* outside the jamming zone, the mercenary destroyers forming a protective triangle around the cruiser, but he'd thought she was still aboard *Oath of Vengeance*.

"Oh, good, people *did* play along," she told him brightly as she hopped up onto his desk. "Saburo said you were having a rough few days."

"You saw the casualty reports," Brad replied. "And Istantinople."

"And I really, *really* want to kill the son of a bitch who decided that political commissars with suicide bombs were a good solution to controlling a cluster, yes," she confirmed. "I believe he goes by *Lord Protector* these days."

That got an unexpected chuckle out of Brad.

"You weren't responsible for the op, though," he pointed out. "None of those people would be dead if I hadn't decided to move here."

"And First Fleet would have had half a cruiser squadron fly up our tailpipes in the battle for Jupiter," Michelle told him. "We needed to deploy. We needed to clean this mess up. I won't let you beat up my husband for that."

"I swear that someone else could have done better," he said quietly, admitting his worst fear. "I'm a mercenary, Michelle. A blade master, a pistoleer, a small force commander. What the hell am I doing in command of a *fleet*?"

"Based off the fact that your crews, mercenary and Commonwealth alike, are starting to think you're an unbeatable god who walks on water?" she asked. "I'd say you're doing okay."

He snorted.

"I've got too many of them killed to buy that," he told her.

"You, my love, need to stop sitting in your office, beating yourself up," Michelle told him. "Conveniently, your wife is aboard and she has *much* better ideas of what to do with your time!"

Brad wasn't sure how long they'd been asleep before a hideous klaxon echoed through his quarters. The sound woke both him and Michelle up, but it took him a good several seconds to realize it wasn't coming from any of the ship's systems or alerts.

The klaxon was coming from his wrist-comp, an emergency signal that was overriding half a dozen do-not-disturb lockouts to get his attention.

Somehow, he wasn't surprised it was an Agency override.

"Brad, this message is priority one, alpha, omega, whatever the fuck tag you want to hang on it," Kate Falcone's voice echoed through the room as he hit ACKNOWLEDGE.

"That itch between my shoulder blades was right. *More* than right. *Hades* and her escorts are moving in to deal with an OWA facility now, but we were too late.

"They had a bunch of crude missile launchers set up, and they were going to use the fuel from Warren's Folly to get them closer to their target, but once they'd confirmed the Folly had fallen, they simply launched from where they were.

"I'm attaching every piece of data I have on the damn missiles they fired, but I can't intercept them from here. I *think* you can...and you have to."

Falcone paused, and he heard her swallow in the recording.

"They duplicated the dirty nukes from the Ceres attack, and they launched them at Ganymede," she said levelly. "They're coming in ballistic now and they might lose a few, given the distance, but if they get even half a dozen warheads into the seas of Ganymede...they'll poison the water supply for the entire Jupiter System.

"You *have* to stop them."

The message ended and Brad stared at his wrist for several long seconds.

"There are alternative water supplies," Michelle pointed out—but she was already dressing.

"Even ignoring that millions will die if they nuke Ganymede, switching to those supplies will take time," Brad reminded her. "Time in which people *will* die."

He had barely even been aware that he was dressing until Michelle leaned in to straighten his stars and kiss his cheek.

"Then we better get to the bridge and feed that vector data to Captain Nah," she told him. "Because I'm with you, love.

"We stopped this kind of bullshit once before. We'll do it again. I promise."

CHAPTER THIRTY-FOUR

FOUR SHIPS BURNED through space at their maximum acceleration, and Brad stood next to his seat on *Incredible*'s flag deck.

The three Vikings destroyers had been sent out to "escort" *Incredible* as an excuse to put him and his wife on the same ship. The only thing that didn't make that an abuse of authority in Brad's mind was that *he* hadn't been involved in that decision at all.

He was grateful they were there now.

"We have confirmation, sir," Captain Nah told him. "*Ajax*, *Achilles*, *Hammerhead* and *Whaleshark* will all be able to rendezvous with us before we intercept the salvo."

Those four ships were two-thirds of the corvettes that Brad had positioned outside the jamming field as relays. Two *Invictus*-class ships and two *Shark*-class ships. It wasn't much—but it was four more hulls, and hulls were going to be key to this task.

"Do we have any way of confirming the presence of the missiles?" Brad asked. "I trust Falcone, but if we can narrow down their location, it will help the intercept."

Nah shook her head.

"From the data the Agency sent us, the missiles went ballistic after about ten minutes," she told him. "We have a good idea of where they are, but we won't be able to detect them at anything above about five hundred thousand kilometers.

"At that point, we'll be able to adjust our courses to intercept, but..."

"But we're going after relatively small targets that are moving damn fast," Brad agreed. "The good news is that they won't be dodging. They burned their fuel to get away from Falcone."

He leaned over his chair and plugged numbers into his repeater screens.

"I make our intercept at impact minus twenty-two hours, with almost sixty hours after that for us to make Jupiter orbit in a controlled fashion," he said aloud. "Any brilliant ideas on the course, Captain?"

"If we try to match the velocities any closer, we risk losing them in the chaos of Jupiter's traffic, rings, and satellites."

"We passed all of the data on to Bailey and Buckley?" he asked.

"As soon as you forwarded it to us," Nah confirmed. "They should have it already and be able to pre-position ships. Any intercept of these things is going to suck."

Brad nodded absently. The data he had suggested weapons identical in purpose to the bombs the Cadre had tried to poison Ceres with a few months before. Major drives attached to a wickedly pointed tip, with a nuclear bomb in the middle coated in tungsten and strontium.

If a single weapon punched through the ice on Ganymede, it would detonate and poison the water for hundreds of kilometers in any direction. Even one bomb would require massive cleanup and safety efforts, even though they would *probably* be able to keep anyone from running out of water.

Multiple bombs would render the entire moon's water supply functionally unusable.

"What about the rest of the task force, sir?" Nah asked quietly. "There's still a pile of ships running around the trailing Trojans."

"Send a com drone in," Brad replied. "Major Papadakis is to retain as many ships as she feels are necessary to complete the mission. The rest are to make their best speed back to Jupiter.

"I imagine the bombs were supposed to launch at the meteor swarm's closest approach to Jupiter, in about a month. With that attack short-circuited, the Phoenix is almost certainly going to decide he's done playing."

"Yes, sir."

And if Jack Mantruso had another string to his bow, Brad wasn't sure he could hang around to see what it was. More and more, it was starting to look like defending Jupiter was giving up the initiative to an enemy with a giant bag of dirty tricks.

———

Brad spent most of the three days en route to the intercept trying not to visibly pace where *Incredible*'s crew could see him. The eight ships with him were a subset of a subset of his fleet, but the fate of the entire Jupiter planetary system could ride on them.

He trusted Bailey to intercept some of the weapons, but the ships he'd left at Jupiter would be intercepting inside the chaos of Jupiter orbit. Their efficiency would be drastically reduced compared to catching them in deep space.

"We've got them," Nah's reported interrupted his determinedly sitting still. "On the course *Hades* projected, four hundred and eighty-five thousand kilometers ahead of us."

"Intercept?" Brad asked grimly.

"We'll enter range in six hours. We'll pass within five hundred kilometers at our closest approach, but we'll only *be* in range for about fifteen minutes."

"It'll have to be enough," Brad replied. He updated his repeater screens, zooming in on the missiles.

Falcone had identified their course perfectly, but she hadn't managed to ID every individual missile. *Hades*'s crew had estimated thirty to forty missiles.

Brad was looking at sixty-two. He couldn't let any of them through.

"I know our hit probabilities suck with the big guns and torps," he told Nah quietly. "We're going to use them anyway. If it can fire, point it at those horrors and pull the trigger. Understand me, Captain?"

"Understood, sir." Nah shook her head. "We're not going to stop them all, sir. Not unless you have a miracle in your back pocket."

"Not that I'm aware of," Brad replied. It was moments like this that he wished he'd sent Bailey instead. Despite his demonstrated success as a fleet commander, he was cold-bloodedly certain that the ex-Martian Squadron Commodore was better than him.

Maybe she'd have seen something he didn't. Right now, he had to hope that she could backstop his failures.

This wasn't even a regular space battle, where he knew there were humans on the other side. The human involvement in this attack was already over. There weren't even computers involved now. The missiles were set on a fixed course and would be set off by a pressure sensor.

No software. No humans. Just cold physics.

And one evil bastard who'd pulled the trigger.

"Firing...now."

Incredible lurched beneath Brad's feet as every one of her multitude of weapons fired simultaneously.

Fifteen-centimeter mass drivers and torpedoes had no place in this mission, but they fired anyway. The seven escorts opened fire as well, their smaller mass drivers joining in with the cascade from *Incredible's* secondaries and their torpedoes joining the swarm.

Brad's ships were hurtling across the missiles' path. When they reached their closest approach, they were right in front of the weapons. Along the way, they laid down a hail of mass-driver slugs and torpedoes that looked almost thick enough to walk across.

The reality of space combat, though, was that there was nowhere near as many rounds out there as it felt like. Missiles died, but for every slug or torpedo that hit, Brad's people fired a thousand useless shots.

They passed the missiles in space and his flotilla rotated, continuing to send fire after the enemy weapons for as long as they could.

When they finally slid out of range, Brad went over the data.

"Eleven, sir," Nah said quietly, before Brad had even finished double-checking his numbers. "We got fifty-one and there are eleven penetrators still headed to Jupiter."

"Send every ship in Jupiter orbit every scrap of data we have," Brad ordered. "Not one missile gets though. Not one."

———

By the time the missiles began approaching Ganymede, Brad hadn't slept in about forty-eight hours. There wasn't anything he could do from this distance—his ships were only starting to reach zero velocity relative to Jupiter—but he had to see.

If a world was going to die on his watch, he owed it to his people to see it happen.

With more time, more hulls, and more deployment restrictions, Bailey had still managed to set up a multi-tiered defense around Ganymede. The destroyers under the Commodore's direct command formed the inner shield, dozens of mercenary and fleet ships forming a screen in front of the planet.

Then the cruisers made the next layer, twenty thousand kilometers farther out.

Then there were four layers of corvettes and frigates. Fleet, mercenary, and militia were hopelessly intermingled, but those hundred-odd smaller ships were Ganymede's best hope.

The first layer wiped out four of the missiles and Brad held his breath for a few seconds, daring to hope that the rest would be as lucky. If they were, this entire threat would be over in moments.

The first layer, though, had been far enough out that the interference of Jupiter's rings and other debris wasn't affecting them yet. The rest weren't.

A single missile died to the second layer. The third layer got two. The fourth didn't get any and the cruisers nailed two more.

Two missiles charged toward the destroyers. They were hard to detect, hard to track, but Bailey's ships gamely tried. The projections on *Incredible*'s screens intersected…and then the missile icons were gone.

"Everlit…what did she *do*?"

Brad heard Nah's murmured comment and focused on the ships—to see a crimson circle around Commodore Sonja Gold's *All That Glitters*.

"Commodore Gold maneuvered her ship to intercept the last missile...*with* her ship," one of the sensor techs reported. "The warhead has *not* detonated—repeat, the warhead has *not* detonated."

But *All That Glitters* now had a ten-meter-long tungsten spike embedded in her hull...and Brad wasn't sure how patient the nuke actually was.

"Get her people off that ship!" he barked.

There was nothing he could do at this range *except* bark orders. Shuttles and lifepods started to spew from *All That Glitters*. Enough for a third of her crew...half...two-thirds.

By any math Brad could run, though, at least a third of the destroyer's crew were still aboard when the two-hundred-megaton nuke went off in contact with her hull.

CHAPTER THIRTY-FIVE

"SHE WAS AN IDIOT," Bailey said bluntly. "An abrasive, rough-edged, tactically clever *idiot*."

"And she saved Ganymede," Brad reminded her. "Did Gold survive?"

He was still ten hours out from Jupiter orbit, but the cleanup effort was done. Only the one ship had been lost. Ganymede went unpoisoned, and as soon as Brad's flotilla returned to orbit, First Fleet was effectively concentrated at Jupiter.

There were still six older frigates in the trailing Trojan cluster supporting the Marines, but Papadakis had chosen her support carefully. *Star*-class frigates were small and under-gunned for even their size by modern standards. They were, however, perfectly capable of dropping mass-driver slugs wherever the Marines and ground troops needed them.

They wouldn't be missed in the fleet action to come.

"Commodore Gold was not aboard *All That Glitters* when the nuke went off," Bailey told him with a sigh. "Instead, she was with the engineering team *outside Glitters*' hull that was trying to disarm the nuke.

"Most likely, she and her engineers never even knew they'd failed," the Fleet Commodore concluded. "Her number two was *Glitters*' captain, and he refused to evacuate his own ship, so *he's* gone. I'm not sure who that leaves in charge of the Goldmisers long-term, but her senior surviving captain has taken temporary command."

"I'm guessing they'll inherit?" Brad asked.

"She doesn't seem to think so," Bailey told him. "And from the woman's record, I wouldn't in her place either. She's a surprisingly decent captain, but a follower by nature. I doubt Gold didn't know that."

He sighed.

"We'll be in place in ten hours," he said. "Make sure the Fleet is fully restocked by the time we arrive. I'll want *Incredible* and her escorts restocked ASAP."

"You can have this damn command back anytime you want," she said. "A few seconds' time delay isn't enough to keep you out of the loop at this point."

He raised an eyebrow at her.

"What, you're not enjoying commanding the largest space fleet ever?" he asked.

"Madrid, if I'm still in charge when your forever-cursed brother makes his move, I'll have to lead the largest space *battle* ever, and I'll pass on that poisoned cup, thanks."

Brad snorted.

"You're probably better qualified than I am," he told her. He was relying on that, in fact.

"I'd agree, but I don't want to hang that millstone around my own neck," Bailey replied. "Get your bestarred butt back to Jupiter and resume command, *sir.*

"And bring some clever ideas with you, or I'm stuck at 'lure *Immortal* into range of the guns guarding Ganymede'."

For the same reason that the OWA had launched the poisoning attack, the Fleet had long ago installed cruiser-grade heavy mass drivers above the main water-refining facilities. Those fifteen-centimeter batteries had twice the firepower of any of Brad's cruisers, but they were still nothing compared to the *fifty*-centimeter batteries aboard *Immortal*.

"That isn't enough," he admitted quietly. "Is *Hades* back yet?"

"She'll be here roughly when you are," Bailey told him. "That'll still leave them with the edge in carriers."

"But we have more cruisers, and nobody thinks this battle is going to turn on the corvettes and frigates," he replied. "Without *Immortal*, everyone knows how this fight would end."

"Yeah, but your brother *has Immortal*. And we don't."

Brad smiled grimly.

"We have a plan," he admitted. "It's even more idiotic than Gold's stunt…but it might be our only hope."

"If you've got an only hope, Madrid, that's one more hope than I've got," she told him.

"It's probably suicide," Brad said.

"*Una salus victis nullam sperare salutem*," Bailey said quietly. "The only hope of the damned is to give up hope for survival."

―――――

Brad watched First Fleet gather around *Incredible* as she entered orbit of Ganymede, and marveled to himself. He'd been amazed enough when he'd first commanded an entire squadron's worth of destroyers.

Now destroyers were barely worth counting in the balance of power. Three drone carriers and ten cruisers formed the core of his fleet, with over a hundred lesser vessels gathered around them—and the third drone carrier had shown up late, with a scratch crew built from the leftovers of *four* carriers.

It was the largest concentration of ships he'd ever seen in his life— and that was *including* both the Martian Squadron and the Earth Defense Force.

The only thing he was lacking to rival either of those forces was a battleship…and unfortunately, his enemy had a similar strength and *had* a battleship.

"I'll want the Fleet Commodores, Buckley, and Kernsky aboard as soon as possible," he instructed his staff. "If we can break Falcone away from her ship as well, that would be best."

"Of course, sir."

Brad studied the moon beneath him and sighed. His charge was to defend Jupiter, but it was almost impossible to defend a fixed target against an enemy willing to engage in attacks with long-range weapons of mass destruction.

Time was his ally in theory, but he didn't know what resources the Outer Worlds Alliance commanded. Even Jupiter had yards that could build destroyers and corvettes—his own Vikings ships had mostly been built here.

They'd expand quickly, he was grimly certain. However this war ended, Jupiter was no longer going to trust the Fleet to protect them. There would be Jupiter-built cruisers soon enough.

The Commonwealth would answer that with Earth-built battle-ships...and Jupiter would match those. Even if the OWA was somehow rendered quiet and cooperative, the next decade would see new fleets and new warships built.

For half a century, humanity had had three battleships. Brad would put a significant quantity of money on the bet that that number would be doubled in a few years...which would also leave him with an unenviable question.

His commission was from the Commonwealth, but his heart was with Jupiter. If the Commonwealth and Jupiter clashed, whose flag would he fly under?

It was a problem for the future...for a future where the Phoenix was defeated and the Solar System made safe. Brad was grimly certain, though, that the genie wasn't going back in the bottle.

By negotiating with Jupiter as an equal, he and Senator Barnes had accepted that there were going to be three nations going forward. The OWA couldn't be brought back into the fold without more bloodshed than Brad was prepared to engage in, and Jupiter was going to walk away now.

It fell to Brad to give those nations a chance to grow and flourish on their own—to let the OWA become a true alliance, not a dictatorship. To let Jupiter decide how they wanted to go forward. To, perhaps, force the Commonwealth to accept a position as first among equals instead of the unquestioned master.

He only saw one way to make that happen...and if the price was his life, what *was* a future for all humanity worth?

CHAPTER THIRTY-SIX

BRAD SAT at the head of the conference room table as officer after officer filed in. Fleet took up one side of the table, with Bailey, Jahoda, and Nuremberg settling in with neat military decorum.

Across from them were Rear Admiral Kernsky, Commodore Buckley, and Commodore Hunt. Two mercenaries and the generally accepted senior officer of the Jovian Militia.

At the far end, facing Brad and looking as shattered as he felt, was Agent Kate Falcone.

"There's a lot of Commodores around this table," Brad said with a chuckle. "Fortunately, that thought occurred to me in advance."

Given the way he knew the rest of this meeting was going to go, opening up with gifts was a good idea from his perspective—and if that should leave his subordinates looking for the other shoe, well, they weren't wrong.

"Firstly, I had Blaze run what should have been obvious by the Council of Governors," he told them. "They gave me the chance to play Santa, so here you go...*Admiral* Buckley."

He slid the doubled stars of a Rear Admiral across the table to Giles Buckley. The rotund man flashed a surprised smile but put on the insignia.

"And, since it would be far too much of a headache to have militia and mercenary Admirals running around Fleet Commodores... Nuremberg, catch."

Brad tossed an identical box of two stars to Iris Nuremberg. Her gaze was suspicious as she put them on, trading a look with Jahoda.

"Nuremberg, you'll take overall command of the cruiser force, with Jahoda commanding your second squadron," he told them. "All of you will be coordinating with Bailey here."

If Nuremberg's gaze was suspicious, Bailey's was outright paranoid. He hadn't handed her stars yet, but he'd just implied that everyone would be working with her.

"I talked to Admiral Orcho," he noted as he met Bailey's gaze. "Only the cloud of suspicion that fell over everyone after *Immortal*'s defection held up your promotion, so bumping you to Rear Admiral didn't make sense to either of us.

"We're officially declaring you the second-in-command of First Fleet, *Vice Admiral* Bailey."

He slid the box of stars over to her and she looked down at it like it was about to grow fangs and bite her.

"This is a trap," she said bluntly. "What are you setting me up for, Madrid?"

"Your fucking job, Angel," Falcone said from the other end of the table. "Shut up and take the stars."

Bailey's suspicion flared to anger, and she glared at Falcone. The women knew each other...but not well enough for either of them to be using the other's first name!

"Both of you, calm down," Brad ordered. "You are the most experienced officer here, Admiral Bailey—and I don't exempt myself from that calculation. I need you at my right hand, not looking for knives in your back. Am I clear?"

"You're clear. *Sir.*" Bailey took the stars and turned her glare on Brad. "And since you've just neatly set up an answer to who is in command if you charge off to do something damned stupid, what are you planning?"

Brad laughed. Bailey, it seemed, knew him well enough to guess what was coming.

He tapped a command that lit up the screen behind Falcone. On one side of the screen were icons representing his First Fleet. On the other was a different set of icons—*also* marked First Fleet, as if the situation needed more confusing.

"Ladies, gentlemen, this is the current estimated order of battle of our First Fleet and the OWA's First Fleet," he said quietly. "We have twice as many cruisers; they have an extra carrier on us. Escorts are a wash—we have a few more, but theirs are more modern.

"In a head-to-head clash of the two fleets, we would win without question," he told them. "Except, of course, for *Immortal.*"

The icon for the battleship was to scale, which meant it was nearly ten times the size of the icons representing the cruisers.

"*Immortal* has as many fifteen-centimeter and lighter mass drivers as any five of our cruisers," he reminded them. "On top of that, she has six turreted fifty-centimeter superheavy guns.

"Nothing in our fleet can take a hit from those guns and survive." He shook his head. "*Immortal* alone could defeat our fleet. The rest of the OWA's First Fleet just makes sure.

"We cannot face the Phoenix's battle fleet and win."

"There are options," Buckley interjected. "We already have facilities working on assembling several seventy-five-centimeter cannons for orbital deployment."

That was the first time Brad had heard about that. It tied disturbingly into his fears for the future, but he doubted it would turn the tide today.

"How long, Admiral Buckley?" he asked gently.

"Fifty to sixty days before the first is ready for deployment," Buckley admitted. "They'll be crude, too. No mobility except for targeting. They're orbital defense guns, not ships."

"Everything we can throw at making Jupiter more defensible is worth it," Brad told them. "But the Phoenix isn't going to give us fifty days. We can be confident that we have been penetrated *completely.* If we might have a battleship killer online in two months, then either he'll make sure it gets sabotaged—or he'll simply make sure he's here before it's ready."

"We are *not* defeated yet," Bailey snarled. "We can win this,

Madrid. I'll stack our Fleet crews up against their pirates and conscripts any day of the week!"

"And if we were facing a remotely even battle, I'd take that risk," Brad agreed. "But *Immortal* makes this beyond uneven."

"Which leaves us no choice: *Immortal* must be removed from the equation." He met Falcone's eyes across the table and gestured for her to begin.

"The Agency has spent the entire time since *Immortal* defected looking for a solution," she said quietly.

From the way heads turned to look at her, many of the officers ignoring the spy as a matter of course.

"We found one. It's…risky. It's uncertain…but it's the only chance we have."

"Everything discussed in this room is classified at the highest levels," Brad told his officers. "It cannot be shared with your military subordinates or your political superiors. If you can't keep that promise, leave."

He smiled.

"I won't hold it against you, I promise. You're in this room because I think you need to know what we're planning, but that plan needs to stay *completely* dark."

No one moved.

"What kind of damned stupid plan are we in for?" Bailey finally asked. "I'm guessing, given Madrid's history, that it's going to involve our Admiral shoving his head into a meat grinder?"

Falcone sighed.

"You're not far off," she admitted. "You were a battleship commander, Admiral Bailey. If your crew had attempted to defect and you didn't think you'd be able to stop them, what would you have done?"

"Triggered the lockdown," Bailey said instantly, then froze. "You can't be serious!"

"The anti-mutiny lockdown override on a Fleet battleship is a genetically locked system that shuts down *everything*," Falcone said calmly. "It is linked to the captain and the admiral, if there's one aboard.

"We know both of those officers from *Immortal*'s original crew are dead. They were murdered before they could even consider triggering an override."

"Then what are you planning?" Buckley asked.

"We have reliable intelligence to suggest that Jack Mantruso is using *Immortal* as his flagship," Falcone reminded them. "He will have put himself in the system as the Admiral, especially given that the presence of his Praetorians as the only armed personnel aboard the ship suggests he does not trust her crew."

"How does that help…"

Michelle trailed off and turned to face Brad.

"No," she told him. "You can't be serious."

"We're serious," he said gently. "Kate?"

"There is a roughly fifty percent chance that Brad Madrid's DNA will trigger his brother's access," Falcone told the others. "We have assembled a hardware system that will link into the override sensor and increase that chance to approximately ninety-nine percent.

"*If* Brad can reach the Admiral's office or flag deck of *Immortal*, that device will allow him to shut down *Immortal*. Completely."

"The override can be turned back off by the same person who turns it on," Bailey pointed out. "You'll need to make sure that the Phoenix doesn't get to a console."

"If at all possible, I don't plan on leaving him alive to disagree with me," Brad said grimly. "Everlit knows, he's earned that fate!"

"Brilliant as this sounds, there is *no way* you can successfully infiltrate a battleship at the heart of a fleet to *get* Brad to the flag deck," Michelle objected.

"The Agency has always needed ways to get agents and personnel into places they aren't wanted," Falcone said in a tired voice. "We have a stealthed boarding vessel that we believe can infiltrate Admiral Madrid and a handpicked assault team of perhaps a dozen soldiers aboard *Immortal*.

"The Phoenix's paranoia means there are only a handful of his elite Praetorians aboard the battleship. His lack of trust in the crew leads us to believe that they should be the only resistance we face."

"That sounds like a one-way trip to me," Buckley noted. "Is that the best use of Admiral Madrid?"

"No one else can do it, Admiral Buckley," Brad reminded him. "It has to be someone closely related to Jack Mantruso, and frankly, the rest of our family is dead." He grimaced. "Usually at the hands of other members of our family."

Including him, though he wasn't going to bring that up. He'd killed his own uncle—though he hadn't *known* the Terror was his uncle or that the man had killed his other uncle.

"It has to be me. No one else can do it—and if I *don't* do it, we can't win this battle."

Brad looked around the room. Michelle still looked argumentative, and he knew he was going to hear a *lot* before the mission actually launched, but he could trust her to raise it in private.

"We've transferred the boarding vessel to *Incredible*," he told them. "We can no longer allow this battle to unfold on Jack Mantruso's terms.

"We will take forty-eight hours to make sure every ship is fully restocked and repaired. After that, First Fleet will deploy forward in an attempt to retake Saturn."

He gestured around the room.

"The entire attack is a cover for getting *Incredible* close enough to launch the boarding ship. We should be able to deploy approximately one day before the battle, allowing us to make contact with *Immortal* shortly before battle is engaged."

"And what happens if you fail?" Bailey asked. "There's no breaking off at that point."

"If this goes to plan, *Immortal* will never fire her guns," Brad told her. "If she *does*, the Fleet will maneuver to reduce the engagement time...but the command will be yours, Admiral Bailey. If anyone can carry the day at that point, it's you."

"There will also be other measures in place," Falcone said. "We haven't established all the details of that yet, but I can promise this: we are almost guaranteed to at least reach *Immortal*...and if we do, she will not emerge unscathed."

"In any case"—Brad cut off further debate—"for all of its flaws, this is the best plan we have. We move out in forty-eight hours. Make sure your people are ready."

CHAPTER THIRTY-SEVEN

MICHELLE FOLLOWED Brad back to his quarters in companionable silence. He knew he was going to get a lecture of some kind from his wife—the mission he'd taken on *was* suicidal—but for now, he simply enjoyed her company.

"Sit down," she told him as the door closed behind him. "You've got two days to poke at guns and blades and bullets, but I have to get back to the Vikings quickly if we're going to attack."

"We have to attack," Brad said quietly. "Every day we wait gives the Phoenix more time to come up with dirty plans to stab us in the back."

"I know," Michelle agreed. "Now stop arguing and sit down, my love."

He obeyed, starting to feel more than a little confused.

"I meant to tell you what was going on when we met outside the Trojan cluster but, well…" She shrugged. "Everything went to hell pretty quickly after that. It just hasn't been the time, but now…now we're running out of time."

"What's going on?" Brad demanded. Now he was *worried* as well as confused.

"I don't expect to change your mind about this mission," Michelle said quietly. "But you need to know.

"I'm pregnant."

It was a good thing Brad was sitting. The world seemed to give way beneath him and reality shifted as he stared at his wife in shock.

They'd talked about children, but—like Michelle had said about telling him—it had never seemed the right time. A child had always been *in* their plans, but the answer was always "not right now."

"That's...amazing," he said in a rush. "And terrifying. And...*how?*"

"I'm not sure," Michelle admitted. "My implant came up for the biannual renewal while we were in Earth orbit and I got it swapped out at a Fleet clinic. According to the implant's data feed, it's still working perfectly, but..."

She cupped her hands protectively over her stomach, looking at him hesitantly.

"Come here," he said gently, holding out his arms to her. A moment later, he was holding her.

"You had to know before you left," she whispered in his ear.

"I did," he agreed, fighting back tears and trying not to audibly choke. "And you're right. It *can't* change anything about mission. I have to go, love. For everyone...and for our child."

He wasn't winning the fight against tears and neither was Michelle.

"Are you going to be safe aboard *Oath*?" he finally asked.

"Angelica insisted on me wearing a weird protective garter/corset thing," Michelle replied, referencing *Oath of Vengeance*'s medic. "It's supposed to shield the baby from any potential rads or similar."

She shivered.

"*Oath* is as safe as anything in the line of battle, but I'm not leaving our people to fight alone. I have a job to do, the same as you."

"I know," he agreed. Part of him wanted to insist that she stay on Io —possibly even Ganymede—behind the fixed defenses of the Jupiter System. Michelle alone was the most precious thing in the Solar System to him...Michelle and their *child* was beyond any value he could imagine.

But while he'd made Michelle Hunt a mercenary, she'd been a

ship's captain long before they met. He couldn't ask her to stay behind —and she couldn't do it if he did.

"I have to go," he repeated.

"I know," she agreed. "I wish you didn't. I wish that your *family* hadn't turned out to be the source of all of this…"

"So do I," he admitted. "But it gives us a chance we wouldn't have otherwise. If Jack Mantruso *wasn't* my brother, we'd have to fight *Immortal* head-on. This is the only way."

"But you have to come back; do you understand me?" Michelle demanded. She took his hand and pressed it against her belly. The baby was far from developed enough for Brad to even feel a noticeable bump, let alone any kicking, but he could feel the warmth of *her* through everything.

"This baby *is* going to have a father," she told him fiercely. "Remember that. No matter what."

"I'll do everything I can," he promised. "I already had plenty to come back for, my love. Our child…" He shook his head in wonder. "I'm coming back, I promise you.

"*Both* of you."

————

Brad had enough self-control and respect for his wife not to make stupid demands or insistences, but he still took time he couldn't neces- sarily spare to walk her down to the shuttle bay.

From the smile Michelle wore the entire trip, she understood completely. He suspected she'd been worried about how he'd react to finding out about her pregnancy—since they'd kept agreeing to delay children, after all!—and his actual reaction had been good news.

They kissed fiercely at the edge of the shuttle bay, gathering a smat- tering of gently teasing applause.

"Go," he told her when she let him go. "We'll see each other soon enough."

"We will," Michelle agreed.

She stepped onto the mercenary shuttle, the ramp rising up behind her. Brad stepped back to clear the safety radius—and almost collided with Bailey.

"Do I get a kiss too?" the newly promoted Vice Admiral asked with an arched eyebrow.

"You should probably talk to whoever you married," Brad told her with a chuckle.

Bailey snorted.

"That's a low blow, Admiral," she warned him. "Did your esteemed wife talk you out of your determination to get yourself killed?"

"I have no intention of getting myself killed, Bailey," he replied. "But I really am the only one who can do this."

She sighed.

"I know. Look…I know it's easy to get carried away thinking that everything rides on you, that you're the only one who can do the job." Bailey's smile was surprisingly self-reflective. "It's what I built my entire career on, after all.

"In this case, though, it's true. But…realize you have to kill him."

"I'm not exactly bothered by that idea," Brad replied.

"Right now," Bailey agreed. "But he's still your brother. The only family you have left. Do you think you can face that man blade to blade and not hesitate? You *need* to pull this off."

She shook her head.

"If you do enough damage, we might be able to carry this if you fail, but even a damaged *Immortal* might still turn the tide. You need to trigger that override and you need to kill Jack Mantruso to make damn sure he can't turn it off."

"I know. And then I'm going to need *you* to come get me," Brad said with a chuckle. "The plan is what it is, Bailey. Got any suggestions?"

She shook her head at him.

"I can command this fleet for you, Brad Madrid," she said gently. "But I'm commanding it *for* you. I don't lead these people. *You* do. You're lending it to me, but First Fleet is *yours*. The wreckage orbiting Mars and the liberated stations in the trailing Trojans won you that.

"Sonja Gold died to save Ganymede, yes, but she also died for *you*.

"Whatever happens, if it's at all possible, you need to come back, Brad. You're the only thing holding this mess together."

Brad was about to be dismissive, but her use of his first name caught him out. She did that rarely…in fact, he wasn't even sure she'd ever done it before.

"I promised Michelle," he told her. "And I made a promise. I'll stop my brother. I'll end this war. And after that, I'm coming home."

"Good."

To his surprise, Bailey hugged him. It wasn't a romantic gesture in the slightest, but it was no less fierce for that.

"Remember that we'll be right behind you, Admiral Madrid," she said formally. "You may be the point of the spear, but First Fleet will be coming—and we'll bring the fire of the rising sun with us!"

––––––––

Brad's apparent daily allotment of hugs from terrifying women was complete when Kate Falcone entered his office moments after him. She got the hug in before he even said hello, and he returned the embrace carefully.

"Does everyone actually think I'm going to die on this op?" he asked her.

"It's more likely than I'd prefer," Falcone told him. She stepped away from him and checked the tray of coffee a steward had left on the table. The carafe apparently passed her test, as she poured two coffees.

"I have a backup plan," she told him. "It's…not pretty."

"Nuke and a deadman switch?" Brad asked. If that *wasn't* her suggestion, they were going to have to scrabble to put it together.

Falcone paused with her coffee halfway to her lips, sighed, then took a swallow.

"Bingo," she conceded. "The warheads on your nukes are theoretically variable-yield, you know?"

He blinked.

"Really? I thought they were fixed at thirty megatons."

"They can be dialed down as low as a third of a megaton," she told him. "I'm not sure why anyone even *bothered*, since I've never seen Fleet fire off a nuke at any setting less than maximum.

"On the other hand, it gave my techs some extra room to play with."

Brad considered that for a second as they both drank more coffee.

"How big?" he finally asked.

"No one has ever rigged up this kind of sequenced multi-initiator bomb out of Fleet nukes before," she warned him. "It's only an estimate, but...three fifty."

"Deadman switches on you and me?" he asked.

"Just you," Falcone said grimly. "If you go down, it's over, Brad. You'll have a manual initiator as well, but we'll hook you up with a bracelet linked to the bomb. You go down, *Immortal*, well, fails to live up to her name."

He nodded. The battleships were big, tough ships. *Immortal* could survive non-direct hits from almost any nuke, potentially even a contact explosion from the thirty-megaton warheads in First Fleet's magazines.

She would *not* survive a contact explosion from a three-hundred-and-fifty-megaton hydrogen bomb.

"Good."

Falcone shook her head.

"I don't like setting up suicide missions, Brad. Especially not for myself and people I like. But if we fail, I want *some* kind of failsafe."

"Why don't we just use the stealth ship to plant that nuke?" he asked. "That seems less risky."

"Three reasons," she told him. "One, the armor on that beast is enough that at least *some* portion of *Immortal* will survive that blast. Two, without human intuition, the stealth systems lose about eighteen percent of their effectiveness, and we'll need every *scrap* of sneakiness we can get to pull this off."

"And third?" he asked.

"Third, we want that damn ship back. Plus, if the Lord Protector is as paranoid about the crew as he seems to be, that suggests we may be able to turn them *during* the battle."

Brad considered that thought. The mental image of *Immortal* turning her fifty- and fifteen-centimeter guns on her former allies at close range was…painful.

"You can't actually expect that," he told her.

"I don't," she admitted. "It's a nice fantasy, but really, I just want *Immortal* intact to be hauled back to Earth. I'm not sure what the future of the Solar System is going to look like, Brad, but I'm from Luna. I *want* those big guns standing guard over my home."

Falcone, it seemed, was having some of the same concerns he was over what would happen after the war.

"First, we have to win the war," he told her. "And that means taking down *Immortal* and the OWA's First Fleet. You'll remain aboard *Incredible*?"

"If you think you're making this damn stunt without me, you're wrong."

"You, Saburo, and the exactly four Marines from *Incredible* who are qualified to use US Army T-51B Power Armor," he confirmed. "We have an extra suit, but neither Saburo or I are qualified to use it and we don't have time to learn. You?"

Falcone laughed.

"No. Not in the slightest."

"Four walking tanks, a spy, and two blademasters," Brad concluded aloud. "Doesn't seem like much to hang the entire future of humanity on."

"I know the blademasters," Falcone told him. "I couldn't risk everything in better company."

CHAPTER THIRTY-EIGHT

IT WOULD HAVE BEEN a surprise to someone who didn't know what to expect, Brad supposed. First Fleet was over a hundred warships, and they all lit off their engines at almost exactly the same time.

The positions of the cruisers, carriers, destroyers, and escorts around Jupiter meant that they were lighting off their engines at different accelerations and different vectors, at least initially, but the mass activation was simultaneous.

From *Incredible*'s flag deck, he had access to the course projections that showed every one of those ships meeting about a light-second out from Jupiter and converging into a single massive formation.

There were tricks they could pull with the formation once battle was joined, but for now, they would assemble a straightforward escort formation. Cruisers and carriers at the center, surrounded by a concentric sphere of destroyers and escorts.

"Think we're surprising anybody?" Captain Nah asked.

"Lots of people," he agreed. "But I doubt we're surprising the OWA. They've been one step ahead of us the whole way."

Which was why even his flag deck crew didn't know the real plan. The only people aboard *Incredible* who knew about the stealth boarding ship were the people working on it.

"I'm counting all the ways this can go wrong," Nah said after a moment. "But still...I can't pretend it doesn't feel good to be moving out. Taking the fight to them."

Brad nodded.

"They've had the initiative so far," he agreed. "Their war. Their offensives. Even our assault on the Trojan was a *counter*offensive. Now...now we write the rules of this particular fight."

The funniest part was that the worst thing the Phoenix could do, from Brad's perspective, was withdraw. If the OWN forced First Fleet to chase them around the Solar System, First Fleet would run out of fuel first. The OWN would almost certainly destroy Saturn's fueling facilities when they withdrew, leaving them with full tanks and Brad's fleet running on fumes in short order.

Their entire plan hinged on Jack Mantruso either coming out to meet them or standing in defense of Saturn.

"He's going to come to meet us," Saburo said behind him. "We've met him."

"He's run from one fight with me already," Brad pointed out. They'd both drawn blood that time—that was how the Agency had realized they were brothers—but the Phoenix had chosen to withdraw that time.

"This time, he thinks he has the advantage. He's got the tonnage, the guns, the ships. In his mind, he has to think he can't lose."

"Then he'll be wondering how I'm planning to stab him in the back," Brad said. "*He'd* have a clever plan—and he knows I'm not one for suicidal attacks."

"So, he'll keep guessing. Right up until it's too damn late."

Brad shook his head.

"Maybe," he allowed. "You're ready for the briefing?"

"Everyone will meet in the bay in twenty minutes," Saburo told him firmly. "Part of me wishes I'd stayed in the Trojans, you know. Goes against the grain to leave a job unfinished."

"And miss this?" Brad gestured to the screen showing the slowly assembling formation of First Fleet. "The greatest space battle in human history. Would you be anywhere else?"

"I'm a ground-pounder, boss. I have a place in this battle, but still..."

not sure 'the greatest space battle in history' is the place for a grunt like me."

Brad snorted.

"I'll meet you downstairs," he told his old friend. "A few last details to sort out here."

———

The shuttle bay they'd taken over had seen its usual occupants transferred to other ships or the stations around Io. In their place was a single spacecraft, slightly smaller than a mercenary or fleet combat shuttle.

Its entire hull was a light-drinking black, so dark it shed the eye almost as effectively as it absorbed radar and other scanners. In its current state, large panels were open and the racks of heat sinks were visible.

Unlike the stealth on, say, *Incredible*, the heat sinks on this craft weren't designed to be cooled via radiators. They could absorb more heat per kilogram than the cruiser's heat sinks, but at the price of being irretrievable once heated up. The sinks could be ejected if there was an appropriate moment, but Brad expected them to have to hang on to the heat sinks as they closed with the OWA fleet.

The heat sinks weren't the only thing designed to be ejected. The spacecraft's built-in engine was a low-heat-signature ion engine, but that lacked the force to get the shuttle moving at a speed that would allow them to move away from the fleet. A pair of high-intensity fusion engines were mounted under the spacecraft. They were the same carefully designed, heat-vectored engines used by the Fleet for the cruisers. With a little careful setup, any extra heat from the stealth ship would be lost in the background of the Sun and First Fleet.

"The bomb is mounted," Saburo told him quietly as the door closed behind him. "I read the specifications, and having that thing on the same *cruiser* as me makes me nervous. Riding it the whole way over to *Immortal*? My blood pressure is going to be a *mess*."

Brad snorted.

"Everybody will fit in around it?" he asked. Past the spacecraft he could see the immense coffins of the storage and charging stations for the T-51B armor his Marines would use to back them up.

"Between the bomb and the armor storage, it's going to be a damn cramped fit," Saburo told him. "I wish I'd had the time to qualify on one of those things though. It took the Marines a while to find guns that the suits could carry that weren't going to punch holes through spaceship hull."

"They're not designed for space combat," Brad admitted. "Any concerns from that?"

"The armor suits have hazardous environment suites that we've modified to function as vacuum suits," Saburo said. "That's probably the biggest concern: they've got the power for an hour or so of combat operation, but we're only going to have canned air for thirty minutes.

"We're going to need them to either breathe *Immortal*'s air until they need to go on canned, or accept that we only really have thirty minutes of operating time. Either way, we can pretty much assume *Immortal* is going to end up a vacuum around us as soon as they know we're aboard."

"Thirty minutes?" Brad grimaced. "That's not a lot of time to take control of a battleship. Or even just to get to the admiral's office."

"The good news is that we have full plans of the ship. We can land close to the target, but…" Saburo shook his head. "That hour is it, boss. The suits have a storage compartment that we've stuck small arms and air masks in, but once they ditch the suits, our firepower and survivability go *way* down."

"So, after an hour, the Lord Protector better be dead."

"Or we will be."

The morbid tone of the conversation was interrupted as Falcone led the four Marines coming with them around the spacecraft.

"Everybody grab a box," she ordered. "We're a minimum of six days from intercept, but most of us have work to do between now and then, so this is the closest we're going to have to a detailed briefing before we stuff ourselves in the flying black box."

"Who's flying this thing, anyway?" one of the Marines asked.

"I am," Falcone replied. "There isn't a pilot in the Fleet qualified on an Agency stealth insertion ship."

She tossed Brad a black bracer, clearly designed to go over his upper left arm.

"Don't turn that on until we're in space," she told him. "It'll be scanning a bunch of vital signs, but as soon as you go down, the bomb goes off."

"So, objective one is keep the Admiral alive, got it," another Marine replied. "I saw that bomb. I don't want it going off anywhere *near* me."

"Objective one is disable *Immortal*," Brad said quietly. "Everything else is a subset of that. If we can get me to Jack Mantruso's office, I can shut her down. If we can't…we set off the bomb and hope that will cripple her badly enough that the Fleet can finish the job."

All four Marines looked at him in silence.

"This is not intended to be a suicide mission," he told them, "but you need to understand the priorities and the risks. We are all expendable going in. So long as *Immortal* is stopped, we win."

"And the best way to stop *Immortal* is to get the Admiral to the override," Falcone cut in. "So long as the Admiral is alive, we have a chance to take her entirely out of the fight.

"If the Admiral dies, the nuke is our only option…and there's no way we're getting off *Immortal* once she's alerted. So, the nuke is wired to the Admiral's life signs."

She studied the Marines.

"You four are the most experienced Marines in First Fleet as far as power armor goes," Falcone told them. "This is a volunteer gig and you all volunteered, but if you want to back o—"

"No, sir!" all four chorused in unison.

"We're in it to win it, sirs," the first Marine told them. "You get us aboard and then we cover the Admiral through to the override. What happens then?"

"Then we hold whatever space we've taken for the override," Falcone replied. "There are at least thirty elite Praetorians aboard *Immortal*, but they're supposed to be the only armed soldiers aboard. If we can hold against them and keep the battleship disabled, it's over."

"It's all over," Brad reminded them. "This is a Hail Mary checkmate, people. Bailey is clever and we've got a lot of smart people building tactics to help turn the battle to come, but if *Immortal* is in the enemy line when the shooting starts, we lose.

"If *Immortal* isn't in the enemy line, we win. It's that simple."

One of the Marines turned to study the coffin-like storage locker behind them.

"Well, then, I think the four of us"—she gestured at the Marines—"need to start doing some virtual drills. The suits will support that and we have *Immortal*'s floor plan, right?"

"The only advantage of her defection is that we know everything about her, except whatever Mantruso's done since he took her," Falcone agreed.

"Then we'll drill," the Marine said firmly. "You do your parts, sir, and once we're aboard *Immortal*, we'll get you to that damned office."

Or die trying went unspoken.

They were Marines…and everybody in the room knew the price of failure.

CHAPTER THIRTY-NINE

"WELL, it seems he's finally made up his mind."

Brad nodded in response to Bailey's comment as he studied the latest sensor reports from Saturn. The OWA had spent several days adjusting their positions around their new conquest, but now they were moving out.

Immortal led the way, with the cruisers settling in on her flanks and the destroyers and light escorts filling in the gaps. The carriers hung back behind the rest of the fleet, farther back than Brad was holding his carriers, in fact.

Of course, Brad was the underdog of this fight. First Fleet couldn't afford to give up the mass drivers and torpedo launchers aboard those carriers.

It took the OWA ten minutes to shake up their formation, but then the sky lit up with energy as they brought their drives online.

"They're coming *fast*," he noted aloud. He'd chosen not to strain any of the systems of his fleet, and they were accelerating toward Saturn at thirty meters per seconds squared.

"Fifty MPS squared," Bailey agreed. "The Lord Protector trusts his engineers more than I'd trust mine...and a *lot* more than I'd trust his."

"His will probably get shot if they have a failure," Brad said grimly.

"You're clear to adjust the fleet course for optimal intercept, Vice Admiral."

He was running an entirely different intercept vector on his wrist-comp, a set of data he wouldn't even let enter *Incredible*'s main systems. If the OWA had continued to hold at Saturn, they'd been three days from contact and less than two from needing to launch the stealth ship.

Now, they were *maybe* thirty hours from combat...and he needed to get the boarding operation underway within the next hour.

"Captain Nah, meet me in my office," he ordered.

His flagship captain looked surprised but nodded her acknowledgement over the video link to the bridge.

———

His office was next to the flag deck but a decent distance from the main bridge. It took Nah two minutes to reach his office, by which time he had coffee poured and waiting for her.

"Bailey sent out the updated course?" he asked.

"Yes, sir," Nah confirmed. "Assuming they're vectoring for a minimum-velocity meeting engagement, we'll do the same and enter range in thirty-one hours."

Brad tapped a command and brought up the course as Nah grabbed her coffee. The assumption was that the OWA would try to extend the engagement time, as would First Fleet. They'd open fire with torpedoes and the big guns at about twenty thousand kilometers, but if they controlled the vectors, they'd be in range for hours. If both of them tried to extend the fight, they could easily end up at zero velocity relative to each other, even as the battle drifted toward Saturn.

The battle wasn't going to last long enough to reach Saturn, regardless of whether Brad disabled *Immortal*.

"Then it's time, Captain Nah," he told her. "Bailey will be relaying through you until the battle is joined, then she'll assume full command." He shook his head. "The confusion is going to suck, but it's necessary.

"I have faith in First Fleet's ability to handle the changeover, but I *don't* have faith that my absence won't leak to the enemy," he admitted. "I trust the flag-deck crew to know I'm missing, but that's it."

"We'll keep it under wraps, sir," Nah replied. She paused. "And if you fail?"

"Then Bailey commands First Fleet and her job is to end the war," Brad told her. Bailey's objectives if the boarding operation failed were brutally simple: cripple the OWA's battle fleet.

At any cost.

The door slid open without any warning and Kate Falcone stepped in.

"You've run the numbers," she said without preamble. "We have twenty minutes."

"I know," he agreed. "Nah, enjoy the coffee," he told his flag captain. "See if you can make it look like we had a meeting. As few people as possible can know I'm gone."

"That isn't a small number, sir," she warned him.

"Then try and keep it to people you trust completely. We're already trusting everyone aboard with the future of the system, but this secret could change everything."

"I'll do what I can."

"I know you will."

He traded a handshake with Nah and stepped out into the corridor. It was dead silent, an unusual emptiness aboard a warship.

"People really trust the software aboard a warship to tell them the truth," Falcone told him. "Right now, the computer says the corridors we're moving through are having minor coolant leaks. People will avoid them until repaired, and Engineering isn't getting any notice of a required repair.

"It will give us enough time to get to the docking bay unseen."

———

Saburo and the Marines were waiting when Brad and Falcone arrived, their trip through the cruiser disturbingly uninterrupted.

"Can you do that on *any* Fleet ship?" Brad asked her as the hangar door closed behind them.

"Sadly, no," she told him. "Captain Nah set me up with special access privileges on *Incredible* so I could watch for active hostile agents." She shrugged. "I didn't find anyone, so this runaround might be redundant, but..."

"We learned never to underestimate the Cadre," Brad finished. "And OWI doesn't seem to have lost any of their edge."

"Given some of the resources the Cadre had deployed over the years, I have to wonder how long the OWA has actually existed in some form," Saburo said. The mercenary had already exchanged his usual casual uniform for a combat vac-suit. The helmet was off, but the suit was still designed to resist small-arms fire.

"Everyone's big question about the first Blackhawk attack was 'Where did the Terror get the troops?' Well, now we know," Brad agreed. "I'm guessing the Cadre already controlled a lot of the smaller settlements by then. Most of them are only a few thousand people, but if you control a hundred settlements, that's easily half a million."

"And conscripting ten thousand soldiers out of half a million people isn't difficult," Saburo agreed. "It can't have helped their control of the outer system when none of them came home."

Brad nodded, burying a flash of guilt as he grabbed his own vac-suit and started changing. Cadre commandos and OWA commandos were volunteers at best, indoctrinated at worst. There was no saving them.

The crews of the Independence Militia and the OWN and the ground troops of the OWA armies were conscripts, trapped by threats to their families and home stations. If he could, Brad had every intention of letting them surrender.

But with political commissars watching over their shoulders and their families held hostage, he didn't think he was going to get many chances.

Wincing as he connected the plumbing of the suit, he looked up to check the others. The Marines were wearing simpler gear, basic emergency vac-suits they'd ditch to fit into their armor when the time came. Falcone was in the same combat suit as he was and had been changing with the same disregard for the audience.

"Are we ready?" he asked.

"T-51Bs are aboard. Guns are aboard. Bomb is aboard," the Marine Corporal reeled off. "Shuttle is fueled; heat sinks are ready to go. I don't know this ship as well as my usual ride, but she checks out by my math."

"I've got a checklist in the cockpit we can run through," Falcone added. "We're running short on time. Ready or not, it's time to go."

There was no point in activating the stealth systems immediately, but there was still enough shuttle traffic around the fleet for Falcone to be able to launch without drawing attention.

"So, what happens if someone in First Fleet sees us now?" Saburo asked.

"They report it up the chain and the chain of command goes, 'Yes, thank you, we're aware of it,'" Brad replied. "Unless an OWA agent sees us themselves and decides it's worth risking their cover to transmit, we should be covered.

"It's not like they're going to assume the *Admiral* has just snuck off on a stealth ship with a giant bomb aboard," he added. "It's not perfect, but it's a lot better than ordering, say, the fleet to turn off all of their sensors."

"I certainly considered the latter, but our luck says that would be the exact moment a bunch of OWA ballistic torpedoes arrived," Falcone said grimly. "Now, the gravity plates on this toy are perfectly fine for her built-in engines, but they can't handle the boosters.

"I'm going to turn them off. Strap in, boys and girls; we get about four hours at five gravities before this show gets boring for about twenty-five more hours. Are we good to go?"

"Never better, Agent Falcone," Brad told her. "Let's go end this nightmare."

No one else said anything and Falcone gently touched a command on her screen. A moment later, over seven times the weight Brad was used to pressed him back into his chair.

He and Falcone were the only ones in the cockpit, though they could talk to everyone else through the open door. He took advantage of the screens to double-check their stealth systems.

A moment later, he shook his head in wonder—then winced and leaned his head back against the rest. That had hurt.

"Built-in heat sinks in the boosters?" he asked.

"Yep. And the only people seeing our heat plume is First Fleet," she confirmed. "That's more vulnerability than I'd like, but..."

"That's what we've got." Brad skimmed through the system. Despite having read the full specifications of the little stealth ship, part of him had still expected to see guns. The only part that would really require human intervention was the stealthy ion engine that would slow them down to board *Immortal*.

"Assuming no one decides to do anything crazy, we'll reach the OWA fleet an hour before the battle begins," Falcone told him. "We'll be maneuvering directly under their guns to board *Immortal*, so pray to whatever you hold sacred that the stealth systems hold."

"Because if they don't, we're dead," Brad concluded.

"Exactly." Finishing up her sentence, Falcone slapped the black armband she'd shown him before around his upper left arm. The band tightened and linked into his vac-suit.

"And now the deadman switch is armed," she told him. "Try not to lose an arm this time; that would probably convince the sensor you're dead and then we all get blown to plasma."

"Trust me, Kate, losing a limb is something I very much want to keep a once-in-a-lifetime experience."

CHAPTER FORTY

"THIS IS INSANE," Saburo breathed, his voice barely above a whisper. "I thought I understood how crazy this stunt was, but this is *insane*."

The stealth ship's engines were silent now. Everything that could leak even the tiniest scrap of revealing energy was now wrapped in a shell of radio-absorbing materials Brad didn't even pretend to understand.

The Agency insertion ship's stealth systems were to a cruiser's what a battleship was to a *rowboat*. Brad had used Fleet military-grade stealth systems to deadly effect throughout his career, but he'd never dream of what they were doing right now.

The First Fleet of the Outer Worlds Alliance spread out across his screen. One of the lead OWA destroyers was close enough that he could *see* her with only minimal magnification. The warship was maybe fifty kilometers distant.

"I want to say we told you, but I agree," Brad admitted. His own voice was no louder than Saburo's.

"Quit it, you two," Falcone snapped. "*Sound* isn't a problem. Energy is a problem, and we've got that wrapped for about, oh"—she checked the systems—"another forty-seven minutes."

"What happens in forty-seven minutes?" Saburo asked, his tone more normal...but still subdued.

"We have to eject about seventeen tons of molten superheated metals to stop the ship incinerating us," the spy replied. "At that point, the heat sink stream provides a giant 'shoot me now' arrow to the entire OWA fleet and someone spares a mass driver from the battle to blow us to hell."

"We should be aboard *Immortal* by then, yes?" Brad asked.

"And if we're aboard *Immortal*, we can dump a lot of heat into her hull," Falcone agreed. "The heat sinks won't be reusable to the same extent as a capital ship's, but at least we don't have to dump molten metal in deep space."

"Time to contact?" he said quietly.

"Twelve minutes, unless whoever's flying that hunk of metal gets unexpectedly fancy."

Immortal and the rest of the fleet were already engaging in basic evasive maneuvers. They'd have to get *much* more evasive before Falcone couldn't get the stealth ship into contact...and they might well do so when the shooting started.

"Twenty-three minutes until Bailey is scheduled to take full command," Brad reminded them all. "Five minutes after that, all hell is going to break loose—and that's assuming that nobody on our side tells OWA about the command change and they get paranoid."

"Well, it'll all be fine so long as we're aboard the battleship by then," Falcone said grimly. "So, I suggest you all shut *the fuck* up and let me fly this. Marines—tin can release in nine! Suit up."

"Oorah."

Behind him, Brad was vaguely aware of the coffin-like lockers being unsealed. The suits opened up and the Marines stripped off and climbed in.

So long as the T-51Bs were in their lockers, they weren't burning through onboard battery and air. The thirty-minute timer didn't start until they unlatched from the coffins.

"Take a look out the window, people," Falcone said, her voice suddenly soft. "Not many people get to see this. That's a battleship in full flight, visible with the naked eye."

It was a slight exaggeration, Brad knew. The shuttle's screens were using digital and optical zoom to show them the battleship, but the range was already under fifty kilometers and dropping fast.

"Initiating final intercept now," Falcone reported. "If you're the praying type, now is *most definitely* the time."

The stealth ship's ion engines were stealthy, but this was something beyond even them. Canisters of carefully chilled gasses were buried at the base of the ship, as far away from the heat sinks as possible to make sure they *stayed* chilled.

Now, those gasses were fired from the ship in carefully calculated jets. They were still going fast enough that impact wouldn't resemble "boarding attempt" so much as "missile hit." Artificial gravity was the only reason they were going to survive.

A velocity indicator popped up on the screen, accompanied by *Distance to target*.

They needed to keep enough velocity that Falcone would be able to adjust for the evasive maneuvers at the last moment—while shedding enough velocity that they didn't pancake on the warship's armor.

"Madrid, pull up the schematics and flag our best landing sites," Falcone said distractedly, her focus on the engines. "Flag deck or his office?"

"Office," Brad said quickly as he pulled the data. A wireframe model of *Immortal* appeared in front of him and he quickly highlighted the target zone. "Flag deck will be more secure, no matter what. And it's easily fifty-fifty on where *he'll* be."

Brad didn't think he needed to specify who he meant by that. This day was going to end with only one Mantruso left breathing...or potentially none.

He marked four locations on the main screen for Falcone.

"Any of those will put us within five minutes of his office," he told her. "I'll keep an eye on her rotation."

She nodded silent thanks, another burst of thrust slowing the ship further as they crossed the five-kilometer line.

At this range, the nuke they were carrying would cause serious damage to *Immortal*'s sensors and targeting. Even if they were detected now, so long as the bomb went off, they'd help tip the odds.

Part of him didn't believe they could make it. As Saburo had pointed out, the plan was *insane*. There was no way this could work.

Four kilometers. This was suicide range. A *mass-driver* round would hit them before they even knew they were under attack. *Immortal*'s defensive maneuvers were now fully visible on the screens, the kilometer-long battleship now clear on the screens.

"Boarding velocity," Falcone whispered.

Two kilometers. One. Brad was holding his breath as the boarding ship dove for one of his marked locations and the jets flared one last time.

Contact.

Plasma cutters flared to automatic life as he clapped Falcone on the shoulder.

"Well done, Kate," he told her. "Let's go find ourselves a dictator, shall we?"

She nodded and he turned to the passenger compartment.

"Marines! This is it. Show me what those tin cans can do!"

———

The plasma cutters had sliced open the hull, clearing the way for the power-armored Marines to lead them forward.

The four hulking suits were carrying massive shotguns with drum magazines, the oversized weapons still looking fragile in the T-51Bs' gauntlets.

The three boarders in regular armor followed them with rifles and blades. The first encounter with the ship's defenders suggested that they might be redundant.

Half a dozen men and women in armored bodysuits with a red phoenix sigil on their shoulders charged around the corner. They were carrying rifles and blades of their own and opened fire as soon as they saw the intruders.

The Marines ignored the incoming fire, forming a wall across the corridor as they opened up with their shotguns. Not one bullet made it past the suits, but they seemed unbothered as they mowed down the defenders.

"They almost certainly called that in," Falcone noted. "We're going to see heavier weapons *fast*. The only good news is that I'm pretty sure these bastards don't have power armor of their own."

"The problem is that if any of the OWA troops *do*, it'll be the Phoenix's Praetorians," Brad pointed out.

His friend glared at him for several seconds.

"You didn't think to mention that before."

Brad shrugged. "Seemed obvious. Office is down that corridor; let's move."

Falcone kept glaring at him as they ran, but they thankfully didn't run into power-armor suits immediately. Two corridors down, they ran into their first crew.

Half a dozen unarmed men and women cowered against the wall, clearly terrified by the immense T-51B suits.

"Bind them," Brad ordered. "Then we leave them. We don't have time for this shit—Marines, scout the way."

Saburo and Falcone were on it immediately, tying the crew's hands behind their back with zip ties. Pushing the prisoners into a side room, they took off again.

By the time they caught up to the Marines, they'd managed to find resistance. Gunfire echoed through the corridor, and Brad grimaced as he recognized at least one weapon: the Praetorians had grenade launchers. And if they'd brought the launchers, knowing they were facing power armor, they'd brought AP grenades.

"On three," he murmured to his companions, holding up three fingers. He counted down, then dove around the corner with his rifle tracking for targets.

The Praetorians had started with at least a dozen troopers, mobile riot shields, and grenade launchers for all them. Several of the shields had been blown aside and at least a third of the commandos were down.

So, unfortunately, were two of Brad's Marines. The armor-piercing grenades were apparently quite effective against the power armor—though the state of the corridor and the armor of the standing Marines suggested they weren't as effective as the Praetorians might have liked.

Focused on evading the rapid-fire shotguns, however, the

defenders weren't ready for three people to open up with precise rifle fire. Brad took a moment to breath and aim...and realized that ready or not, the Praetorians were *very* good.

A bullet hammered into his shoulder and sent him reeling back, the moment to aim clearly a moment too long. The round failed to penetrate his armor, however, and he bounced back around the corner and opened fire.

Falcone had already taken down one, and Saburo had shot two more. Brad dropped a fourth, and the last two went down to the Marines.

"We have to leave them," one of the Marines told Brad as he went to check on the downed Marines. "Suit telemetry says they're dead and we don't have time. Combat range for the fleets is in under two minutes."

Brad nodded grimly and checked his map. The intersection they were currently standing in wasn't the only way to the office, but it was one of two...and the one more convenient to the bridge.

"Hold here," he ordered. "I'm guessing the bastards cut the entrances to the office down to one to protect the Phoenix better.

"Falcone, Saburo, you're with me—in case I'm wrong."

One of the Marines traded out his shotgun for one of the Praetorian grenade launchers, checking its systems as Brad spoke.

"We'll hold, sir," she told him. "Semper fi."

———

The two Praetorians holding the door to the office turned out to have a tactical network with the others or *something*. They were ready and waiting when Brad and his companions came around the corner, opening fire with assault rifles instantly.

Saburo took several solid hits and went down, but not before emptying half a clip down the hallway. One Praetorian went down; the other managed to duck for cover and keep firing.

Brad tried to return fire, only to realize he'd survived the initial fusillade because several rounds had hit his rifle instead of him. He tossed the weapon aside and dove under the incoming fire.

He was scrabbling for his pistol as he came up and found himself facing the business end of a bayonet. The Praetorian, however, froze when she caught sight of his face—a moment of hesitation at the familial resemblance, Brad presumed.

Whatever the reason, it was enough for Falcone to put a three-round burst into the woman's head.

The Praetorian collapsed and Brad rushed back to Saburo.

"He's alive," Falcone told him crisply. "I think I can stabilize him, and we're secure here. Look."

She gestured at the crude new wall blocking off the corridor, emblazoned with the same phoenix sigil as the Praetorians.

"That room has the override. It's up to you now," she told him. "Go!"

Falcone knelt over Saburo, pulling a compact emergency medkit out of her belt as she did.

Brad hesitated.

"Go!" she snapped.

He went. The door attempted to resist him for a few moments, but he was out of time and patience alike. The control panel failed against several bullets and the door slid slightly open—enough for him to get the mono-blade through.

Brad sliced a gap in the door and barged through.

Then an alarm sounded, and he dove away from the door, both his weapons skittering away as a security hatch slammed shut behind him. There was no way out now, but he hadn't activated anything...

"I'll admit, brother, I wasn't quite expecting this," a familiar, cultured voice said calmly. "I'm not even sure I know what your plan is, but this seems...appropriate."

Brad looked up from the floor as Jack Mantruso stood up from his desk. The Lord Protector was unarmored, wearing an elegantly cut black suit, but he held a massive pistol in his hand.

"I was content to know you died when we vaporized your flagship, but this..." Mantruso grinned. "No audience, no stupid games. Just you, me, and one gun."

CHAPTER FORTY-ONE

BRAD PROMPTLY DOVE for the gun he'd dropped, only to watch it skitter away as a bullet slammed into the weapon. There was no way the pistol had survived that, but he'd almost never seen aim like that.

Stopping, he turned to face his brother and rose, waiting for the bullet that would take him down. Now that he took a moment to study Jack Mantruso, he saw the problem: the other man was wearing a targeting eyepiece that was talking to the gun. So long as he had that, he wouldn't miss.

The good news was that it seemed to be making him overconfident. He didn't appear to notice Brad catching his mono-blade between his feet. Safety protocols had disabled the weapon when he'd dropped it, but it was within reach now.

"So shoot me," he told Mantruso. "It's not like that toy will let you miss."

And when he killed Brad, his whole ship was going to go up in smoke.

"Oh, believe me, brother, I have no intention of being goaded into giving up any advantage," the older man told him. He tapped a command on the desk and the wall behind him lit up with a view of deep space around them.

"There's your fleet, you know," the Phoenix said conversationally as icons populated the screen. "I figured you had a plan, clever tricks to try and even the odds. I wasn't expecting you to show up on my ship."

"Maybe you should have watched the security better." Brad was watching the other man's hand...and the desk. The desk held the hardware to activate the mutiny lockdown.

"Or maybe part of me knew you were coming," Jack Mantruso said quietly. "A final chance. We're all that's left of our family—at least, until your wife gives birth."

Brad stared at his brother in shock.

"Oh, I know about that," the dictator told him. "*I* arranged for her to get the defective implant, Brad. I need an heir, but I'm sadly lacking in a partner these days. There are all sorts of games I could play, but, in all honesty, they all feel a bit too much like rape."

He grimaced.

"I will be emperor of mankind," he said flatly. "Many will call me evil. I can live with that...so long as *I* know that I am *not*."

The line between directly raping someone or forcing them to bear a child and overriding someone's contraceptive implant seemed fuzzy at best to Brad. It seemed pretty damn close to rape in *his* head, at least.

"Whereas you and Michelle, adorably happy and murderous, weren't going to really mind if she ended up pregnant. Your child, my niece or nephew, would serve quite well as an heir."

Mantruso shook his head.

"I really wish you'd convinced her to stay behind though," he noted. "The order to spare *Oath of Vengeance* is probably going to get some of my people killed." He shrugged again. "A sacrifice for the future. They may not understand, but their deaths will have meaning regardless."

Anger rippled through Brad and he took a step closer to the desk. Despite his anger, he kept the blade between his feet.

He was expecting the perfect snap-to-deadly-aim reaction from the gun. It was a very large gun, he concluded, and the barrel looked like a gateway to hell.

"Last chance, Brad," Jack Mantruso said very quietly. "A good chunk of that fleet out there will stand down if you order it. They'll get to live if you do. If enough of them listen, well, quite possibly *everybody* gets to live. Isn't that worth your pride? Your self-righteous *honor?*"

"I will never join you," Brad told his brother. "How much blood is on your hands? How many innocents? Commissars and hostages and mass poisoning attempts...you *are* evil."

"Everything I have done has been to purchase a better future for all mankind," the older man said. "From the day I joined the Cadre as an adult, President Mills's plan was already underway. That man was going to break the Commonwealth no matter what I did.

"Everything I did was to provide an alternative once that happened. Join me, Brad, and we can usher in a golden age. We can make all of this *worth it*."

Brad's brother was insane. Or self-deluded; he wasn't sure which.

It didn't matter.

"I think killing each other off appears to be the family tradition," he told the Phoenix. "Why break it now?"

The emergency transmitter in his wrist-comp had a thousand intended uses. A jammer wasn't one of them, but in a small space, sealed against electronic transmissions to guard the admiral's security, it could serve.

Jack Mantruso's eyepiece went mad, lights flickering across it that were visible to *Brad* as Mantruso dropped the gun to tear at it.

Brad kicked his mono-blade up off the floor and charged. The glowing blue blade activated as he leapt across the desk—and then bounced off another one as Mantruso grabbed the other weapon off the surface.

"Fine," the Phoenix spat. "You killed our uncle, but you took him by surprise. I am *not* surprised, brother mine."

———

Brad *was* surprised—when the Phoenix leapt over the desk with a sharp series of potentially deadly cuts. He parried each of them, years of practice and combat carrying him from defense to defense...but his brother was moving fast enough and skillfully enough to *keep* him on the defensive.

"Did you think Armand never taught me anything?" the older man asked as he drove Brad aback. "The Terror taught me everything: how to fight, how to lead, even how to torture. It took our treacherous other uncle *thirty-six hours* to die; did you know that?"

Brad snarled, focusing on staying alive.

"I only have one uncle," he spat. "The man who saved me from becoming like *you*."

Boris Mantruso might have arguably kidnapped Brad as a preteen, after his parents had been killed by the Mercenary Guild, but he'd seen Brad into a life where he *wasn't* a criminal. A life where he got to choose who he got to be.

"You know, for most of those hours, you were all Armand wanted from Boris."

Brad could tell that the other man was trying to distract him, to create a weakness in his defenses. He pinned the blades for a moment and then leapt backward, clearing a space to allow him to circle Jack Mantruso.

"I didn't know I had a brother then, but Armand did," the Phoenix told him as he circled in turn. They were just out of reach of each other; the office was large enough to let them dance out of the way of the careful testing swings both took.

The office was overkill in Brad's opinion, but he supposed a battle-ship was a kilometer long.

"Thirty-six hours he tortured Boris to find out where you were, and Boris told him nothing." Jack laughed.

"The funniest part is that if he'd just *told* Armand, it would have saved your life. We didn't know who he'd kicked out of the spaceship. We'd have gone back for you if he'd told us! Sheer bloody Mantruso stubbornness almost killed you!"

"It also kept me alive," Brad replied, testing his brother's defenses while he stepped on his anger. "Through everything you and the Terror threw at me."

He pressed in, pushing his own attack as Jack chose not to retreat.

For a few moments, he pushed his brother back, blue blades glittering in the light of the office, but only for a few moments.

Then the Phoenix twisted the blades through a deadly riposte Brad couldn't block. He dodged backward, reducing what could have been a deadly blow to a glancing strike that peeled away a layer of his body armor.

They'd both be in trouble if *Immortal* took a bad hit and lost atmosphere now, but that didn't slow the older Mantruso. He turned the riposte into a series of strikes, and the balance shifted against Brad again.

This was *nuts*. Brad had trained with the mono-blade every day for years. He was an unquestioned blademaster with few equals—but his brother, who'd spent most of his life as a *politician*, was pushing him back.

Then the ship shivered underneath them, the big fifty-centimeter guns firing for the first time, and everything changed. Bloodily earned battle experience kept Brad on his feet through the tremors…but Jack Mantruso didn't *have* that experience.

The other man was probably the best-*trained* blademaster Brad had ever faced, but he didn't have the battle experience and the trail of dead bodies Brad and his mono-blade had left behind them.

Brad took advantage of the moment, driving inside the older Mantruso's defenses. The Phoenix reeled, unable to regain his footing, struggling to defend himself.

And then a strike slipped past the older man's defense. Jack was twenty years older than Brad, into his fifties, and age cost him a moment of balance, a moment of speed that changed everything.

The glowing blue blade went flying away—only active because Jack Mantruso's hand was still attached to it.

"No!" Jack Mantruso shouted as he scrabbled backwards. "I'm your *brother*."

"No. You're the bastard who tried to poison two worlds," Brad said calmly. "And it ends *now*."

He didn't even register that the Phoenix was grabbing the gun from the table as he struck. The weapon didn't matter, would *never* matter… as Brad's final strike removed Jack Mantruso's head.

CHAPTER FORTY-TWO

BRAD FROZE FOR SEVERAL SECONDS, watching a man who looked like an older version of him fall to the side in several pieces. The big pistol dropped to the floor with a clatter—and then the vibration of the main guns ran under his feet again, reminding him of what he was there for.

The screen the Phoenix had pulled up told him the state of the battle. Bailey had concentrated all of her heavy ships on one side of her formation—the side away from *Immortal*. Javelin drones were diving into the chaos around the battleship, hammering torpedoes into the escorts even as the Commonwealth cruisers smashed their way through the OWA's weaker flank.

It was a clever plan and might even be enough to balance the odds. If Bailey crushed the OWA's cruisers and most of the lighter ships before she had to directly engage *Immortal*, she'd have a chance.

It was up to Brad, however, to make sure that wasn't needed.

He crossed to the desk and found the concealed button he'd been told to look for. A part of the apparently wood surface popped up and slid aside, revealing a standard palm and DNA scanner.

Instead of putting his hand on it, however, he put his wrist-comp on it. A wireless override program provided by the Agency woke up, linking into the system.

A few seconds later, text popped up on his screen.

PALM SCAN OVERRIDDEN. DNA SCAN VARIABILITY INCREASED. DNA
SCAN REQUIRED.

The moment of truth...and Brad placed his hand on the scanner.
There was a tiny pinprick of pain as it took its blood sample, and he
held his breath.

The light above the panel flashed from amber to blood red. For a
cold moment, Brad thought everything had failed.

Then he realized the vibration of the ship had stopped. *Immortal*'s
engines had shut down. He checked the main screen displaying the
battle and swallowed a cheer.

Immortal was dead in the water, the rest of her fleet leaving her
behind as she stopped accelerating. Stopped firing. Stopped dodging.

The override had worked.

The panicked reaction was clear in the fleet around her. Escorts
reversed their courses, attempting to match the velocity *Immortal* had
frozen at. Long-range torpedo fire tore through them, but Brad saw
that someone on his side was paying attention.

The Javelins were now tearing into the escorts. None of their torpedoes or mass-driver fire was being directed at *Immortal*.

A communicator icon beeped. Brad ignored it, watching as the
battle unfolded. The communicator chimed again—and then someone
overrode it.

"What in Everdark are you *doing*?" a panicked voice demanded.
"Lord Protector, the ship is telling me *you've* shut us down. We're
going to lose the battle if *Immortal* doesn't engage. Everlit, we still have
boarders aboard."

Brad considered things for a few seconds—seconds in which he
watched a pair of OWA destroyers get blown apart by the Javelin
drones. At least three hundred people had just died...they might be
the enemy, but the dictator they had been enslaved by was dead.

"Bridge," he said into the communicator. "This is Admiral Brad
Madrid of the Commonwealth. Jack Mantruso is dead and I have
assumed control of this ship.

"This war is over. It's only a question of how many people are
going to die today."

"Turn that off!" a new voice barked. "It's the boarders; we need to—"

A gunshot echoed on the communicator…and then silence.

"As a matter of fact, what I *need* is to stop listening to your bullshit," the first voice said. "Admiral Madrid, this is Captain Karsten Solyom. I was *Immortal's* executive officer, but these sons of bitches kidnapped my daughter.

"Can you save her?"

Brad swallowed.

"I don't know," he admitted. "It's going to depend on what the OWA does in response to this. If you help me, Captain, we can save your fleet—and if we turn this fleet on the Cadre's commissars, *you* might be able to save your daughter."

There was a long silence.

"I swore an oath to Jack Mantruso. Rumor has it you're his brother."

"Long-lost and estranged as soon as we met," Brad replied. "I can't make you any promises, Captain."

"But if we fire a few warning shots from *Immortal* at the OWA, they'll panic," Solyom replied grimly.

"That would require me to give you back control, Captain."

"I have no way to disable that override, Admiral," the Captain replied. "You can stop me anytime. I owe my daughter…" He swallowed. "I owe my daughter and my crew the chance to try."

"You have thirty seconds, Captain," Brad replied.

He disabled the override. *Immortal* leapt to life, her engines flaring to maximum power as she suddenly charged toward her own cruisers. The fifty-centimeter guns each targeted a cruiser or a carrier, then fired.

From the screens Brad had, they *hadn't* missed…except that the targets were still there. Solyom had to have missed his targets by mere *meters*.

"All ships, this is Captain Solyom of *Immortal*," the Captain's voice echoed. "I have sworn allegiance to the *new* Lord Protector, *Brad* Mantruso—and his orders are for the Fleet to stand down and surrender."

Brad stared in shock at the speaker. That was *not* the tack that he'd expected Solyom to take, and it spoke to future problems…problems that, right now, Brad had no choice but to *leave* to said future.

"Any ship that continues to resist will face *Immortal*'s guns. We are the flagship of the Outer Worlds Alliance and we are ordering your surrender!"

For a moment, everything froze—and then one of the cruisers swung about and charged *Immortal*, her guns opening fire at their full power.

As the battleship rang under the hits, Brad realized he hadn't locked Solyom out—and *Immortal*'s fifty-centimeter guns spoke once again.

Six slugs hit the cruiser. She didn't even manage to dodge, suggesting that there was more going on aboard her bridge than was seen from the outside. Each of those slugs was a weapon of mass destruction that could devastate continents.

Six of them *obliterated* a three-hundred-meter-long cruiser.

"This is your final warning," Solyom barked. "Stand the *fuck* down."

Engines began to cut out across the fleet, fireflies winking out across the night as OWA ship after OWA ship shut down their drives. Ship after ship went dark until only *Immortal* remained.

"Thank you," Solyom said softly. "And one final order from our new Lord Protector." There was a vicious glee in his tone. "All commissars are to be interned *immediately*. If the OWA survives this, it will be as *our* country…and without the Phoenix's reign of terror."

CHAPTER FORTY-THREE

SIX WEEKS CHANGED...WELL, everything.

Brad was still aboard *Immortal*, the crew of the battleship apparently having decided that he was the only thing keeping them safe from both sides. The news out of the OWA suggested that there was some serious confusion over who was in charge now—but everyone was *damned* certain it wasn't the Cadre remnants who'd been acting as Jack Mantruso's enforcers and commissars.

Enough governors were still intact that they'd managed to find a trio of representatives to send to the peace conference that Brad had demanded.

With the two largest fleets in the Solar System tentatively, if strangely, under his command, no one had argued when he'd told them they were going to make nice.

Jupiter's delegation had arrived first, with Arbiter Blaze in the lead. They could have beaten everyone else by weeks, but Blaze clearly hadn't seen the point.

The Commonwealth and OWA delegations were arriving within hours of each other—mostly because it had taken so long for the OWA to sort out *who* was coming!

If anyone was objecting to the peace conference being held aboard a battleship, well, no one was entirely sure who was going to claim the battleship. Captain Solyom had accepted that the ship was going back to the Commonwealth, but Brad had told him to keep his mouth shut on that.

Returning the battleship was a huge concession, one the OWA was going to have to make but one that could also help buy a fair peace.

Brad didn't want to have to do this all over again in a different uniform in ten years.

Michelle squeezed his hand to interrupt his distraction. Six weeks had changed things there, too. She was now into her second trimester and visibly pregnant.

Her anger over *why* she was pregnant hadn't faded, but at least they'd decided they couldn't hold that against their baby. The child to come wasn't responsible for their monster of an uncle.

Blaming people for their uncles would end badly for Brad.

"Commonwealth delegation is two minutes out," she told him. "Saburo is rolling the honor guard out now."

That was perhaps a bit more on point than she'd intended. Brad looked over to the honor guard—Vikings, not troops from any of the three powers gathering today—and their wheelchair-bound commander.

He was quite sure there was something terrifying hidden under the blanket covering Saburo Kawa's legs, but that didn't change the fact that the mercenary couldn't walk. Kate Falcone had saved his life, but one of the bullets had severed his spine. Neural regeneration, as Brad's arm could attest, was a long and messy process.

It would be at least a year before Saburo could walk again. That didn't seem to slow him down, though.

"Commonwealth, arriving," Saburo's voice bellowed across the bay as the shuttle slipped through the hangar doors and coasted to a gentle stop.

Brad was about to argue that that declaration should have been reserved for the President when the shuttle ramp dropped.

Someone had warned Saburo but the note hadn't made it to Brad.

President Barnes led the way down the ramp with two Senators

Brad didn't know trailing him. The President returned the salutes of the honor guard and passed through them to reach Brad.

"Admiral Madrid, you've done us all proud," he said quietly. "Thank you."

"Hold the thanks till after the peace conference," Brad replied, equally quietly. "I don't think the Senate is going to be a fan of the results."

"Not my problem," Barnes replied. "As we speak, the election is being called on Earth. I'm not running for Senate or President. I gave them you and you're giving them peace. I'm done."

"One last duty, Mr. President," one of the Senators said. "You have a fiduciary duty to the Commonwealth today, after all."

"I do," Barnes agreed. "But a bigger one to humanity, I think."

Brad's wrist-comp buzzed and he checked it.

"Michelle, can you see the President and his companions to their quarters?" he asked his wife. "The OWA shuttle is right behind you, President Barnes, and we don't want to keep anyone waiting today."

"Of course not. Good luck, Madrid."

Brad exchanged a nod with the leader of the Commonwealth, then turned his attention to the big doors as they slid open again.

———

To his shock, Brad recognized the head of the Outer Worlds Alliance delegation. Lynda Eden had been one of the members of the Council of First Oberon, the effective rulers of Uranus's largest moon, when he'd visited that planetoid.

"Councilor Eden," he greeted her cheerfully as he offered her his hand. "I'm afraid I presumed you were dead."

"I might have been the only one of us to see your brother coming," the old woman said bitterly. "Thanks to Envoy Lathrop, I got into hiding and survived the initial purges. The rest of the Council was far from as lucky.

"Once things started coming apart again, well, I still had my resources and connections." She grimaced. "Until we sort out something better, I'm the Governor of Oberon—and since I've got the steadiest hand on the largest world, everyone else is deferring to me."

"Better you than many others, I think," Brad told her. "It's nice to see someone speaking for the Outer Worlds that I know has a brain."

Her laugh was sharp and bitter.

"That's pushing it. I'm here, aren't I? Stepping on Jack Mantruso's flagship at the invitation of his little brother—for a peace conference that may as well be my nation's surrender."

"Better that you speak for the Outer Worlds than someone who might sell them out," Brad replied. He knew that Eden had reached her Council seat by hook and by crook—all of the Councilors had been ruthless merchants and businesspeople—but she already had enough wealth to live out her life in luxury.

It was hard to buy someone who had everything they wanted.

"We must speak in private, Admiral Madrid, as soon as possible," Eden responded. "Now would be better than later."

"Unfortunately, I'm running two fleets and a peace conference," Brad admitted. "I'm swamped. I can probably break some time free for you once the conference is underway, though."

She grunted, but nodded her acceptance.

"Understand that it's important, Madrid," she told him. "To you and the Outer Worlds alike."

"I will have my staff contact you to set up a time," he replied. "May I have Lieutenant Muhammad here show you to your quarters?"

Marja Muhammad was one of the OWN officers who'd been added to *Immortal* to thicken up her crew after the mutiny. She was about as young and innocent as the OWN came.

A lot of OWN officers had blood on their hands, but if pardoning them was the price of peace, Brad was prepared to pay it. There were enough officers like Lieutenant Marja Muhammad to give him hope, though.

"That will be acceptable," Eden allowed. "I look forward to meeting my counterparts."

Brad shook his head as the Councilor was led away.

Unless he missed his guess, "Governor" Lynda Eden was the functional leader of the Outer Worlds Alliance. There was no question in his mind at all that Arbiter Kenna Blaze was acting as the effective head of state of the as-yet-unnamed Jovian nation.

And no one was going to question that President Barnes led the Commonwealth.

The conference was going to be *fascinating*.

CHAPTER FORTY-FOUR

KENNA BLAZE DIDN'T BOTHER TRYING to set up an appointment or going through Brad's staff. She just walked into his office as he was trying to coordinate a logistical transfer from the closest Jovian ships to a group of OWA ships about to hit their minimum oxygen reserves.

"You know I have a staff, right?" he asked the Arbiter.

"And they're damned good at running interference," she agreed. "Not so good at stopping a senior delegate who isn't willing to be slowed by anything short of bullets."

Brad gestured at the screen.

"I'm buried, Arbiter," he told her. "You're familiar with the feeling, I'm sure."

"I am. But I also know you can make time when you're buried, when you need to. When it's critical—but your staff wouldn't even let me get to you to *tell* you something was critical."

With a sigh, he pointed her to a seat.

"Fine," he conceded. "Talk, Arbiter. The conference starts in the morning. You've got twelve hours left to be ready."

"I'm ready," she said without hesitation. "But there are two ways I can approach that conference, and I know which way I want. And that leans on you."

"On me?" he asked. "Arbiter, everyone is here, safe, and protected. I've done my part!"

"You need to understand the opportunity that lies before you," Blaze told him. "Tell me, do you see a way to guarantee peace if we come out of this with three separate nations?"

"A lot of ways," he replied. "They did it on Earth for decades, centuries. Trade, commerce, shared information networks. We can't force people back under the Commonwealth. Would Jupiter kneel to the Senate again, even if concessions were made?"

"That's not the point. You're not wrong," she allowed, "but that's not the point. Everyone has come to this conference assuming we're walking out with three major powers. My own orders are clear on that.

"But there *is* another path."

"You've lost me, Arbiter," Brad admitted.

"That's why I'm here, in your office, having bull-rushed your staff," Blaze told him. "Because you *can't* see, and we need you to. We need you to see the opportunity before you, the chance to make humanity safe."

"I think I did that already," he pointed out. "I'm done, Arbiter Blaze. My letter of resignation from the Commonwealth Fleet is already on file. It's effective the moment the peace conference ends and will go back to Earth with Senator Barnes.

"I won't."

She sighed.

"That's probably for the best, but again…you're missing the point."

"Then what is the point?" Brad demanded.

"Brad, half of the damn OWN already calls you Lord Protector," Blaze said quietly. "Eden is here to offer you the title formally."

It was a damn good thing he was already sitting.

"You can't be serious," he told her.

"Why do you think she wanted to meet with you? You're Jack Mantruso's logical heir, and the OWA is in shambles. You control their fleet. Even when you send those ships home, it's still going to take them time to rebuild, to establish elections, to come back together.

"They need a symbol of unity and continuity, and you're the best— the *only*—candidate on the range."

"I won't take it," Brad said. "I don't want it."

Blaze visibly rolled her eyes.

"Even though refusing might cost lives?" she asked him. "The OWA needs you. You're their best hope for a peaceful transition."

He exhaled.

"I can't do it," he told her. "I was a born on a spaceship, but Jupiter's my home.

"And that's what I mean by you being *blind*." Blaze shook her head.

"My orders from the Governors were clear," she continued. "I was to encourage you to resign from the Commonwealth Fleet and come home to Jupiter. It sounds like that's your plan."

"And the OWA isn't going to deter me from it," he told her.

"If that's the case, then the second part of my orders comes into play," she told him. "The Governors found having the Arbiter Guild standing as a final overriding vote far too useful in a crisis. Their current plan going forward is a constitutional monarchy."

Brad stared at her. He had to be missing where she was going.

"We don't even have a name or a title yet, but my orders are to offer you the crown of Jupiter."

He kept staring. He couldn't be hearing her right. It wasn't *possible*.

"Both us and the OWA would happily let you take both crowns. Certainly, I suspect both Eden and I would smack down any dissenters thoroughly enough. Two of the three nations united, a guaranteed peace."

He swallowed, but she held up a hand before he began to speak.

"If you took the crowns, it would take us more effort to *keep* Mars from defecting to us than it would to get them to come over. Barnes knows that. And he knows that both fleets here would follow you.

"The massed fleet you gathered couldn't have stopped *Immortal*. There is no force in existence that could stop the combined forces around this ship, the forces that would follow *you*. There'd be little enough objection regardless, so long as you promised Earth's nations the same autonomy they have under the Commonwealth.

"If we have three nations, Brad, we're going to have a three-way cold war," she said finally. "The only way I see to stop that is to prevent that schism, right here, right now. That requires a symbol, a leader everyone will follow.

"You're the only one who can do it," Blaze told him fiercely. "Eden and I can push it through the conference; it's what we're both after. The only way to make this peace conference *truly work* is to make the coronation of humanity's new ruler.

"We need a symbol of unity if we are to stay united. It has to be you.

"It can only be you."

Brad swallowed again, then laid his hands on the table and faced Blaze as he marshaled his thoughts. She had raised every fear he'd had about the future, every concern about what might follow this war and peace conference...but...

"My entire family is dead," he said quietly. "We killed each other. I'm a fratricide and I murdered my own uncle. I killed them both with my own hands. I'm not putting that bloodline anywhere near anything resembling a hereditary position.

"I'm not putting my *child* in a position where they're expected —*required*—to twist their entire life to the service of this Frankensteinian nation you want to forge.

"This schism is inevitable. If we force a unity over it, we simply paper over the cracks and guarantee a worse war down the line. People *must* find their own way. We must accept what is, not what we want to be."

He shook his head as Blaze opened her mouth to speak.

"No, Kenna," he told her gently. "My answer is no. I will resign my commission and I will return to Io with my wife, where I will see my daughter born in peace.

"In a year, if Jupiter's leaders want one washed-up mercenary as an officer, you can come knocking. But I won't take a crown or a throne. I'm not qualified...and I don't think we need one."

"And if you're wrong?" she asked in a small voice.

"Then we have all failed. But it falls to us to build a better future, Kenna, and if we try to bind that future in the form of dictatorship, regardless of how benevolent, we can only hold humanity back.

"You have my answer, Arbiter Blaze," he concluded formally. "It will be the same answer I will give Councilor Eden. I won't be humanity's safety blanket. We can and will stand on our own two legs—and by the Everlit, I intend to live to see it."

ABOUT THE AUTHORS

#1 Bestselling Military Science Fiction author **Terry Mixon** served as a non-commissioned officer in the United States Army 101st Airborne Division. He later worked alongside the flight controllers in the Mission Control Center at the NASA Johnson Space Center supporting the Space Shuttle, the International Space Station, and other human spaceflight projects.

He now writes full time while living in Texas with his lovely wife and a pounce of cats.

————

Glynn Stewart is the author of *Starship's Mage*, a bestselling science fiction and fantasy series where faster-than-light travel is possible–but only because of magic. His other works include science fiction series *Duchy of Terra*, *Castle Federation* and *Vigilante*, as well as the urban fantasy series *ONSET* and *Changeling Blood*.

Writing managed to liberate Glynn from a bleak future as an accountant. With his personality and hope for a high-tech future intact, he lives in Kitchener, Ontario with his partner, their cats, and an unstoppable writing habit.

OTHER BOOKS BY TERRY MIXON

You can always find the most up to date listing of Terry's titles on Amazon at author.to/terrymixon

Scorched Earth

The Vigilante Duology with Glynn Stewart

Heart of Vengeance

Oath of Vengeance

Bound By Stars: A Vigilante Series with Glynn Stewart

Bound By Law

Bound by Honor

Bound by Blood

Want Terry to email you when he publishes a new book in any format or when one goes on sale? Go to TerryMixon.com/Mailing-List and sign up. Those are the only times he'll contact you. No spam.

OTHER BOOKS
BY GLYNN STEWART

For release announcements join the
mailing list or visit **GlynnStewart.com**

STARSHIP'S MAGE
Starship's Mage
Hand of Mars
Voice of Mars
Alien Arcana
Judgment of Mars
UnArcana Stars
Sword of Mars
Mountain of Mars
The Service of Mars
A Darker Magic
Mage-Commander (upcoming)

Starship's Mage: Red Falcon
Interstellar Mage
Mage-Provocateur
Agents of Mars

Pulsar Race: A Starship's Mage Universe Novella

DUCHY OF TERRA
The Terran Privateer
Duchess of Terra
Terra and Imperium
Darkness Beyond
Shield of Terra
Imperium Defiant
Relics of Eternity
Shadows of the Fall
Eyes of Tomorrow

SCATTERED STARS
Scattered Stars: Conviction
Conviction
Deception
Equilibrium
Fortitude (upcoming)

PEACEKEEPERS OF SOL
Raven's Peace
The Peacekeeper Initiative
Raven's Course
Drifter's Folly (upcoming)

EXILE
Exile
Refuge
Crusade
Ashen Stars: An Exile Novella

CASTLE FEDERATION
Space Carrier Avalon
Stellar Fox
Battle Group Avalon
Q-Ship Chameleon
Rimward Stars
Operation Medusa
A Question of Faith: A Castle Federation Novella

SCIENCE FICTION STAND ALONE NOVELLA
Excalibur Lost

VIGILANTE
(WITH TERRY MIXON)
Heart of Vengeance
Oath of Vengeance

Bound By Stars: A Vigilante Series
(With Terry Mixon)
Bound By Law
Bound by Honor
Bound by Blood

TEER AND KARD
Wardtown
Blood Ward

CHANGELING BLOOD
Changeling's Fealty
Hunter's Oath
Noble's Honor
Fae, Flames & Fedoras: A Changeling Blood Novella

ONSET
ONSET: To Serve and Protect
ONSET: My Enemy's Enemy
ONSET: Blood of the Innocent
ONSET: Stay of Execution
Murder by Magic: An ONSET Novella

FANTASY STAND ALONE NOVELS
Children of Prophecy
City in the Sky

Made in the USA
Las Vegas, NV
22 September 2021